Out of the corner of her eye, she saw Dr. Reit's panic-stricken face as he leaped forward. For an instant his hand closed about her wrist. But before he could pull her free, an unearthly wind seized her. Sheila screamed as she was dragged away from Dr. Reit—

Then she was tumbling helplessly down and down into a dizzying world of stormy blue . . .

—from *Swept Away!*

"[The Secret of the Unicorn Queen books] still stand the test of time today, and conjure up a wonderful place to escape to! I fell in love with the books when I was younger, and still treasure them today!"
—LORNA REID, fan, Kent, England

The Secret of the Unicorn Queen Series

Swept Away!
Sun Blind
The Final Test

THE SECRET OF THE UNICORN QUEEN

Volume I

SWEPT AWAY!
JOSEPHA SHERMAN

SUN BLIND
GWEN HANSEN

BALLANTINE BOOKS • NEW YORK

A Del Rey® Book
Published by The Random House Publishing Group

www.delreydigital.com

A Library of Congress Control Number is available from the publisher upon request.

ISBN-13: 978-0-345-46849-9

Manufactured in the United States of America

First Edition: August 2004

OPM   9   8   7   6   5   4   3   2   1

Contents

Swept Away!

1

Swept Away

"I still don't see how you can like that weird old Dr. Reit, Sheila." Cookie Rogers, who was fourteen, plump, and an aspiring actress, gave a melodramatic shudder, hugging her schoolbooks to her. "He gives me the creeps."

Sheila sighed, shifting her backpack to a more comfortable position. Sheila was Cookie's age, but they weren't at all alike in anything else. Where Cookie was short and plump, with curly brown hair and big blue eyes, Sheila was tall and slim. But she was in great shape thanks to running and softball. Her face freckled in the sun no matter what she did, and her hazel eyes usually sparkled with warmth and good humor.

But her eyes weren't sparkling right now. She liked Cookie, she really did. They had a lot of fun together. But sometimes her friend could be such a pain! "Dr. Reit is not weird. Just because he's a scientist—"

"Sure! A *mad* scientist!"

"He is not!" Sheila stamped her foot angrily. "Dr. Reit is a famous inventor. He also happens to be my friend."

3

"I thought *I* was your friend."

"You are!"

"Well? You promised to come home with me after school so we could go over the math homework together, and instead you're going off to that creepy old house to look at some creepy old books."

"I told you. *I* need them for my paper. The one on parallel worlds in science fiction and fantasy."

"What does *that* mean?"

"Parallel worlds? It's a theory that there might be thousands of different dimensions, with a different Earth in each one. You could have a world where no one ever discovered America, or where magic works, or just about anything!"

Cookie shrugged. "I don't know how you can read that stuff. Spaceships and sorcerers and—and Things . . . Ugh. I'd rather read a play any day. Or a love story." She sighed romantically, pretending to swoon, and Sheila grinned.

"Love stories are okay, but science fiction's fun and exciting, too. Look, I've got to look through those books, but it won't take me more than an hour or two. We'll still have time to study. Okay?"

"Well . . . okay." Cookie grinned. "Give my regards to Dr. Reit."

Sheila looked up at Dr. Reit's house. She supposed some people really might call it creepy. It was one of those old Victorian mansions—all funny angles and shapes, as if rooms had been added at whim. Every edge and corner was covered with that busy ornamental woodwork called gingerbread. Dr. Reit had inherited the house from his father. He had inherited a lot of money from his father, too, but most of it had gone into the laboratory attached to the house. It was a beautiful laboratory, with strange shining machinery and mysterious gadgetry. Sheila loved it when the scientist let her watch him at work, even if she didn't always understand what he was trying to do. In fact, there were times when she wasn't sure if even Dr. Reit knew what he was trying to do!

Sheila rang the bell. As she waited at the door she wondered about what Cookie had said. Just why *did* she like the scientist? He was old enough to be her grandfather, and he didn't know anything about popular music or anything like that. But he treated her like an adult. He let her ask all the questions she wanted and listened to her ideas. He liked to read science fiction, too. And he never made fun of her when she daydreamed about other worlds, worlds where she could be someone exciting, like a heroic adventurer out of one of Dr. Reit's old fantasy magazines.

Sheila pressed the bell again and laughed as the theme from *StarWars* rang out. That was another thing she liked about the scientist: he had a great sense of humor.

Dr. Reit's voice, sounding metallic and far away, said over the intercom, "Sheila? Is that you? Yes, yes, I see it is, the camera's working properly. Wait a minute, now. I'll get the door open. . . . There."

With a whir and a click, the door swung open.

"Did it work?" Dr. Reit's voice asked urgently. "It's a new invention, a sort of remote-control door-opener."

Sheila giggled. "It worked fine. Hey, hi, Einstein!"

Dr. Reit's orange cat had come running to greet her, meowing happily as she bent to scratch him under the chin. Dr. Reit's voice continued, "I'm in the laboratory, Sheila. Come on back. I want to show you what I'm working on now!"

"Gee . . . I'm really sorry, but I can't. I promised Cookie . . ."

But Dr. Reit had already shut off the intercom. With a sigh, Sheila started down the hallway to the laboratory, Einstein padding along silently at her side.

"Einstein! Watch it!"

The purring cat had started to twine affectionately about her legs as she walked, nearly tripping her.

"Einstein! Look, cat, I know you like me. I like you, too, but— Oh, all right." She scooped him up into her arms. "Oof. You're putting on weight, cat."

Einstein only purred.

"Ah, there you are!" Dr. Reit's tall, skinny figure appeared in the doorway to the lab, a grease-stained white lab coat not quite reaching far enough to cover all of his lanky height. His mop of white hair stuck up in wild tufts; Sheila knew the scientist had a habit of absently running his hands through it while thinking, even if his hands were covered with grease. "Come on, I've got something exciting to show you."

He caught Sheila by the hand. Einstein spilled to the ground with a startled yowl, giving Dr. Reit a reproachful look. "Sorry," he said absently. "There, now, what do you think of that?"

Sheila entered the laboratory cautiously, looking around. Nothing much seemed to have changed. Tools and bits of unfinished machinery were still lying all over the place. Plans scrawled in Dr. Reit's wild handwriting and blueprints of mysterious devices covered every flat inch of desk and walls. She also noticed a calendar—a year out of date—showing photos of galaxies, a worn-out poster from *The Day the Earth Stood Still*, a misplaced bag of kitty litter, and a sketch she had once drawn of Einstein as a kitten.

"I don't see anything different . . ." Sheila began hesitantly, reaching down to pet Einstein, who had forgiven her for dropping him and was weaving about her ankles.

"No, look over here. What do you think of this?"

In an alcove stood what looked like the framework for a doorway, a rectangle of shining metal, taller than it was wide. Sheila blinked. "I don't—"

"Doesn't look like much, does it? Aha, but watch this!"

Dr. Reit darted to a console near the "doorway." As he pressed buttons and moved gears, a low hum filled the air and grew more and more shrill. The vibration of it quivered through Sheila till she winced. "The doorway!" cried Dr. Reit. "Watch the doorway—there!"

Sheila gasped. What had been empty space a moment before was now a mass of swirling blue, as though the opening had become a window onto a stormy sky. "What *is* it?"

Dr. Reit grinned. "That, my dear, is the prototype for my grandest invention: my Molecular Acceleration Transport Device. I intended it to be a teleportation device. You know, put a package into one station in New York, press a button, and—zip!—it appears in San Francisco the next moment."

"That—that's fantastic! Does it work?"

"Ah. Well. Not exactly the way I intended. You see, Sheila, I may have stumbled across something very fantastic, indeed." The scientist absently ran a hand through his already tousled hair. "Remember that paper on science fiction you were writing for school? It may no longer be mere fiction." His voice trembled with excitement. "I think you may be looking at a gateway into another level of time and space." As Sheila stared at him, he added gleefully, "In short, I have every reason to believe you're looking at a portal that can take you right into another dimension!"

Sheila gasped. "I can't believe . . ."

"I didn't, either, at first. Go take a look for yourself. If the blue clouds are just some sort of bizarre electrical discharge, you should be able to see through them to the wall beyond. But you can't! Go ahead, take a look. But be careful!"

Heart pounding, Sheila took a wary step forward. Could it be true? Could that simple doorway really lead to the magical worlds of which she had dreamed? Chewing nervously on her lower lip, she peered into the mysterious blue swirling, looking for the wall that must be there, just a few inches behind the doorway. But all she saw were swirling clouds that seemed to go on for miles.

"Be careful!" warned Dr. Reit again. "Don't get too close. Remember that we don't know what's on the other side!"

Maybe there wasn't *anything* on the other side! Sheila shuddered. What if there were only clouds? If you fell through there, you just might go on falling and falling forever. . . .

She hastily turned away, saying, "Maybe you'd better shut it down until—Einstein!"

The cat, unnoticed, had twined himself between her feet. Sheila stumbled over him and fell—right toward the doorway!

"Sheila! No!"

Out of the corner of her eye, she saw Dr. Reit's panic-stricken face as he leaped forward. For an instant his hand closed about her wrist. But before he could pull her to safety, an unearthly wind seized her. Sheila screamed as she was dragged away from Dr. Reit—

Then she was tumbling helplessly down and down into a dizzying world of stormy blue.

2

Arrival

Something was tickling her nose. Sheila groaned in sleepy protest. "Einstein? That you?" she muttered. "Cut it out, cat."

The tickling continued.

"Einstein! Stop!"

Sheila sniffed, then gave a mighty sneeze. Her eyes popped open. Jolted awake, she stared blankly, realizing all at once that she was lying full length on something hard and bumpy, her head cushioned by her arm. It hadn't been Einstein tickling her nose at all, but what . . .

Sheila blinked in bewilderment. This wasn't the laboratory, was it? She was lying on what seemed to be a shaggy, mangy, dusty green carpet, a twist of which had been rubbing against her nose. Carpet? It didn't smell like carpet. In fact, the air smelled funny, too, full of a sweet, dry, desery sort of scent. The lab had certainly never smelled like this!

Sheila closed her eyes again, trying to clear her dazed mind. *This is really weird,* she thought groggily. Wouldn't Dr. Reit have moved her to a bed if she had fainted? She *had* fainted, hadn't she?

It wasn't easy to remember what had happened. The last thing she could recall was tripping over Einstein and falling. . . .

Yes! Falling for what had seemed forever through all those weird blue clouds!

"Where—where am I?"

Sheila sat up sharply, then winced as her head throbbed. After a moment things settled down again, and she glanced warily down, half afraid she would find parts of herself missing. But to her relief, everything seemed to be in place. No missing pieces. And she was still wearing her shirt, jeans, and sneakers; she even had her backpack.

But she wasn't sitting on a carpet. She was sitting on thin, spiky blades of grass scattered over bare, sandy earth.

"This is impossible." Sheila struggled to keep her voice steady. "This is absolutely impossible."

Carefully she got to her feet and looked around.

Nothing. No lab, no house, nothing but mile after mile of rolling, empty grassland reaching to the horizon in all directions under a wide, clear blue sky. There wasn't a sound, except for the hissing of a dusty wind and the faint, thin cry of what she guessed must be some kind of hawk.

"I'm dreaming, that's what it is. I must have hit my head on something, and I'm having a weird dream."

But she ached from lying on the rough ground. And she was growing thirsty under the intense sun. Sheila wondered uneasily if you could feel any discomfort in a dream.

"If this is a dream, it's an awfully real one. And I don't know how to wake up and get out of it, either."

What if it wasn't a dream? That could mean only one thing: the doorway, the Molecular Acceleration something-or-other, had really worked. It had thrown her right out of her own world and into . . . wherever.

Sheila swallowed dryly. "All—all right," she said. "If it's a dream, I'm bound to wake up after a while. And if it's not a dream, I'll just wait here till Dr. Reit brings me back again."

Could he bring her back? After all, he had hinted that his invention was still in the experimental stage. Maybe when she had fallen through the blue clouds, she had somehow broken the whole machine! Maybe she was trapped here! Sheila blinked, fighting back her tears. She wasn't going to start bawling like a baby! And she wouldn't let herself be scared! Not yet, anyhow.

Time passed. The hot sun moved slowly across the sky till it was almost directly overhead. Nothing else happened, nothing at all. At last Sheila sighed and stood up.

"If Dr. Reit could have gotten me back, he would have already done it. Whatever this is, dream or reality, I guess I'm not going to get out of it by just standing around."

Which way should she go? She spun around, trying to find something to give her a clue, but the grassland still looked the same on all sides. The sun beat down on her head so strongly that Sheila wished she had a sun hat.

"Wait a minute! Somewhere in my backpack there should be . . . yes, here it is. I knew I'd put a scarf in here."

It wasn't as good as a hat, but it was better than nothing. Sheila looked around again. Nothing had changed, not even the dusty moan of the wind. She shrugged. Shouldering her pack once more, she randomly picked a direction and started on her way.

By the time the sun had moved three quarters of the way across the sky, Sheila was too hot and tired and thirsty to care about any more hiking. For all she knew, this empty grassland went on forever, all the way around whatever world she was on. She had a quick, scary mental image of herself trudging on and on till she collapsed from exhaustion. Maybe she would die here, and her bones would lie bleaching on this plain forever. . . .

"No, wait! I think I see something on the horizon!" If only there was a tree she could climb to get a better view! But there wasn't so much as a bush, so Sheila tried jumping up as high as she could. "There—it's smoke—I'm sure of it." Panting, she stopped jumping to catch her breath. "Maybe the smoke is coming from a campfire! That means there are people on this world after all! I'm not alone!"

She started to run. But suddenly a shadow passed swiftly overhead, and Sheila staggered to a stop, staring up. What was that? It looked something like the golden eagle she had seen on a trip out West. No eagle she had ever seen was that huge! It was as big as a man, and its wings looked as wide as those of a small airplane. Bright, fierce eyes studied her for a moment, and Sheila wondered nervously what she was going to do if the eagle decided it wanted her for its next meal. But then, with a sharp cry that sounded almost like a mocking laugh, the eagle flew away, spiraling up to rejoin a whole flock of its kind.

"But eagles don't fly in flocks!" Then Sheila caught herself. "Well, maybe they do in this world."

The eagles were swiftly soaring off in the direction of the campfire. Shading her eyes with her hand, Sheila stared after them, then started forward again. She hadn't gone far when a sudden cloud of dust erupted on the horizon.

Sheila's eyes widened in alarm. "That's not a cloud! Those are horsemen—and they're galloping right toward me!"

For a hopeful moment she thought they were coming to rescue her. But those shrill, savage yells didn't sound like the yells of friendly rescuers! And now she could see that the riders were brandishing swords and spears!

Frantically Sheila looked for a place to hide. But there wasn't any! And she certainly wasn't going to be able to outrun galloping horses!

As the riders bore down on her, Sheila froze, staring in wonder. Those five fierce riders weren't men, but women—warrior-women dressed in a rainbow of bright silks and leather and pieces of armor glinting brightly in the sunlight, like something out of a fantasy story. And those weren't horses they were riding—

They were *unicorns!*

3

Captured!

Before Sheila could catch her breath, the warrior-women on their swift unicorns had surrounded her in a blur of color and noise. Choking on the dust the prancing hoofs raised, Sheila spun around and around, seeing fierce faces glaring at her on every side, trying to ward off the warriors' weapons, terrified that she was going to trip and be trampled.

A hand grabbed her arm, clamping down with painful force.

"Hey! Let go!"

Sheila, struggling wildly, glared up at her captor, a woman with wild red hair, a broad-featured face, and a solid body that reminded her of the gym teacher she had had in sixth grade. *I never did like that teacher!* thought Sheila. She punched at the hand holding her as hard as she could. The woman grunted, but didn't release her. As the other warriors laughed sharply, Sheila was pulled off her feet and thrown across the saddle of the red-haired warrior's palomino unicorn. One warrior, a beautiful young black woman whose armor glinted with gold, called out something in a melodious language. The others shouted in agreement. With that, the unicorns eagerly leaped forward.

14

For a time Sheila was just too dazed to move. But the saddle's pommel was digging painfully into her middle, cutting off her wind. And the sight of the ground whizzing by under her helplessly dangling head wasn't helping her stomach at all. Sheila squirmed around till she could slap her captor's leg.

"Let me up!"

No answer.

"Hey, come on, please, just let me sit up!"

The woman muttered something that was plainly "no," her voice as rough as the rest of her.

Sheila took another look at the dizzying blur of ground and groaned.

"You'd better let me up, or—or I'm going to be s-sick all over your leg!"

Her captor glanced down at her. Even if the woman didn't understand her words, one look at Sheila's green face got the message across. To her relief, she was dragged up to sit sideways on the saddle, her captor's arm like a bar of iron holding her in place. Sheila glanced warily around. The first thing she noticed was that the palomino unicorn wore no bridle. In fact, none of the unicorns wore more than simple saddles. *And the saddles don't even have stirrups!* thought Sheila. The women didn't seem to miss them, sitting their mounts with practiced ease. In addition to her gruff captor and the black woman, Sheila noticed a brown-haired archer, quiver slung over her back, and a slender, dark-haired girl of about her own age who kept giving Sheila hostile stares.

"Don't blame me!" Sheila said to her. "This isn't *my* idea!"

Her captor gave her a shake and a frown that clearly meant "Keep quiet."

The unicorns streamed down a gulch and into a flat little valley. Sheila saw a few earth-colored, patched tents before her captor gave her a shove that sent her tumbling off the palomino to the ground.

"Hey! What's the idea?"

But the red-haired woman wasn't paying any attention to her. "Pelu!" she called. "Ho, Pelu!"

A slender young woman appeared out of one of the tents. Unlike the warriors, she wore no armor, only a simple white tunic and worn leather sandals, and her ash-blond hair was coiled up in braids on top of her head. As the others spoke to her, she studied Sheila with quiet blue eyes, then approached the girl. She said something in that melodious language, and Sheila sighed and shook her head.

"Sorry. I don't understand."

Pelu nodded thoughtfully. Reaching into a pouch at her belt, she took out a gleaming blue gem. Before Sheila could move, the woman touched the gem to the girl's head, lips, and heart.

"Can you understand me now?"

"I—hey! Yes, I can! What did you do?"

"The touch of the Gem of Speaking gave you our language."

Sheila stared, thinking wildly, *Boy, I'd love to have something like that in school!* "But—but how does it work?"

Pelu looked at her as though she had asked something stupid. "Magic, of course."

"Oh, of course," echoed Sheila weakly. "How foolish of me not to have known."

But she was speaking to the air. Pelu had rejoined the others, who were arguing fiercely. Sheila heard her captor, who apparently was named Myno, insisting, "She is *my* prisoner."

"Ridiculous!" cut in the black woman, Nanine, with a haughty toss of her head. "We all found her."

"Who found her isn't important," said Pelu quietly. "I vote we simply hold her till Illyria returns."

"Don't *I* have any say in the matter?" began Sheila, but she was drowned out by Myno's shout:

"No! She's *my* prisoner."

The dark-haired girl, Dian, gave Sheila a withering glance. "Why would you want someone like *her?*"

"Because . . ." Myno's voice dropped to a mutter. "Because after all my years of slavery, I want a servant of my own."

"Hey, I'm not going to be anyone's servant!" said Sheila indignantly. "Look, who are you? What makes you think you can just kidnap me?"

The women ignored her.

"I think we're making a mistake." The archer, Kara, plucked at her bowstring suggestively. "Think about it: a girl, all alone in the middle of nowhere, just happens to be walking right toward our camp. Sounds strange, doesn't it?"

"She's no warrior," Dian said in contempt.

"Maybe not. But who knows what weapons she's hiding in that pack of hers? I say she's some sort of spy."

"I'm no spy!" Sheila shouted. "Listen to me, will you? I don't even know where I am!"

The warrior-women huddled, murmuring. Sheila overheard uncomfortable words like "Death to spies" and thought nervously, *I don't think I'd better hang around here any longer.* No one was paying any attention to her, so she began to edge carefully away. She turned to run—and found herself facing a living wall of unicorns, all of them with their heads down and their long, spiraling horns pointed right at her.

"All right," said Sheila softly. "I—uh—get the point."

She backed carefully away, turned—and found herself facing a line of cold-eyed warrior-women. "Look," Sheila began, "I don't want any trouble. I only—"

With a roar, they rushed her. Frantically Sheila rummaged in her pack, trying to find a weapon, any weapon. Her hand closed around something circular—soda! A can of orange soda! *Wish I'd remembered I had this when I was out on the plain!* thought Sheila wryly. Now the soda was much too warm to drink—

Too warm! Of course!

Hastily she shook the can with all her might, pointed the opening at her attackers, and pulled the tab. A geyser of hot, sticky orange soda shot out, fizzing madly, and the startled women shrieked and jumped back.

"Sorcery! She's a sorceress!"

Is that good or bad? wondered Sheila.

It was bad.

"Hurry," shouted Nanine, "kill the witch before she works more evil magic!"

"No!" yelled Sheila. "I'm not a witch, honest!"

But they weren't listening to her. Myno raised her sword. Kara fit an arrow to her bow—

"Stop!"

The command rang out like a bugle call. Heads turned sharply. Weapons were lowered. Sheila, heart racing, whirled to find herself staring up at a magnificent unicorn stallion, shining white as moonlight. On his back sat the most gorgeous woman she had ever seen, tall and proud in the saddle. The woman, evidently the warriors' leader, the missing Illyria they had mentioned, was clad in what had once been an elegant tunic of fiery red silk, now travel-stained and mended in several places, over which she wore armor consisting of a leather breastplate and a sort of skirt of leather strips that reminded Sheila of pictures she'd seen of Roman legionnaires. Silver glinted from ornamental inlays in that armor, and from the woman's elegant armbands. Her legs were protected by bronze greaves, and at her side hung a dangerous-looking sword in a worn sheath and an equally dangerous curved dagger. The woman's tanned, fierce face was framed by masses of silver-blond hair come partly free from what Sheila guessed must have been yards of braids wound about her head.

She's like a heroine out of a fantasy book! thought Sheila, awed.

Piercing blue eyes held Sheila's gaze, staring at her until Sheila felt sure Illyria knew all about her.

The woman turned to glare at her warriors. "What is the meaning of this?"

Kara said uneasily, "Ah . . . Illyria, the eagles warned us that something was wrong. We rode out, and sure enough, we found the girl out on the plain—and heading right toward our camp!"

"Sure I was!" cut in Sheila angrily. "I saw the smoke from your campfire. It was the only sign of life in the whole place!"

"Be silent, girl." Illyria's voice was calm. "You will have your turn to speak. Now, what about you, my comrades? Since when do we make war on girls?"

"She's not just a girl!" said Dian. "She's a sorceress!"

"Come now, Dian. She's even younger than you."

"It's true!" the dark-haired girl insisted. "She tried to kill us with a magic potion. It's probably some deadly poison!"

"It's not poison." Sheila couldn't help giggling. "It's only soda. See?"

She licked the last drops from the can she still held. Everyone stared. When nothing happened to her, they all drew back, murmuring in wonder.

Oh, great, thought Sheila. *They think I just used magic to keep the soda from poisoning me. They still believe I'm a witch, all right: they're just trying to figure out whether I'm Glinda or the Wicked Witch of the West.*

Kara seemed determined to prove that Sheila was an evil sorceress. "I've seen enough magic in my time—remember Mardock and his foul spells?"

"Yes, of course," argued Pelu. "But magic can be worked for good, as well as evil. You've watched my healing spells and seen the Gem of Speaking."

Dian shook her head. "Those are just small charms, everyday spells. You told me so yourself!"

"That's not the point, Dian! If the girl really does have Power, can we afford to lose a magical ally?"

That sparked a wild debate.

"You don't understand! I say get rid of her, now!"

"First we should learn who sent her and—"

"No! We mustn't wait!"

"That's ridiculous! We mustn't—"

"We must—"

"We—"

"Enough!" said Illyria at last. "The sorceress comes with me. I will learn the truth from her. Alone."

"And I," muttered Sheila, "will finally get some answers!"

4

Questions

Illyria slid down from the back of her unicorn. He turned his head to nuzzle her affectionately, then trotted off to be unsaddled by one of the warriors. Illyria signaled for Sheila to follow her, then started toward the largest of the few worn, patched tents. Inside the tent were only two camp chairs, the sort that fold up flat, a wobbly table consisting of a plank set on two rocks, and a pack that Sheila suspected held Illyria's spare clothing.

Illyria raised an eyebrow. "Not luxurious enough for you, sorceress?"

"I'm not a—" began Sheila, then stopped short. By now there wasn't any way she could pretend to herself that this was all only a dream. Oh no, this was all quite real. Like it or not, she was stuck, without a clue as to how to get home, getting firsthand information on an alternative world where magic worked. Maybe, for safety's sake, she had better play along and pretend to have magical powers of her own. Magical powers for good, not evil, of course.

Illyria seated herself in one of the chairs, chin resting on

steepled hands. Her fierce eyes studied Sheila without blinking.
"Sit, girl."

"My name isn't 'girl' or 'sorceress,' it's Sheila."

"So. Sheila. Now, tell me what you're doing here."

"Ah." Sheila thought frantically for an answer. "Not much,
really. Just trying to figure out a way to get home again."

"Don't play games with me, girl. The very fact that you didn't
speak our language proves you're not from around here."

"No," agreed Sheila honestly. "Believe me, I'm from far away.
Very far away."

"Then how did you get here? Sorcery? Why are you here?" The
blue eyes blazed. "Did Dynasian send you?"

Sheila shrank back from the attack of questions. "Who?" she
asked in bewilderment.

"Come, come, I'm not a fool! Everyone knows the name of the
tyrant who usurped the throne of good King Amar!"

"Everyone but me!"

Illyria paused, studying her, then frowned slowly. "I could almost swear you were telling the truth."

"I am! Look, I didn't want to come here; I don't even know
where 'here' is!"

"These are the Steppes of Arren, many days of hard riding
away from Campora."

That didn't mean much to Sheila. "Oh," she said blankly.

Illyria's frown deepened. "Why, you really don't know what I'm
talking about, do you?"

Sheila shook her head. "Sorry. The only thing I can tell you is
that I was on my way home from school."

"Wizards' school?"

"Not—not exactly. Anyhow, I stopped off to see Dr. Reit. He's
a scientist friend of mine."

"A . . . scientist." Illyria pronounced the word carefully, as
though it were foreign to her. It was foreign, Sheila realized after a

moment; she'd had to say it in English because there wasn't any such word as *scientist* in Illyria's language.

"Oh. Well, I suppose you probably would call him a wizard. His cat tripped me—"

"Deliberately? This cat-creature is the wizard's familiar?"

"No, no, he's just a pet! And it was an accident, that's all! He tripped me, and I fell right through the . . . the . . ." But there weren't any words like *Molecular Acceleration* in this language, either. Sheila ended up lamely, "Let's just call it a spell that wasn't tested yet. Only in the place I come from, we don't use magic. We use science instead. You know: airplanes, television . . . no," she added sadly, seeing Illyria's bewilderment, "you don't know, do you? Hey, wait, I'll show you!"

Sheila rummaged around in her backpack, trying not to notice that Illyria was keeping a wary hand on the hilt of her sword.

"Ah, here it is! This is something from the world of science: a cassette player."

She pressed the "on" button, and the tent was flooded with the sound of Bon Jovi. Sheila grinned.

At the first note Illyria sprang up, sword drawn. Eyes wide, she murmured, "Sorcery!"

"Hey, it's all right! Don't be afraid! It can't hurt you," Sheila said quickly.

She turned off the player. "It's just something kids like me use for fun."

Illyria sighed. "I'm willing to believe you're not a spy, Sheila from the World of Science, where even mere children wield magic. Your sorcery has nothing of the foul taint of Mardock about it."

"That's the second time someone's mentioned Mardock. Who is he?"

The woman raised a surprised eyebrow. "Didn't you know? I thought surely all magicians would know the name. He's Dynasian's pet sorcerer, and his spells are all of the Darkness."

"But I still don't know who Dynasian is!"

"Later. First, you still must prove to me that your own magic really does no harm, and—"

The sounds of quarreling outside the tent interrupted her.

"Now what?" the woman muttered under her breath, and moved to the tent's entrance. "Stay where you are, Sheila. Pelu! What's going on?"

"Myno and Kara are arguing over the—ah—the sorceress."

Illyria let out her breath in an angry hiss. "Come inside and guard our . . . guest. I will be back."

The tent flaps swung shut behind her. "Uh . . . Pelu," Sheila began after an awkward silence. "What *is* all this? I mean, who are you people? What are you doing here? And—and those really are unicorns, aren't they?"

Pelu gave her a quick grin. "I know how you feel! When I first met Illyria's unicorns, I thought I must be dreaming. But yes, they are unicorns, and they are quite real." She hesitated. "As for what we're all doing here, I can only speak for myself." Pelu paused again, toying with memory. "Since I was a little girl, I've always loved animals. At first my parents only laughed when I'd want to take care of stray dogs or wounded birds, even though they couldn't deny that I seemed to have a true healer's touch. But when I told them I wanted to train to become a professional healer of animals, they stopped laughing and beat me instead."

"Why?"

Pelu shrugged. "In our village women are forbidden to work with animals. That is men's work. A woman's place is at home, taking care of her children and obeying her mate."

"But that's ridiculous! If you're good with animals, what difference does it make if you're male or female? Where I come from, a woman can do anything she wants! We have plenty of women veterinarians, women who are healers of animals."

Pelu sighed. "You must come from a strange land, indeed. Here, the only way for me to follow my dream was to run away. But no one would hire a woman healer. I would have starved had I not met Illyria and joined her band. And when I was befriended by my own dear unicorn—"

A sudden crash outside the tent made Sheila and Pelu both jump. Pelu let out a little cry of pain.

"What is it?" asked Sheila. "Oh, you've cut yourself!"

"It's nothing, a scratch. I was careless with my dagger and—" Pelu stopped abruptly, staring, as Sheila rummaged around in her pack. "What are you doing?"

"Hunting for . . . ah, here it is!" The girl smiled at Pelu. "Hey, don't look so scared. This is only a . . ." But the language didn't have a word for *Band-Aid*, so Sheila finished, "This is a sort of a sticky bandage."

Nervously, Pelu let her put it over the little cut.

"See?" said Sheila. "Nothing to be afraid of."

Pelu looked at her bandaged finger in wonder. "You *are* a sorceress! But . . . this is healing magic. No evil sorceress can work with any of the healing arts. Nor would she stoop to doing a good deed."

"Uh . . . no. I guess she wouldn't."

"Then it's true. Your magic is good, not evil."

"Well . . . if I have any magic, it's good magic," said Sheila carefully.

Pelu studied her for a moment. "But you're still a very young sorceress, aren't you?" the woman asked gently. "And very far away from home."

Sheila swallowed hard. "F-farther than you think."

"Poor thing! You really don't know what's going on here, do you?"

"No."

"Very well. While we wait for Illyria to return, I shall tell you a story: the story of the Unicorn Queen. Listen carefully. . . ."

5

The Quest

Pelu was a fine storyteller. As she spun her tale, Sheila found herself listening so intently that pretty soon she forgot everything around her. Instead of a ragged tent, she seemed to see the adventure itself unfold before her eyes. . . .

The village was a peaceful place of thatched cottages set in a small green valley high in the mountains. It was a perfect place to raise the swift, sure-footed horses for which the village was known. And the finest horses were bred by a man called Sandrous. Sandrous had two children, Illyria, even then already tall and beautiful as a goddess, and Darian, her younger brother, brown of hair and eye, and daring of heart. Their mother had died when they were very young. But Sandrous taught them many things, from the proper way to handle a frightened colt to the method for taming a horse without breaking its spirit.

That was a good, happy time. But far beyond the mountain village, the world was changing. In Campora, capital city of the vast kingdom in which the village lay, the wizard-king, Amar, a good and kindly man, had been deposed (some said by dark and devious sorcery), and Dynasian, ambitious and cruel, had usurped the throne.

Sandrous thought that since Campora was so far away, the problems there could not possibly affect him. Still, he decided, better to be prepared. Sandrous had been a warrior when he was younger, and now he taught his daughter and his son weaponry, the ways of sword and spear. Illyria soon became as skillful with the sword as any warrior Sandrous had ever seen.

"That's very interesting," Sheila cut in, "but what about the unicorns?"

"Hush, little sorceress. I'm getting to them."

Pelu continued:

One fine day Illyria and Darian went riding. They were enjoying an ordinary ride through the clear mountain air. Suddenly Illyria's horse shied, and the young woman found herself looking down at the bloody, beaten body of a handsome young man.

"Hurry, Darian! We've got to get him to shelter!" she cried.

The young man was badly hurt, but Illyria nursed him back to health. His name was Egael. He told her to beware of Dynasian; it was the tyrant's men who had beaten him and left him to die.

As Egael healed, he and Illyria grew close.

But one night Illyria woke suddenly, sensing that something strange was happening. Alarmed, she ran to the room in which Egael slept. But he was gone! Illyria ran out into the night, frantically shouting Egael's name, but the only answer to her calls was the wild cry of an eagle. Far in the distance she saw the fading shadow of great wings. And somehow, she didn't know how or why, Illyria knew that Egael had vanished from her life.

As she stood in the moonlight, wondering, blinking back tears, Illyria felt a soft muzzle brush her arm. *One of the horses has gotten loose*, she thought, and turned—to find herself facing a magnificent white stallion. A unicorn stallion. That was Illyria's first meeting with Quiet Storm. And he is with her still.

In those days Quiet Storm lived a peaceful life, siring handsome unicorn foals with Sandrous's mares. The horse foals were sold at market as always; the unicorns—Sandrous being a wise man—were allowed to run free and happy, as unicorns must. And the village flourished. No one fell ill. The harvests were bountiful. And everyone knew this was due to the magic of the unicorns.

Pelu paused. "Storytelling is thirsty work. Illyria usually keeps a water jug in here . . . ah, yes."

As the woman drank, Sheila prodded her eagerly, "Go on! What happened next?"

"What else? Trouble. Listen. . . ."

Word of the valley full of fabulous unicorns reached Dynasian's ears. Or, rather, it reached the ears of his favorite sorcerer, Mardock. A foul and cruel man, Mardock is as dark of heart as he is of beard and hair. An exile, it is said, from some mystical land to the east, Mardock is a fine companion to his tyrant master.

Mardock looked through his magic window and saw that while the unicorns roamed free, strange things began happening to Dynasian's legions. Whenever they'd try to collect taxes, the taxes would turn to rocks, or bright blue butterflies. Whenever they would try to arrest an innocent soul, their swords would shatter. People began to laugh at them, and at Dynasian.

It is never wise to mock an evil man.

One terrible day Illyria and Darian returned home to find the village destroyed and Sandrous slain. The unicorns were gone. Dynasian had stolen them all—all except Quiet Storm and Darian's own mount.

Dark times followed, full of plague and misery. But then Illyria had a dream; in it a great eagle, large as a man, told her that the land would prosper once more only when the unicorns—those beings of Light and Goodness—were freed. Upon waking, Illyria swore a solemn vow: she would free the unicorns from Dynasian's snares, or die in the attempt.

Pelu stopped.

"And?" insisted Sheila.

"And she's been traveling ever since. Campora is very far from here. Some of the captive unicorns have managed to escape Dynasian's men; those are the ones we ride. As for us . . . well, now, we are a band of seven, counting Illyria and Darian, all of us escaping tyranny of some sort. You already know my story. Redheaded Myno, whom you've—ah—met, is a runaway slave." Pelu winced. "She never talks about her former life, but I've seen the scars of whips on her back. You can imagine how she hates Dynasian and all he stands for! She's the only one of us who's actually been in Campora. And if ever there was a genius for figuring out a sly, clever plan, it's she."

"What about the black woman? She seems so proud."

"Ho, she should! Our Nanine is a princess in her homeland to the south. She ran away from the foppish pig of a prince she was being forced to wed. She claims to like our rough life far better than any silken prison of a harem, even though she complains about having to sleep on the ground 'like a commoner' and eat food that's 'barely fit for swine'!"

Sheila giggled. "And what about the archer?"

Pelu's smile faded. "Kara's our archer, and she doesn't laugh very much. You see, she has her own mission: Kara is looking for her sister, who was carried off by Dynasian's soldiers. Poor thing, she may or may not be alive in Campora."

"What about the black-haired girl? The one who's about my own age?" Sheila asked.

"Dian? Oh, she's our 'baby.' She found one of the unicorns lost and hurt, and took care of it. When the unicorn recovered, and rejoined our herd, Dian came along with it. She's showing signs of becoming a fine warrior. And she's got a lovely singing voice, too, very comforting at night when we're all gathered around the campfire and feeling sorry for ourselves." Pelu smiled. "So. There you have our story."

"And a fine story it is, too!" said a sudden voice.

6

Sheila Enlists

Sheila and Pelu both sprang to their feet in surprise, Pelu with her dagger ready. At the tent's entrance stood one of the cutest boys Sheila had ever seen. He was tall and lean, and looked as though he had been working out with weights. *But in this crazy world he's probably been working out with a sword!* Sheila thought. Shoulder-length brown hair framed a strong, suntanned face that reminded Sheila of Illyria—

"Darian," said Pelu with a sigh, sheathing her knife. "Don't startle me like that. I might have stabbed you."

"Sorry." He gave her a quick, dazzling smile, then turned to look at Sheila.

"Darian?" she asked. "Oh, of course. You're Illyria's brother."

"And you're the sorceress." He took a swaggering step into the tent, looking Sheila up and down. "Kind of young to be a sorceress, aren't you, little girl?"

Sheila straightened angrily. How could she have thought that this arrogant boy was cute? "Kind of young to be a warrior, aren't you?"

Darian flushed. "A child like you should be with your mother. Learning to stay in the kitchen, where you belong."

"Why, you—you—" Sheila sputtered. Oh, why didn't this language have words like *male chauvinist pig* in it? "You spoiled little boy!"

Pelu, chuckling softly, murmured, "Oh, no. I don't want to get in the middle of this! Excuse me, you two."

She slipped out of the tent, but neither Sheila nor Darian saw her leave. "What's that?" the boy asked sharply. "Your pack of magic tricks?"

"It's my pack, yes. What about it?"

"Then it really does have magic stuff in it? Hey, that's nothing for a girl to carry around! Let me have it before you hurt yourself."

"I will not! Leave me alone!"

Laughing, he reached for the backpack—and Sheila kicked him sharply in the shin. There was a roar of laughter from the tent's entrance, and Darian and Sheila whirled to see Illyria standing there, eyes bright with amusement.

"My, my, what a brave little sorceress you are! Brother, I do think you've met your match! And I think you just might have had it coming, too."

Darian, rubbing his shin, glared at his sister. But then he gave a rueful grin and muttered, "I guess maybe I did." As he left the tent with a limp, he shot Sheila a quick, grudging glance of respect.

Once the tent flaps had swung shut behind him, Sheila, blushing, turned to Illyria, more than a little awed at the quiet power radiating from the woman. She was a true leader!

Oh, great! And I just kicked her brother in the shin! "I'm sorry, I didn't mean to—"

"No need to apologize." Illyria gave a deep sigh, but her eyes still twinkled. "Poor Darian! It's not easy for him, being both the only male in our warrior band and the second youngest. He still has a good deal to learn." The humor vanished from her face.

Coolly, the woman added, "As do we all. And one thing I mean to learn right now, my dear, is whether your magic is good or evil. Pelu seems to like you. That's a point in your favor. But humans can make mistakes. I have a better judge of character, one who is never fooled."

"I—I don't understand."

Illyria pulled aside a flap of the tent. "Storm!" she called. "Quiet Storm!"

The magnificent white unicorn trotted up, his coat and long spiraling horn glinting bright silver in the sunlight. His large, amber eyes studied the girl almost thoughtfully.

"Storm, come closer. Meet Sheila."

The unicorn stuck his head into the tent. Sheila drew back a little at the sight of that long, sharp horn so close to her head, but the unicorn's eyes were gentle. And he was so beautiful! His head was lovely, as fine-boned and graceful as the head of a deer, reminding her a little of an Arabian stallion she had seen in a movie. His small ears pricked forward in curiosity. He had a small beard of whiskers beneath his chin, and his breath was as sweet as fresh clover as he nuzzled Sheila. After a moment she dared to stroke his cheek. His coat was warm and soft beneath her hand, softer than velvet.

"So," said Illyria softly. "Thank you, Storm. You may go now."

With a snort that sounded almost like an amused chuckle, the unicorn withdrew his head from the tent, carefully turning sideways so he wouldn't snare his horn in the fabric, and trotted off again.

It seemed to Sheila that she had been holding her breath all this time. Now she gave a long, awestruck sigh. "He's beautiful!"

"He is, isn't he?" Illyria smiled. "More important, he's just told me what I needed to know. No unicorn would tolerate the presence of a worker of evil magic. Welcome to my camp, Sheila of the World of Science."

It was said so formally that for a moment Sheila wondered if she should curtsy or something. "Uh, thank you."

The twinkle of amusement was back in Illyria's eyes. "Come, be honest now. You're not really a sorceress, are you?"

Sheila started. How should she answer that one? "Well . . . no," she began warily, then stopped in panic.

Oh, boy! What did I say that for? I just ruined the only chance I had to defend myself!

But Illyria was continuing casually, "I thought not. You're just too young to have completed the years of study a sorceress needs. Unless, of course, you aren't truly young. Do you happen to be wearing a Disguise of Youth?"

Sheila blinked. "You mean, am I really an old woman who's turned herself into a girl?" Could there really be such a spell? "Ah . . . no. I'm a girl, honest."

"So. You must be an apprentice. Perhaps of this wizard you mentioned, this—Dr. Reit, I believe you named him."

"Yes. I mean, that's his name." Sheila thought quickly. "And I . . . have helped him with a few experiments," she said truthfully.

"You must make a fine apprentice." The woman's voice was as matter-of-fact as if she had complimented Sheila on her bike riding. "Already you wield your powers well." Illyria paused thoughtfully and looked the girl up and down appraisingly. "And you do seem fit enough, if not as fit as a true warrior. Tell me, now, have you ever studied any form of weapon-craft?"

Sheila bit back a wild giggle at the thought of herself in full armor in gym class. "Well, I cover third base on the school softball team. That can get pretty wild sometimes. And I've hit a couple of homers, too."

"That is a form of combat unknown to me. Still . . . Sheila of the World of Science, my warriors and I could use the help of a sorceress of good magic in our quest, even a sorceress-in-training. Particularly one who wields objects of great magical power such as that far-speaking box and the foaming potion."

Objects of power! thought Sheila in amazement. *My cassette player and that can of soda?*

"Come now, Sheila, look at me. I'm asking you a question. Will you join us?"

"Oh. I—I don't know. I've got to think about it for a moment."

Illyria nodded in understanding. Sheila turned away, chewing nervously on her lower lip.

Defeating an evil tyrant . . . freeing trapped unicorns to return good fortune to the land . . . it certainly did sound like a worthy cause. In fact, it sounded like every heroic daydream she had ever had.

It also sounded awfully dangerous. You couldn't get hurt in daydreams, but these people weren't carrying swords just for fun!

Still . . . it *was* a worthy cause, and besides, she really didn't know what else to do except wait and hope that Dr. Reit would find her and take her home.

"All right. I'll join you," said Sheila. "At least until I find a way home."

Illyria, pleased, nodded solemnly. "I'm glad to hear that. But I must tell you this, Sheila: it won't be easy. There will be many challenges, from the land itself, from Dynasian's forces, from dark sorcery. Many women have wanted to join me along the way. I accept only those who can endure the hardships of a warrior's training. Do you think you can endure, and triumph?"

For a moment the sheer strangeness of it all nearly overwhelmed Sheila. Such a wave of homesickness washed over her that she wanted to shout *No! I can't! Just leave me alone!* But instead she swallowed fiercely and managed to get out, in an almost level voice:

"I guess I won't know until I try." Sheila paused. "But I've got to warn you, I've never been on a horse in my life."

"Unicorns aren't horses," Illyria replied. "You'll learn. One way or another. Come, I'll introduce you—formally, this time—to the others."

7

Warrior-in-Training

Sheila looked around the camp. It was late afternoon. Everyone seemed to know exactly what they were doing—from Myno, skillfully mending a saddle girth, to Kara, who had returned to camp with bow in hand and a brace of rabbits over her shoulder. The unicorns wandered freely, stopping to graze every now and then on sparse grass or thorny bushes; Sheila was fascinated as she watched how delicately the unicorns twisted their lips in the leaves to avoid getting stuck.

Watching unicorns was fun, but it wasn't something she could do all day. What *was* she supposed to be doing? Sheila wondered. Everyone else seemed to have some task or another. But no one paid any attention to her. She hadn't even been told where she would sleep, or if she was going to have to stand guard like the others. Though there was still plenty of light, the sun was already slipping behind the horizon, and a chill was rising from the rapidly cooling earth. Sheila shivered and gratefully pulled the cloak Pelu had lent her more tightly about herself. Weird! This was all so weird! Had it really been only a few short hours ago she had been talking with Cookie about studying?

Sure. A few short hours ago—in another world—in another dimension!

Sheila shivered again, and this time it wasn't from the chilly air. How was she ever going to get home?

"Uh . . . Sheila," said a hesitant voice.

It was Darian. *Oh, fine*, thought Sheila. The last thing she wanted right now was to get into another fight with him!

"Darian, I—" she began, just as he started:

"Sheila, I—"

They both laughed nervously and stopped.

"Sheila," began Darian again, not meeting her gaze, "I . . . What I mean is . . ." He gave an exasperated sigh. "Look, what I'm trying to say is, I acted like an idiot before. I don't know why I did it. I'm not usually so . . . obnoxious. Sorry."

Sheila eyed him warily. "Did Illyria make you say this?"

"No!" He glared at her indignantly. "I'm trying to apologize to you! Are you going to let me or not?"

"Hey, what happened wasn't *my* fault! You don't have to yell at me!"

To her surprise, Darian only grinned. "Yeah. You're right. I've got an idea. Why don't we just forget the whole thing and pretend we're just meeting for the first time now? Okay?"

"Okay," she said with a smile. "My name is Sheila. What's yours?"

"I'm Darian. Pleased to meet you, Sheila."

"Pleased to meet you, too, Darian."

They solemnly shook hands, then burst out laughing. "Friends?" the boy asked.

"Friends," agreed Sheila. "Ah . . . why are you staring at my wrist?"

"That bracelet you're wearing—it's moving!"

Sheila glanced down at herself and laughed. "That's just my Mickey Mouse watch."

She had to say *Mickey Mouse watch* in English, of course, and Darian gave her a blank stare. "Magic," he said at last.

"It's not magic, it's just a way to tell time."

"Tell it what?"

"Very funny. This is a device to let you know what time of the day it is." *Assuming, of course*, she added to herself, *that this world has the same twenty-four-hour day as mine!*

"The sun tells you that."

"Suppose it's a cloudy day?"

Darian grinned and shrugged. "You've got a point. But if that—that 'watch' isn't magic, how does it work?"

"You wind this little knob, and gears turn, and—"

"Yes, but how does it *work?*"

"Well . . ." It dawned on her that she really didn't know; a watch was just one of those things you took for granted. She sighed. "All right. Call it magic."

"Fine!" His grin widened. "You're lucky you found us when you did. When we were stopping for a day, I mean, to give the unicorns a chance to rest. That gives you time to get the feel for riding."

"In only a day . . . ?"

"It shouldn't take longer. They're easier to sit than horses. You'll see."

Darian's voice was casual. *Of course*, realized Sheila. This world didn't have any automobiles or subways or anything like that. Everybody here would take horseback riding very much for granted.

"Now," said Darian cheerfully, "let's see about getting you a unicorn."

Sheila suddenly felt someone watching her, looked up to see Dian staring at her, dark eyes filled with rage. *Great!* thought Sheila. *She's Darian's girlfriend, and now she thinks I'm trying to steal him!* Well, she couldn't worry about that right now. "How do you go about getting a unicorn?"

"Well, you don't exactly. You wait until one of them picks you."

"What happens if none of them wants me?"

Darian looked at her in dismay. "But they will. They must."

Sheila thought about being left here, in the middle of nowhere, and shuddered. "I hope you're right."

"Here, we're far enough away from camp now. Sit."

"Wait, where are you going?"

"I'll be back, don't worry. Just sit."

"And . . . ?"

"And wait."

With a wave of his hand, he hurried off, and Sheila was left all alone. Wondering if this was Darian's idea of a practical joke, she sat. And sat. And sat. It was growing really dark now, and chilly, and she was beginning to realize it had been a long time since she had last eaten. She looked at her watch. Just a few minutes more and she was going to give up on the whole thing and—

Something warm and soft brushed her cheek. Sheila yelped, and something large let out a startled "Whuff!" and jumped aside. Then it moved warily forward again, and the girl held her breath. A unicorn! More than that. This was a lovely young unicorn mare, reaching down to sniff delicately at Sheila's face.

"Oh, you beautiful thing!"

The mare seemed to like that. She pushed gently at Sheila's shoulder, then suddenly folded her legs and lay down beside Sheila, resting her head in the girl's lap.

"Oh. You—you've chosen me, haven't you?"

Wonderstruck, she stroked the silken coat, and the unicorn gave a faint, contented sigh. Even in the fading light, Sheila could see that the unicorn was a lovely creamy-white, with a black mane, tail, and slim, elegant horn. Her big blue eyes were shaded by long white lashes. As the mare got to her feet again, Sheila saw that all four legs were black, too, from hoofs to knees:

markings like that were called stockings, she remembered, on horses anyhow.

"Hey, great!" Darian's voice said suddenly. "This is the sister to my own unicorn, Wildwing. Be nice to her, eh?" he told the mare, who whuffled at him.

"Isn't she beautiful, Darian? But what's her name?"

He laughed. "Who knows what unicorns call each other? You'll have to name her yourself. Don't worry, a name will come to you. Now let's get back to camp or we'll miss dinner. Aren't you hungry?"

All at once Sheila remembered just how hungry she was. "Yes!" she said.

The unicorn leaned her head on Sheila's shoulder, almost as though she was saying "Don't go," and Darian grinned. "All right. You too!" he told the mare.

The unicorn nodded her head vigorously and whinnied at them. Darian and Sheila burst into laughter and laughed all the way back to camp.

Finding a place to sleep, Sheila learned, was a simple thing on such a clear night. You merely found a level spot, curled up in your cloak, and closed your eyes. She was tired enough to be glad not to have to move any more today. But sleep was another matter. For a long time she lay staring up at the night sky. Without any pollution or street lights to interfere there seemed to be more stars than she had ever seen: the sky was blazing with light. It was incredibly beautiful. But something about it wasn't quite right. . . .

Oh no! Sheila thought. All at once she knew. Dr. Reit had taught her the constellations, but she didn't recognize any of the star patterns she saw now. The stars blurred as Sheila's eyes filled with the tears she had held back all day. But she was here, however far away "here" was, and she would just have to make the best of it! She wiped her eyes with the corner of her cloak. Besides, she had that lovely unicorn mare to think about.

Have to find her a good name, Sheila thought.

She shut her eyes.

And this time she slept.

Sheila groaned. Was it morning already? It didn't seem possible. But birds were singing loudly, and people were moving about all around her, doing things that seemed to make an awful lot of noise and shouting a lot. Sheila groaned again, reluctant to open her eyes, every muscle aching. She'd been camping before, but there was a big difference between sleeping in a nice down sleeping bag and having only a cloak between you and the ground. The hard, cold, bumpy ground—

A sudden snort made her open her eyes with a start. Something large was standing between her and the brightening sky, and for a moment, heart racing, she thought of fearsome monsters. Then the creature gave a friendly horsy little whicker, and Sheila laughed.

"Oh, it's you."

The unicorn mare snorted again, and Sheila smiled. Beyond the spiral of her horn glinted the last star of early morning.

"Why, that's it! That's your name. Morning Star. Do you like it?"

She giggled as the unicorn tossed her head as if nodding in agreement. Sheila got to her feet, stretching, trying to get her muscles to limber up. After a moment she became aware of eyes on her, and realized that all the others in the camp were watching her, almost as though she were some kind of exotic animal that might do something dangerous.

Great. They still think I'm a sorceress. And they're scared of magic.

Pelu was sitting nearby, toasting something over a small fire, looking as calm and settled as though she had been awake for hours. "Good morning," Sheila said to her with a determinedly cheerful smile, and was a little relieved to see the young woman return the smile. Pelu, at least, wasn't scared of her. Or not so it showed, anyhow.

"Good morning, Sheila. Come have some breakfast."

"Yes," added Darian, stopping by Pelu's side. "And then, Sheila, you can start learning how to ride."

"And to use a bow," Kara joined in.

"And a sword," said Illyria. Sheila looked dismayed. "I *told* you it wasn't going to be easy, didn't I?"

It wasn't.

Sheila stood next to Morning Star, looking up at the unicorn's back. It seemed impossibly far away. "How do I get up there?" she asked Darian plaintively.

The boy gave her a puzzled look. "We found you a spare saddle. What more could you want?"

"Stirrups, for a start!"

"Stirrups?" He echoed the unfamiliar word carefully.

"You know, sort of loops that hang from the saddle. You put your foot in one to help you climb on, then keep both feet in them while you ride."

"Whatever for?"

"Well . . . to keep you from falling off, for one thing."

Darian shook his head impatiently. "You don't fall off that easily. Look, all you have to do is vault onto a horse's back, and then just sit his gaits. It isn't difficult."

"Maybe not for *you*!" muttered Sheila. "All right, here we go."

She took a running start, made a graceful leap—and smacked right into the unicorn's side. Morning Star gave her a reproachful look.

"Sorry."

On her second attempt she leaped a little higher—and found herself dangling foolishly half on, half off the unicorn's back.

"Darian! Help!"

But he only cheered her on. "That's it! You're getting it."

"Oh, I am, am I?"

She gave a mighty heave, lost her balance, and slid back down to the ground in a heap.

"Oh, rats!"

Gritting her teeth with determination, she got to her feet, backed off, gave a mighty leap up—and found herself sailing right over Morning Star's back, landing with a thud on her backside. The unicorn turned her head to watch, and Sheila could have sworn she was laughing.

"All right," she said grimly. "One more time."

She leaped. For a moment she was hanging on for dear life— and then she found herself sitting astride Morning Star! Sheila laughed. It was so high up here, but so wonderful! She could feel the warm strength of the unicorn under her, and the long black mane felt like silk in her hands.

"I did it! Hey, Darian, look. I did it!"

"Sure." He grinned at her. "Now you only have to learn to ride."

By the end of her first lesson, Sheila was so stiff she could barely slide from Morning Star's back.

"But I stayed on," she told the unicorn, hugging the glossy neck. "I stayed on at the walk and the trot and even the canter!"

"So you did," said Kara calmly. "Now let us see if you can handle a bow as well."

"Handle it," said Sheila a little later, when they were standing before a makeshift target made out of some straw tied into a rag. "I can't even *draw* your bow!"

That actually got a faint smile out of the grim Kara. "I thought you might have trouble. Don't feel bad about it, though; it's an expert's weapon, after all. Pelu can't draw it, either. Let's try something else. Hey, Dian! You and Sheila aren't that far apart in size. Lend her your bow."

Dian glared at Sheila. "Just don't go putting any spells on it," she said.

"Hey, I—"

But Dian had already stalked away.

"All right, Sheila. Pay attention. We don't have any blunt target arrows with us, so we'll have to use the real thing. I don't like the idea, but . . . Come, you hold the bow like this."

The lesson came pretty close to being a disaster. Sheila, who had thought her arm was strong enough, found out that holding a fully drawn bow was very different from throwing a softball to first base. As hard as she tried to keep her arm steady, something always went wrong each time she loosed an arrow. The first one dropped right off the bow. The second shot straight up into the air. The third missed the target altogether and landed in a tree. Kara was very plainly holding in her temper, keeping her voice just a little too calm and quiet. But when the fourth arrow shot off at a wild angle, making the other women dive for cover, the archer shook her head.

"Looks like the bow just isn't your weapon," she said with great restraint. "Well, try once more. *Carefully* this time!"

Shaking, all Sheila did this time was shoot down the target.

"Give me that!" Dian snatched the bow from her hands, examining it for scratches, then glared at Sheila. "Stick to your spells, sorceress!" she hissed. "You'll never make a warrior!"

That night, too sore and tired to sleep, Sheila silently agreed with her. Oh, Illyria had tested her with the sword, and told her she showed definite promise as a swordswoman, but still . . .

I want to go home! Sheila thought. *Dr. Reit, wherever you are, I just want to go home!*

8

Rivalries

The next day the warrior troop moved on, headed for Campora and the rescue of the captive unicorns. And Sheila, aching in every muscle, went with them. There wasn't any choice. It was either ride with them or stay behind in the middle of nowhere. She endured what seemed an eternity astride Morning Star. She was so sore she could barely stay in the saddle and wondered if she would be able to walk again. When they finally stopped for the night, Sheila almost fell out of the saddle, clinging to Morning Star for support, then sank gratefully to the ground, exhausted.

"Hey, what's this?" It was Myno's rough voice. "Resting? Not yet! We have work to do!"

"Myno, please . . ."

"Come on, lazy girl, up!"

And Sheila forced herself through the agony of a rigorous workout with the sturdy ex-slave, running, climbing, lifting. At last it was over. Myno dismissed her with a disapproving shake of the head, and Sheila gladly began to sit down once more.

"Oh, no. Not yet." It was Illyria, looking down at her with a wry smile. "Come, girl. Take up your sword."

Groaning, Sheila obeyed. No wonder Illyria had said that many women couldn't endure a warrior's training! She wasn't so sure *she* could endure!

But if she failed . . .

Dian expected her to fail. In fact, Dian *wanted* her to fail! Sheila pictured the smug look on that dark-eyed face and clenched her fists in anger.

Sorry, Dian. I don't give up so easily.

Just because of that, Sheila vowed, just because Dian thought she was nothing but a—a weak little girl, she *refused* to fail! She *would* become a warrior.

Even, thought Sheila wearily, *if it kills me!*

Gradually, much to her amazement, things began to get better. After two days of misery Sheila found herself feeling quite at home on Morning Star's back, even without stirrups. No longer aching with every jolt, Sheila realized she could keep her balance easily even when the high-spirited young unicorn threw in a good-humored buck or two.

Things were getting easier when she was on foot, too. One amazing day she actually found herself outracing Myno, and not even panting—well, at least not too much.

"Good," the ex-slave told her. "Very good!" and gave Sheila an encouraging slap on the back that nearly knocked the wind out of her.

As time went on, Sheila really began to look forward to the lessons in swordplay she received from Illyria. At first, of course, the woman would easily knock aside the girl's weapon, rapping her sharply on her shoulder or chest. But little by little it dawned on Sheila that the grace and speed needed to be a good swordswoman weren't all that different from the skills needed to be a good third baseman. Once she realized that, she picked up fencing moves so swiftly that both she and Illyria were delighted.

At last the day came when Sheila was able to hold her own in a duel for so long that Illyria called a halt, grinning, and said:

"At first, I admit, I had my doubts about you. But—here, Sheila. This was Darian's sword until he outgrew its grip. It's a good blade. Wear it with honor. You are a warrior after all!"

The days that followed passed in a blur for Sheila. To her secret wonder and delight, she no longer spent her time exhausted and aching. And when she chanced to catch sight of her reflection in a pool, she was stunned. Who was this lean, hazel-eyed girl? She recognized herself only by her freckles! Fat had disappeared, re-placed by hard muscle, and though her skin had burned painfully in the hot sun at first, now it had tanned to a smooth golden brown.

Sheila drew back a little, studying herself. Her jeans were hold-ing up pretty well, but her shirt had been patched so many times with so many different colored scraps of material that she looked like a character out of a fantasy tale.

Well, I am! she realized with a shock.

Gone was the soft city girl. In her place, Sheila realized with some pride, was a strong young warrior-woman who could ride all day and do what needed to be done without complaint. She rested a hand on the sword hanging at her hip and smiled.

Of course, the heroic life still left a lot to be desired. Just once it would be nice to sleep on something softer than the ground. And as for provisions: well, at least clean drinking water was no problem. The power of Goodness was so strong in the unicorns that all Quiet Storm had to do when they came to a pond or stream was touch his silver horn to it, and the water instantly be-came sparklingly clear.

Too bad my own world doesn't have unicorns! thought Sheila sadly.

But even with clean water to drink, the problem of food remained. There was little to eat save what the warriors happened to catch along the way: rabbit and lizard mostly.

Sheila had to stop herself from daydreaming about cheeseburgers and ice cream . . .

But at least the others were beginning to treat her as one of them, almost as a friend.

All of them except Dian, of course. She continued to be hostile, until Sheila cornered her at last.

"All right, Dian. I've had just about enough of this. I don't hate you. Why do you hate me?"

The other girl gave her a contemptuous look. "I don't hate you."

"Oh, no. You just go out of your way to try to make me feel like—like something you want to step on! Look, Dian, I'm not stupid. Every time you see me, you either glare at me—particularly if I dare to crack a joke with Darian!—or talk to the person next to me as though I'm invisible!"

"I don't know what you're talking about. Excuse me. I have to go take care of my unicorn."

"Dian!"

"All right! I don't like you. You don't like me. Let's just leave it like that."

Sheila sighed. As Dian stomped away, Sheila thought, *Spoiled brat! Before I came, you were the youngest. Everyone babied you. But now I'm here, and you're so-o-o jealous!*

Well, that was just too bad. From now on, Sheila decided, she would simply ignore the girl, and that was that.

But it wasn't so simple. The next day, while Sheila was running with Myno, a loose rock rolled into her path, sending her sprawling.

"An accident," Myno told her, but Sheila, rubbing a scraped knee, wondered.

*   *   *

The day after that Sheila and the others were tying the tents onto one of the pack horses when the rope she was pulling suddenly snapped in two; all the carefully packed bundles came tumbling down on top of her.

"An accident," Pelu assured her, but Sheila realized that the women were watching her uneasily.

Great. Now they're wondering if I'm a jinx!

There didn't seem to be much she could do about it.

The next day Sheila was with Morning Star, trying to groom the playfully fidgeting mare, when a furious Illyria came storming up to her.

"What do you think you're doing?"

Sheila blinked. "Grooming Morning Star. Why—"

"Here you've been after me to give you something important to do. Fine! I told you to go out with Kara and Nanine on a scouting mission this morning. But they couldn't find you! What are you doing here?"

"But—you never—nobody told me—"

"Don't try to lie to me! I sent Dian to tell you—"

"Dian!"

"Yes! I sent her on the mission instead of you!"

"But, Illyria, you don't understand. Dian never said—"

"Are you trying to put the blame on her?"

Sheila sighed. "No." What good would arguing do? It was just her word against Dian's, after all.

Oh, Dian, Sheila thought, *somehow I'm going to get you for this!* But how?

She found out that afternoon, when it dawned on her that everyone in the camp was surreptitiously watching her. Did they know Dian was to blame for what had been happening? Were they testing Sheila to see how she would react?

And just where *was* Dian? Suddenly suspicious, Sheila decided to find out. She wouldn't have gone very far from the camp, not by herself with night coming on.

Wait a minute. What was that flicker of motion, there in the shadows? Sheila pretended not to notice, but she knew . . . that was Dian, all right, holding what looked like a saddle girth.

Sheila straightened. *I'll say it is! It's Morning Star's girth! I'd know that weave anywhere! I'll bet Dian's up to no good!*

Carefully Sheila stalked forward as she had been taught, moving silently as a cat, till she was right behind the other girl.

"What do you think you're doing?" she asked coldly, and was delighted to hear Dian actually scream with shock.

"Oh . . . I . . . found this lying around, and—"

"And you were picking it up with your knife? Oh, come *on*! What were you really doing? Cutting the girth just enough so it would snap? So I'd go tumbling off Morning Star and make a fool of myself?"

"No!" Dian drew herself up haughtily. "Besides, there's no mark on the girth. You can't prove a thing."

Sudden inspiration made Sheila laugh. "Oh, I don't have to," she said, trying to make her voice sound cold and mysterious. "The spirits will do that for me."

"I—I don't believe you."

"Have you forgotten I'm a sorceress?"

"You don't have any magic, not any powerful magic!"

"Don't I? Apologize now, Dian—"

"I won't!"

"Then the spirit voices will get you—*tonight!*"

She shouted the last word. Dian gasped, and fled.

The night was still and calm. The only sounds to be heard were the faint chirpings of insects. The camp slept. And then . . .

"Dian. Waken, Dian."

The voices were shrill and ghostly.

"*Dian. We call to you. Waken.*"

The girl sat up with a gasp. "Who . . . who are you? Where are you?"

"*We were summoned,*" whispered the voices. "*You know by whom. We were summoned from the Other World. We are here for you, Dian.*"

"N-no. Go away."

"*We are coming to get you. We are all around you.*"

"No! Don't—"

"*We are coming closer . . . closer . . . We are HERE!*"

At that, Dian screamed in sheer terror. The others jumped wildly to their feet. Swords flashed. And amid all the confusion, Sheila stood up calmly and switched off her cassette player. The "ghostly" voices she had recorded stopped immediately. She smiled sweetly at Dian.

"I *did* warn you," Sheila said calmly.

There was a moment of startled silence. And then all the camp burst into laughter.

"Well done, Sheila!" called Pelu. "Oh, well done!"

"Clever, indeed," said Illyria. "But I think we've had enough of feuding between you two. Sheila. Dian. Come here, shake hands and have an end to it."

Triumphant, Sheila held out her hand. Dian hesitated, then turned and rushed off into the night.

Illyria sighed. "She'll be back. All right, everyone. The excitement is over for the night. Go back to bed."

But Sheila couldn't sleep. The memory of Dian's hot, hating eyes remained in her mind. And she couldn't help but wonder, had she just made a very bad enemy?

9

The Rescue

As the days passed, Dian made a point of avoiding Sheila, turning away whenever she saw her, pretending to be very busy whenever Sheila happened to come near.

Well, that's just fine with me, thought Sheila.

Still, she couldn't help but wonder if this truce meant that Dian was plotting some sort of weird revenge.

Never mind, Sheila decided. *I'm not going to worry about it!*

After all, things were getting far too interesting for her to waste time thinking about a silly spoiled brat. Now that the warrior-women had finally accepted Sheila as one of their group—though they were still wary of her magic—she was learning a lot of fascinating stuff. Pelu was teaching her the names of the proper herbs to heal a sword cut or a sprained ankle. Myno was showing her all sorts of tricks: like how to toss a dagger into the air and catch it neatly by the hilt. And even haughty Nanine was unbending enough to tell Sheila some of the exotic tales of gods and heroes from her homeland far to the south.

The land had gotten more interesting, too. They had finally

left the last of the grassy plains behind and were climbing through a maze of thickly wooded hills and meadows so lush with grass that those unicorns who weren't being ridden frolicked, tails in the air, like a bunch of colts, trying to decide what to eat first. Sheila giggled.

"They look so silly!"

Illyria smiled. "They certainly do." She glanced at Sheila, who was sitting easily on Morning Star's back, one leg hooked comfortably over the pommel of the saddle as though she was riding sidesaddle. "Be careful. Don't forget she's a living animal, not some overstuffed chair."

Sheila patted the unicorn's silky neck. "Oh, she wouldn't even think of bucking me off. Would you, girl?"

Morning Star flicked an ear back to listen to her, and snorted as though in agreement.

"You miss the point, Sheila. This is the sort of terrain snakes and bears love, but that unicorns, like horses, don't like."

"Smart unicorns!" said Sheila, patting Morning Star again. She didn't notice Dian watching her. If she had, she might have seen the girl's eyes brighten at the mention of snakes. But Sheila had no warning at all for what was to come next.

They were climbing a steep, rocky stretch, a tangled forest of bushes on their right, the land falling away on their left, down to a wooded ravine through which a wild river roared its way.

It was Pelu's turn to act as advance scout. "Come on," she called down. "We're almost at the top. And things level out nicely up here."

"Fine," said Illyria. "We'll be able to give the unicorns a chance to catch their breath."

It got a little confusing, as those who reached the plateau first hurriedly dismounted, trying to leave enough room for the rest of the troop. Sheila, nearly last because she had let Morning Star stop for a quick bit of a tasty shrub, was still sitting the unicorn when she saw Dian spring to the ground ahead of her and snatch something out of a bush. A *snake!* Sheila realized in horror.

And Dian flung it right in front of Morning Star! With a squeal of terror, the unicorn shied away in one violent leap. Sheila lost her balance completely and went flying!

The cliff! I'll fall all the way to the river—I'll die!

But strong arms caught her just in time, pulling her away from danger.

The arms belonged to Darian. "Are—are you all right?" he stammered.

She nodded, too dazed to do more than look up at Darian, whose eyes were warm with concern, and realized that it wasn't at all unpleasant to be held by such a handsome boy. . . .

Then her senses returned, and Sheila scrambled to her feet. "You—you saved me. I don't know how to thank you."

He reddened. "I didn't do it for a reward."

"I know, but . . . ah! Here. I want you to have this."

Quickly she unfastened her watch and handed it over to him. Darian's eyes lit up. "I will cherish this magic gift forever!"

"Oh, Darian, it isn't magic, really it's—"

But by now they were the center of the whole worried troop of warriors, all of them asking at the same time: "Are you hurt?" "Is everything all right?" "Did you break anything?"

"I'm fine, really," Sheila began, "thanks to Darian. I—" But then she saw a white-faced Dian standing to one side and shouted at her, "You! What sort of a stupid—"

"I—I didn't mean any harm!" the girl stammered. "I only—"

"Didn't mean any harm!" echoed Illyria grimly. "You could have killed her! If she had fallen just a little farther to the left, or if Darian had been just a little slower to react . . ."

Dian's eyes widened in horror. "I never thought . . . I only wanted . . ." Her voice rose hysterically. "Don't you see? It's all *her*

fault! Everything was fine until *she* joined us! You think she's so
sweet, so innocent—ha! She's bewitched you all with her magic!
Well, I'm going to put a stop to it, right now!"

Sheila's backpack had slipped off in her fall. Dian snatched it
up and went racing madly down the steep, wooded slope toward
the rushing water.

She's going to throw my pack into the river! thought Sheila.

She hurried after Dian, scrambling down the steep embank-
ment, slipping and sliding down the crumbling earth, getting
scratched and snagging her clothes on thorns and branches, stub-
bing her toes on rocks. Once she tripped over a root and nearly
tumbled all the way down.

"Dian! Don't!"

The roar of the river drowned her out. Dian was all set to hurl
the backpack into it, so Sheila lunged at her, grabbing for the
pack. The two girls struggled fiercely there on the river's edge.
Sheila tore her pack out of Dian's hands. But the other girl, kicking and hitting, wasn't giving up. Part of the bank crumbled under her feet and splashed into the river during the fight, and
Sheila gasped.

"Dian, stop it! There isn't room—"

"Sorceress! I don't care!"

She swung wildly at Sheila—and the earth gave way completely! With a scream of terror, Dian plunged into the raging
river!

"Dian!" Sheila threw herself down on the bank, reaching out as
far as she could over the water. "Give me your hand!"

"I—can't! The—the current's too strong!"

Struggling desperately, Dian was swept downstream, white water breaking over her head again and again.

She's going to drown! Sheila looked frantically up the embank-
ment, but the others were just beginning to make their way down

to her. They would never get down in time! *I've got to save her! But—how? If I go in there, I'll drown, too!*

She wouldn't panic. She refused to panic. Heart pounding painfully, Sheila stared downstream. That tree . . . it hung way out over the river. If only it was sturdy enough!

There wasn't time to worry about it. Sheila raced to the tree and shinnied out onto a branch. Ugh, it was slimy, and slippery from waves hitting it. Sheila gasped as the cold water struck her, too, and held on with all her strength. She would have only one shot at this. Here came Dian . . . a little farther . . .

Now!

Clinging to the branch with one arm and both legs, Sheila grabbed wildly for the girl. Her hand snagged something—Dian's tunic! In the next moment Dian's hand had closed about her wrist, and Sheila began to carefully work her way back down the slippery branch. It was creaking—it was going to break!

Not yet! she pleaded with it. *Oh, please, not yet!*

But suddenly arms were reaching for her, drawing Sheila and Dian to safety.

"It's all right," said Illyria quietly. "It's over."

Dian, gasping for breath, stared at Sheila. "You . . . saved my life."

"I guess I did."

"Why?"

"You're kidding, right? I wasn't going to let you die over a—a backpack! Which reminds me . . ."

She scrambled back along the bank to where the pack had fallen and gladly slipped it into place once more, then rejoined the others. Dian was still staring.

"Thank you," she said grudgingly.

"Gee, I'm thrilled by your enthusiasm."

"I said thank you. What more do you want?"

Sheila sighed. "I was kind of thinking of friendship. But forget it. I'll just settle for a truce."

"Good enough," said Illyria. "Come, let's get you into some dry clothes."

But as they climbed wearily back up, a shadow crossed Sheila's face. She craned her head back and gave a little cry of surprise.

"The eagles! The giant eagles! They're back!"

Illyria nodded curtly. "They've been following us ever since— ever since we started this mission. They almost seem to be trying to protect us. And who are we to argue with them?"

She smiled. But for a bewildering instant Sheila saw sorrow, sheer heartbreaking sorrow, on the woman's face.

And she wondered.

10

Illyria's Story

They traveled on through the rugged region all that day, till Sheila was sick and tired of hills. Every time Morning Star came to the crest of one, Sheila sat as tall as she could in the saddle, hoping to see something new. But each time all she saw was yet another ridge before her.

"But there *is* something different now," she said to Pelu, who was riding beside her, "something about the air." The girl took a deep breath, then nodded. "Salt. And fish. Ocean, that's it. I could swear I'm smelling the ocean."

"You are." Myno's voice was grim. "Campora's harbor lies on the coast just beyond the last of these hills. We haven't too much farther to go."

Campora. Suddenly Sheila felt a chill run up her spine. Up to this moment she had almost completely forgotten the real reason for their journey, caught up as she was in learning the skills of warrior-women. But this wasn't any simple little crosscountry pleasure trip!

Campora. The girl thought of the tyrant of that city, the

59

Emperor Dynasian, and winced. Judging from the stories she had heard from Myno and the others, he sounded very much like someone she never wanted to meet. And what about Mardock, his sorcerer?

Sheila shivered again. Magic was real here. It worked. Oh, everyone might think she had powers of her own, but it was all just a game! If it came down to a fight between her and Mardock . . . how could she, with only things like a—a harmless flashlight to help her, ever hope to defend herself against an honest-to-goodness evil sorcerer?

Maybe it won't come to that, she told herself. *Maybe we'll be able to find out where the captive unicorns are held and free them without having to fight anyone.*

Sure. And maybe Superman would fly down out of the sky to help them.

Morning Star was sidling nervously under her, and Sheila forgot her own fears and concentrated only on calming the mare. Now that she noticed it, all the unicorns were uneasy, snorting and prancing, for as long as the wind blew from the sea—and Campora.

"They sense evil," murmured Pelu softly. "They do, indeed."

Knowing their goal was so near, Illyria pushed her troop on without pause all the rest of that day, her eyes cold, her face grim. As the sun began to slip behind the ridges to the west and twilight came on, she still showed no sign of wanting to stop. Sheila brought Morning Star up alongside Quiet Storm, who was as uneasy as the rest of the unicorns, and cleared her throat cautiously.

Illyria didn't respond.

"Uh . . . Illyria? If we don't stop soon, it's going to be too dark to see where we're going. We'll get stuck halfway down this hill, without any place to camp."

"We'll camp." The woman's voice sounded distant. "There's a little valley, right down there."

There was. But by the time the troop reached it, it was too dark to do anything more than unsaddle the unicorns and settle down for the night as they were. Sheila thought back on all that had happened that day, from the adventure at the river's edge, to all the riding they had done, and sighed wearily. Her eyes closed. Before she knew what was happening, she was asleep.

Sheila came awake with a jolt, staring blankly up into the night sky ablaze with stars.

What . . . Was I dreaming?

She thought she heard a voice calling plaintively. . . .

Silence.

It must have been a dream.

Sheila closed her eyes, only to open them again at the sound of a groan. Now, *that* was no dream. Or, rather, it wasn't *her* dream. Illyria, asleep beside her, was moaning, tossing restlessly about. She murmured a name, "Egael," and Sheila was shocked to see tears glint on her face.

She's having a nightmare. Guess I'd better wake her up.

"Illyria?" Sheila said softly, not wanting to wake up everybody else. "Illyria."

When the woman didn't stir, Sheila reached out gingerly to give her a gentle shake. And that woke Illyria up, all right! The woman came springing up with a warrior's trained reactions, flinging Sheila aside. The next thing the girl knew, she was lying flat on her back, Illyria's knife at her throat!

"Hey! It's only me, Sheila."

After a tense second recognition flooded Illyria's eyes. Fully awake, she slid the knife back into its sheath.

"Don't ever, ever do that again, Sheila," she said softly. "I might have killed you."

"Sorry. It's just . . . you seemed to be having such a bad dream, I thought you would want to get out of it."

Illyria sagged wearily. Her braids had come loose during the night, and sitting there as she was, surrounded by the long, silvery-blond waves, she looked much younger than the fierce warrior-woman of the daytime. *Why, she can't be more than . . . oh, maybe nineteen or twenty!* Sheila realized in surprise.

"Yes," said Illyria after a moment, "it was a foul dream. Thank you. Go back to sleep now, Sheila."

She pulled her cloak about her, looking so unhappy that Sheila couldn't obey. "You called out a name," she began hesitantly. "Egael."

Illyria flinched but said nothing, and Sheila continued:

"Isn't Egael the name of the man you once helped?"

Illyria glared, as though angry at her for prying. But as fast as it had come, the anger faded. Head drooping, Illyria sighed and nodded. "I see Pelu told you part of my story," she said slowly. "Now let me tell you the rest and get it over with. It began simply enough, a pleasant spring day, Darian and I out riding for our pleasure. . . ."

When we first found the injured man, he lay so still I felt certain he was dead. And a part of me wept inside at that thought because, even with the bruises of his beating on him, he was still so young and handsome that my heart sang. But then Darian cried:

"He's still alive! I saw his chest move!"

The two of us struggled to bring him safely down to my father's house. It . . . was a fair, comfortable home in those days, clean and neat and smelling sweetly of hay and herbs. A fine place to tend a wounded stranger.

He woke soon after I had bathed him and tended his injuries, his eyes the piercing eyes of some wild thing. "Don't be afraid," I told him. "You're among friends."

"You must know—I must warn you—" he gasped, then fell back into an exhausted sleep, leaving me full of sudden unease.

Nor was I any more at ease when the stranger woke again after a time and told me his story:

"I am . . . call me Egael," he said. "And, as I see you have guessed from my accent, I am not from these mountain lands. I am a wanderer, seeing something of the world. But I made a mistake, a bad one: I insulted the soldiers of Dynasian. Ha, your reaction tells me that you've heard of *him* even up here in the countryside."

Egael's tone was light, but his eyes were ablaze with a fierce, barely controlled rage. Just then, they weren't the eyes of a common wanderer at all.

"And what did I do that was so terribly insulting," Egael continued, "me, a man afoot, while they were riding so proud and fine up there on their steeds? I didn't step aside quickly enough to suit them. I didn't grovel deeply enough in apology. So they beat me and left me for dead." Those fierce, handsome eyes burned into mine. "And dead I would have been, lady, alone and wounded as I was, after a night without shelter out there in the chill of the mountain air, if it hadn't been for you. All my gratitude to you."

"Hush," I told him. "Enough talking for now. Rest."

But when he closed his eyes once more, I was more troubled than before. A man who had drawn down the wrath of Dynasian's soldiers on himself might draw it down on us, too. Our village was isolated enough to have had little to do with the emperor or his men, and after hearing some of the horrible tales of Dynasian's cruelty that were filtering out of distant Campora, I wanted to keep it that way.

And I doubt that he's just a simple wanderer, I told myself. *His way of speaking is too fine for that.*

Egael. What manner of name was that? I had rescued a mystery man, indeed. Surely I should turn him out and be done with him!

And yet . . . Egael was so handsome . . .

More practically, to throw him out now, before he was strong enough to take care of himself, would almost certainly mean his death.

So Egael stayed, and healed with great speed that was almost supernatural. And a miracle blossomed between us. I'm not even sure when I first realized the truth of it, but—though our time together was all too brief, though I knew nothing about him, and he knew little about me, Egael and I fell in love.

But then one night I awoke to the sound of a door slamming. I knew in an instant that he had left, as suddenly and mysteriously as he had appeared. "Egael?" I called, then again, "Egael! Where are you?"

I ran outside into the night, searching wildly, calling his name—

Fruitlessly.

Egael was gone, gone as totally as if he had never existed. And only the wild, lonely cry of an eagle answered my call.

And as I stood in the moonlight crying for my lost love . . . Quiet Storm appeared. Almost as if he had been sent to comfort and help me.

Illyria stirred restlessly and the spell of her words was broken. Sheila knew the rest of the story.

"And the giant eagles?"

"As I've told you. They've been following us at a distance ever since we set out to free the unicorns that Dynasian has imprisoned."

Illyria turned away abruptly. Sheila stared at her, shaken. Sheila had felt the stirrings of romance already; she had enjoyed being held by handsome Darian, for one thing. And once, pretty much by accident, she and a boy at school, tall, shy Steve, had kissed. But Illyria's continuing love for Egael was stronger, finer, more romantic than anything Sheila had ever dreamed.

She's still looking for him, the girl realized. *She's still seeking him everywhere she goes.* "I hope you find each other," she told Illyria softly.

"What's that, Sheila?"

"Oh, nothing."

But to herself she added silently, *I hope you and Egael get to live happily ever after.*

11

Campora at Last

As the troop of warrior-women rode on, the scent of the sea grew ever stronger. If Sheila listened carefully and the wind was right, she was sure she could make out the distant sound of waves. And surely those birds soaring by overhead were gulls, just like the ones at home.

Home. With a pang of guilt, Sheila realized she hadn't thought about her own world for days. *This* was the real world now; that other one of homework and softball games, that place without magic where she was only Sheila McCarthy, schoolgirl, seemed more and more like a dream.

But just then Morning Star gave a nervous little buck, jarring Sheila out of her bewildered thoughts.

"Hey, easy, girl! Nothing to be afraid of."

Morning Star wasn't alone. All the unicorns were growing more and more uneasy with every step they took.

"They've caught the scent of their captive friends," said Nanine. "And of Mardock and his evil sorcery, I think."

Illyria nodded. "Even Quiet Storm is nervous. I doubt the unicorns will let us ride them much farther."

"Well, we're not that far from the city now, are we?" asked Sheila.

"Not far at all." Myno's eyes were dark with memory. "I should know," she added under her breath. "I escaped from Campora over these hills."

Sheila winced at the bitterness on the ex-slave's face. Poor Myno! How she must have suffered! "Well," Sheila said with forced cheerfulness, "we could hardly ride the unicorns right down Campora's main street, anyhow."

Myno only grunted. Sheila tried to think of something else to say to rouse the woman out of her unhappy memories. But just then Morning Star reached the top of one particularly steep hill, and everything Sheila was going to say went flying out of her mind. All she could do was sit her unicorn and stare.

The land fell sharply away from where they paused, sweeping away to the rolling sea which glittered sapphire blue in the sunlight, a blue sea dotted with ships bearing wide sails of bright white, and yellow, and red. At one point the land curved in to form a wide harbor. And there, where sea met shore, stood a city that could only be Campora.

Sheila gasped. Maybe the capital of the empire wasn't as large as New York or Chicago, but—oh, how beautiful it was! Campora was a confusing mixture of sweeping walls and elegant palaces, graceful towers, domed pavilions and buildings with so many columns that they reminded her of pictures of Greek temples she had seen. All the city seemed to be made of marble, or at least of some type of smooth, sleek stone that gleamed white in the sunlight. Ornamental traceries of gold reflected the bright light back again, till Sheila, dazzled, had to blink and look away.

"It—it's like something out of a fairy tale!" she breathed.

"Sure," muttered Myno grimly. "From up here. Down there, thanks to Dynasian the usurper, that pretty fairy tale turns into a horror story."

Sheila stared at her. "What do you mean?"

Myno shrugged. "Where do I start? Only those with a lot of gold live comfortably there. And even they, the nose-in-the-air aristocrats, can't relax altogether. They never know when Dynasian may decide one or the other of them is a traitor, fit only for the executioner's ax. As for the poor—well, it's not difficult to wind up poor in Campora, because even those with only a few copper coins to rub together still are taxed heavily by Dynasian. He has to find *some* way to pay for his pretty games."

"Games?" asked Sheila warily.

"Why, gladiatorial games, girl! Man against man, man against beast, to the death, all for the amusement of the emperor. And those who can't pay his taxes wind up sold on the market block as slaves."

Something in Myno's eyes told Sheila that that had been her fate. Sheila shivered. "I—I see."

Myno grunted. "The only people who wander Campora's streets freely are robbers and beggars—until Dynasian's soldiers round them up, too—for the games."

And we're going in there? Sheila thought wildly. *To get the unicorns away from Dynasian?*

Heart racing, she fought a fierce battle with the panic that was screaming to her to drop everything and run for her life. But running wasn't going to solve anything!

Sheila braced herself and calmly took stock of her condition. Her jeans were still in pretty good shape, although they were ragged in some places and patched in others. Her shirt, though, was so shabby and stained that even a punk rocker would have scorned it. She glanced around at the others.

They didn't look much better. Only Illyria and the elegant Nanine had ever had anything like full armor. The others wore whatever unmatched bits and pieces they had been able to pick up along the way, though Kara had managed to add some turquoise ornaments, and Myno did wear a few pieces of bright copper. There were a few other brave attempts at beautification. But beneath those weatherbeaten leather scraps of armor and ragged cloaks, nobody seemed to be wearing anything that didn't have at least five patches. Even Illyria's once-elegant red tunic had been mended to the point where the sleeves were now barely long enough to cover her shoulders. They looked like beggars themselves.

That's it! Sheila thought. "Robbers and beggars, eh? Well, we may not be robbers, but we're certainly dressed like beggars! We shouldn't have any trouble getting into the city."

"Some of us," Illyria corrected. "The smaller the group, the less attention we're likely to attract. We'll split up. Yes," she said over the chorus of nervous comments, "we will split up. Myno, I'll need you with me; you know where to find the royal stables. And Sheila, you will be coming with me, too. I know you're still an apprentice sorceress, but if we have the misfortune to run into any of Mardock's spells, you just may know how to cancel them."

Sheila almost choked. "But I don't—I can't—"

"I might have known you'd be afraid," said Dian contemptuously. "Illyria, take me with you instead. *I'm* not afraid!"

"Then you're foolish," Illyria told her shortly. As Dian stared, openmouthed with shock, the woman continued. "I want you and Pelu to stay with the unicorns. Try to get them down to the beach if you can; if we're cut off on land, we still may be able to make a break for it by sea."

"Assuming, of course, that we can convince a herd of frightened unicorns to board a ship," murmured Pelu wryly.

"As for you, Kara and Nanine," said Illyria, "and—yes, Darian, you, too, I haven't forgotten you—you're to wait."

Darian frowned, disappointed. "Wait? Just wait? How long?"

Illyria stared hard at the city. "It should take us a day to get into Campora, another day to find the captive unicorns. . . . Give us three days' grace. If you haven't heard from us by then, I want you to forget about us—"

"No!"

"Yes, brother. Forget about us and try to rescue the unicorns."

She looked at them all. "Any questions? No? So be it. Remember this, my friends, for the sake of the land and everyone on it: Whatever else happens, those unicorns must be freed!"

As Sheila went off with Illyria and Myno, her thoughts were fixed on Campora and the dangers of their mission. She did not look back at Darian and the others who waited with the unicorns.

"I still don't like this," Darian said as he watched Pelu and Dian prepare to drive the unicorn herd to the sea.

Pelu sighed, sitting her unicorn comfortably. "I know you don't. I don't either. But your sister usually knows what she's doing. And with any luck at all, we'll all be back together again— with the unicorns—soon enough. Till then, good luck to you, Darian, Kara, Nanine. Dian, let's go."

Pelu and Dian hadn't ridden very far before Dian gasped. "Pelu, look! The eagles!"

"You've seen them before, Dian."

"Not this close!"

Pelu glanced up and gasped in spite of herself. The great birds *did* seem to be diving right toward them.

"They're curious, that's all. Come now, Dian, you've seen them at fairly close range before."

But Dian was staring up into the heavens. "Look out!" she screamed, and whipped out her sword.

Deadly beaks gaping open, sharp talons outstretched, the eagles were attacking! Pelu hastily drew her own sword, wondering how two swordswomen were going to be able to beat back so many winged attackers. Their fierce screams rang in her ears, the wind from their wings buffetted her, but every time she tried to strike at an eagle, it managed to fly up, just out of her reach.

It—it's almost as though they're trying to keep us from leaving, the woman realized, *almost as though they're herding us!*

Just as she thought this, the leader of the eagles, a magnificent, fierce-eyed bird, shrieked out a sharp cry.

Now, that sounded like a command! thought Pelu, wondering.

It was. All the unicorns, including those she and Dian were riding, turned as obediently as trained ponies, despite the warriors' frantic protests, and trotted nicely back to where Kara, Nanine, and Darian stood stunned, their mouths open. Kara grabbed her bow, hastily fitting an arrow to the string. She drew the bow—

And a unicorn gently pushed the weapon aside with his horn.

"I—I don't believe it!" the archer gasped.

"Believe it," Pelu told her dryly. "Come on, Dian. Better dismount. I don't think we're going anywhere just yet."

The eagles continued to circle, skimming so low that the wind they raised stirred the manes of the unicorns. But now there seemed to be a definite pattern to the way they were moving.

"It looks almost as though they were trying to tell us something!" exclaimed Nanine.

"Campora!" cried Darian suddenly. "That's it! They want us to go to Campora!"

"We don't know that for certain," said Pelu. "What about Illyria's orders?"

"These eagles, or whatever magical birds they might be, have followed us all along to be sure we accomplished the mission. They know something about what's happening in the city and they're trying to tell us. They're telling us to go to Campora and help Illyria rescue the unicorns!"

To the women's surprise, the eagles all screamed in unison at that, as though they were trying to say, *Yes! That's it!*

"I . . . think I'm beginning to believe this," said Kara slowly.

Pelu nodded. "The eagles *have* been mixed up in this from the beginning. And I can't believe they're creatures of evil." She sighed. "Well, are we all in agreement? Yes? Then, Campora it is." Half in jest, she turned to the unicorns who had been following them. "Here's where we say good-bye, my friends. We can hardly take you into the city with us."

To her astonishment, the unicorns snorted, nodded their heads as though they understood exactly what she was saying, and galloped happily off into the hills. Only Quiet Storm and the other unicorns the warriors had been riding remained, prancing nervously.

"Ah, it's kind of you to stay," Pelu told them uncertainly, wondering just how much human speech unicorns did understand. "But what are we going to do with you? Any unicorns who enter the city are going to be in danger."

"Not if they don't enter as unicorns," said Nanine slowly. "In my land, we have all sorts of festivals involving masquerades. Wait, now . . ."

Her deft fingers began weaving long grasses together into something that looked like a long, hollow pyramid. "With your permission," she said to Quiet Storm, and slipped it on over his horn, tying the cone in place with more strands of grass. "There! As long as he keeps his cloven hoofs hidden in the dust, he can pass as nothing more than a white horse wearing a unicorn disguise!"

Quiet Storm snorted, tossing his head uneasily. He caught sight of his reflection in a small pool and stared. Then he turned sharply away, obviously insulted, and the women laughed. "Sorry, my friend," Pelu told him. "But you're going to have to put up with being just a horse, at least till we free your mistress."

Nanine was quickly plaiting disguises for the other unicorns. "But what about us?" she asked. "What are we supposed to be?"

Pelu looked down at her ragged self. "Why, poor wandering actors, of course! What else? We'll be . . . Ha, I have it! From now on, friends, we're the Marvelous Magical Unicorn Troupe!"

Illyria had been right, Sheila thought wearily. It *had* taken the three of them a full day to reach Campora by foot. At least they really did look like beggars now, dusty and travel-stained as they were, armor and weapons hidden under their tattered cloaks.

She craned her head back, staring up and up at the massive city wall, seeing the guards patrolling the top of it. As far as Sheila could tell, the only way into Campora was through those huge, heavy gates of what looked like gleaming bronze. The gates were guarded by grim, spear-bearing soldiers in bronze-studded armor.

"Are they going to let us in, just like that?" Sheila asked uneasily.

Myno gave a short, sharp laugh. "Of course not. Campora has enough beggars of its own!"

"Then how . . . ?"

Myno glanced up at the sky. "Nearly sundown. That's just about the time of day we want. See the crowds all around us, all headed toward the city? There'll be a storm of people pretty soon, all trying to get in before the gates are shut for the night." She grinned. "The guards aren't going to have time to check everybody too carefully. And that's how we'll get in."

It was, indeed. The merchant who brought his cartload of goods into Campora never noticed the three figures who slipped silently out of the back of his cart and stole away into the night-dark streets.

Sheila glanced eagerly around. Despite the danger, she had been looking forward to her first glimpse inside this exotic city. What wonders might there be? After all, there'd been such a wild mixture of costumes and languages in the crowd making its slow way through the gates! Peeking warily out of the burlap sacking under which she had burrowed in the merchant's cart, she had caught glimpses of men and women and children of all colors and types, from poor farmers clad in simple brown or gray tunics, to wealthy folk barely visible through the heavy silk coverings of their elegant litters borne by sweating slaves.

But now that night was here, there was nothing to see but a maze of unpaved streets, smelling unpleasantly of horses and drains and things Sheila didn't want to think about, faced on either side by whitewashed houses with barred, shuttered windows. Everyone but the three warriors seemed to have vanished up those streets or into those mysterious houses.

"Campora, here we are!" whispered Sheila. "Now what?"

Illyria tugged the hood of her cloak farther forward to hide the glint of her silvery hair. "Now," she said, "we find the stables and hope that the unicorns are there."

"*And* hope we can get 'em out without rousing Dynasian's whole army," muttered Myno. "Come on, let's get this over with."

It was an eerie walk. The moon had risen, casting a cold, silver light over the quiet city, making the empty streets look like something out of a horror movie, Sheila thought. The warriors kept to the shadows as much as possible, walking as warily and silently as cats. But then, all at once, a hand snaked out from an alleyway! Sheila gave a little shriek as it closed about her arm and pulled her into darkness.

"Eh, what have we here? A girl!"

Oh, great! thought Sheila, seeing the glint of a knife. *A Camporan mugger!*

"C'mon, Raggas, what've you caught?"

Muggers, corrected Sheila, *a whole gang of them!*

She couldn't get to her sword in the cramped space, so instead she brought her knee up sharply and got the thief right in the pit of the stomach. As he doubled up, gagging, Sheila managed to pull her sword free, just as the other thieves tried to rush her. Illyria and Myno joined her, steel flashing in the moonlight.

"Swords! They've got swords!" hissed one of the thieves. "Run!"

"No, fool! Only nobles carry swords. That means they've got gold, too! They're just women. Get 'em!"

As one ruffian rushed Illyria, she skillfully parried his thrust, his long knife sliding up the blade of her sword with a painful screech of metal, till the two hilts locked. For a tense moment Illyria and the man strained against each other, breath hissing with the strain, each trying to tear the weapon out of the other's grip. Then, with a mighty effort, Illyria uncoiled her arm and sent the thief staggering back.

"You—witch!" he cried, and made another rush at her, knife raised. Illyria lunged. Sheila winced and turned away as the shining sword pierced flesh. She heard the man shriek, and looked back just in time to see Illyria quickly pulling her weapon free from his crumpled form.

"'Just women'?" Illyria asked wryly. "Come, fools. Come and die."

But suddenly there was a wild commotion from the street behind them. "The guards!" yelled one of the thieves. "Let's get outta here!"

"Good idea!" muttered Myno. "But there's no place to run. The guards are all around us!"

Trying not to panic, Sheila glanced up and gave a little cry of relief. "Look! Those balconies should hold our weight."

Illyria nodded. "Hurry!"

Scrabbling frantically, trying not to make any noise, the three warriors climbed up and up, all the way to a slippery tiled roof.

"Down!" hissed Illyria, and they lay flat, watching the guards searching the streets below.

They didn't see us! thought Sheila in relief. *We're safe!*

"Myno," said Illyria softly as the baffled guards dispersed, "aren't those the stable roofs I see, over there?"

Myno nodded, and Illyria grinned, her teeth flashing white in the darkness.

"How conveniently close together the houses all stand. I see no reason for us to risk our necks down there . . ."

"When we could be risking them up here, instead," whispered Sheila.

"All right, let's try it," Illyria ordered.

As the guards continued to patrol the streets, the three warriors moved silently over the rooftops, leaping lightly from house to house, till at last they had slid over the stable wall down to the ground again. There in a large, well-guarded corral were—

"Unicorns!" breathed Sheila.

She started forward, but Myno caught her by the arm. The three warriors huddled in shadow against a wall as a new squadron of guards approached to relieve the men on duty. The new guards were full of gossip, and the three warriors stole forward to listen. What they heard filled them with horror.

"Too bad about the unicorns."

"Yeah. Pretty beasts. Feels good just to be around them. Too bad they have to die."

"It's that Mardock's fault." The soldier dropped his voice to a wary whisper, looking nervously about him. "Encouraging Dynasian to make pacts with King Kumuru of Samarna."

"Kumuru of Darkness, you mean. Everyone knows he worships the Dark Gods! What does Campora need with the likes of him?"

The first soldier shrugged. "Kumuru has an army. Dynasian wants to join it to ours and conquer the world. It's not our affair."

As they strolled past the spot where the three warriors were hidden, the second soldier, the man who liked unicorns, muttered, "Not our affair, no. Not our affair that to seal the alliance,

Dynasian's going to send half that pretty herd to Kumuru in the morning—for sacrifice!"

As the soldiers disappeared beyond the stable wall, Illyria straightened. "Sacrificing unicorns to the Dark Gods! I never imagined that even Dynasian would stoop so low!"

"We've got to free them!" gasped Sheila.

"What a pity you won't succeed," said a smooth, sly voice.

As the warriors whirled in shock, a shadow seemed to move forward out of darkness. It wasn't a shadow, Sheila realized after the first, startled moment. It was a man—tall, lean, handsome in a cold, harsh sort of way—clad in elegant, silky, black robes. His long hair and beard were black, too. And his eyes were as hard and cruel as ebony.

"Mardock!" cried Myno.

"Ah, I see you know me," the sorcerer purred. "How flattering. Especially since I shall be the last person you see before you die!"

With that, he raised his arms, the wide sleeves of his black robes fluttering like the wings of some terrible night creature. Sheila stared in sheer disbelief as she saw blue lightning flash and crackle about him. But then she heard Mardock begin to murmur twisted, ugly, alien words. And though she couldn't understand them, she knew that this was the beginning of a spell—a spell that would mean her death!

12

Trapped!

The dark power of the building spell held the three women stunned and helpless.

As *though we're stuck in glue!* thought Sheila. But even though she couldn't move, she could still use her brain. Her mind raced wildly, trying to come up with some way to fight back. As soon as the spell was finished, it would be the end of the three of them, she knew it, but she couldn't think of a thing. Already the air seemed so thick . . . it was so difficult just to breathe . . .

No! I'm not going to give up! There's got to be something I can do!

"Uh . . . wait!" she called to the sorcerer. "You mustn't do this!"

Cruel humor flickered in Mardock's eyes. With a commanding wave of his hands, he held the growing force of magic in check. "Why not, little fool?"

"Because—because . . ." Because *why?* Sheila hadn't the vaguest idea of what she was going to say next. But she had better keep talking, because Mardock's patience wasn't going to last forever. "Because I—I have some magic, too."

"Do you?" mocked the sorcerer with a sneer.

"No, I—what I mean is that I'm a—a sort of an apprentice. Of science."

Mardock frowned at the unfamiliar word, puzzled. "Science?" he echoed warily.

"Yes." Sheila hurried on, "I—I work with Dr. Reit on things like the Molecular Acceleration Transport Device."

Mardock blinked, confused by what must have sounded to him like alien sorcery, indeed. "Small magics," he said after a moment, but he was plainly bluffing. "My spell cannot be held in check much longer. What are you trying to say, girl?"

"Well, I . . . I've seen Dr. Reit's science. But your sorcery is the most amazing I've ever seen!" *True enough*, thought Sheila. *After all, I've never seen any sorcery!* "I—I might like to learn it, too."

"Indeed."

The cold black eyes stared at her as if trying to pierce right through her mind. Sheila desperately tried to keep her thoughts a blank. She had read a story somewhere about a man who kept someone from reading his mind by reciting the multiplication tables.

Let's see now . . . one times one equals one, two times two is four, three times three is . . . is . . . I can't hold him off much longer! Three times three is—

"Clever child!" said Mardock, and the terrible pressure vanished from her mind. "Oh, I could break you easily enough. But why bother? Besides, you just might make a cunning apprentice. Come here, girl."

"Uh, not—not yet. First let my friends go."

"So that's the game, is it? Fool! The first thing a sorcerer learns is that he *has* no friends! Forget those two. Come to me and you shall live—but only if you watch them die!"

Sheila swallowed, her throat dry, aware of Illyria and Myno staring proudly ahead. They weren't going to beg. She must make her own decision. If she went over to Mardock's side, she would be safe. But . . . to see Illyria and Myno die . . .

"No," Sheila said, amazed at the steadiness of her voice. "Sorry, Mardock. I can't do it. I'm not going to let them die."

"Then die with them, fool!"

And he began the black chant anew. As Mardock's evil magic flashed and crackled about him, Sheila's thoughts circled and circled, and kept returning to: What do you fight darkness with? Light, of course, but—

Light! Sheila gasped as the idea struck her.

Yes! I've got it!

It was a slim chance, but it was the only chance they had. She began rummaging frantically through her backpack, her fingers feeling hopelessly clumsy and slow. Mardock was concentrating too hard to notice her movements.

Where is the thing? Where is it?

Out of the corner of her eye, Sheila saw Illyria fighting off the heaviness of the building magic, then with a groan of effort, draw her sword and lunge at the sorcerer. But before she could reach Mardock, she was thrown violently back against a wall, the weapon flying from her hand.

"Now," hissed the sorcerer, "you all die!"

At that very moment Sheila's hand closed about a familiar object. With a triumphant cry she pulled it out of her pack and flicked a switch—

"Aagh!!" Mardock cried out in shock as the flashlight's beam blazed right into his eyes! The blue lightning of his spell dissolved into nothingness as he staggered back, clawing at his face, terrified of this new, alien magic.

"Come on!" whispered Sheila. "Let's get out of here!"

She started backing warily away, holding the sorcerer transfixed by the beam of light. A little farther, now, and she could just turn and run. . . .

But suddenly the flashlight's light flickered.

Oh, no! thought Sheila. *Not now! Please, not now!*

The light flickered on again. And then it went out. Sheila shook the flashlight. "Come on!" she cried. But nothing happened.

"I knew I should have put in new batteries!" the girl wailed.

The three women raced for their lives. Expecting at every moment to be struck down by some terrible sorcery, Sheila risked a quick glance back over her shoulder. Mardock, hand over his dazzled eyes, was in no condition to cast a spell. Yet. They just might make it—

But the light and noise had attracted guards! Their bronze-studded armor clashed loudly as they hurried after the three warriors, swords flashing in the moonlight. But a cloud suddenly covered the moon, and all at once it was too dark to tell friend from foe. Sheila stifled a hysterical giggle as she heard one guard yelp and shout at another guard who had just accidentally jabbed him right in the backside. It really wasn't funny, not when she realized the next wild swing of a sword might get her.

"Don't kill them, you fools!" came Mardock's angry shout. "Just stop them! Surround them!"

Sheila bit her lip in terror. How were they going to get out of here? All around her were dimly moving shapes—where were Illyria and Myno?

"Sheila!" It was Illyria's tense whisper. "This way!"

The woman caught her hand, pulling her toward safety—

Too late. In the confusion Myno made it to safety; but just at the wrong moment the moon came out from behind the cloud, pinning Sheila and Illyria in a silvery spotlight.

"There they are!" someone shouted.

Before they could move, the two warriors were surrounded by guards, a circle of deadly spearheads pointed straight at them.

"Put down your swords," said a grim voice.

Illyria sighed. "One of the important lessons in becoming a

warrior," she told Sheila, as calmly as though they were alone, "is knowing when to surrender."

They were dragged through the streets of Campora, up a steep, winding hill. The houses on either side grew more elegant with every step, set back from the street, surrounded by high walls. Through ornate ironwork gates Sheila caught glimpses of tantalizing marble pavilions, magnificent gardens, and palaces. She wasn't surprised that the most splendid palace of all stood on the very crest of the hill. It was a huge building. Buildings, really, thought Sheila, staring—a collection of them all joined together, each one built in a different style. Some had steep, peaked roofs covered in many-colored tiles, some had golden domes, and there were even a couple that seemed to consist mostly of columns. All the buildings were of gleaming white marble covered with bizarre, elegant carvings showered in gold.

But this was no time for sightseeing. She and Illyria were pushed roughly forward through the front gates and down a long pathway lined with grim-faced statues and paved with slippery marble. At the end of the path a guard rapped three times on a huge bronze door. It swung silently open on well-oiled hinges; they entered a large room, bright with candlelight reflected off gold, silver, and gems that encrusted the interior. On a dais, at the far end of the room, a man lounged idly on a crimson and gold brocade sofa. He was wearing the ugliest, most wildly colored silk robes Sheila had ever seen. The guards led the warrior women toward him. When they were a foot from the dais, the guards forced Sheila and Illyria to their knees and stood with swords drawn all around.

This must be Dynasian, Sheila realized with a shiver. The emperor sat upright slowly, studying his prisoners lazily through a small crystal lens on a golden chain. Despite the danger, Sheila felt disappointed.

This was the terrible Dynasian? She had expected a tall, dark, majestically evil figure. Dynasian was rather short, and fat, and balding, clutching his gaudy robes about him with a clumsy hand. His eyes were small and piggy, nearly lost in the folds of his pudgy face. But when those eyes met her gaze, Sheila knew fear as if for the first time. They were gray as ice, cold and hard, and absolutely without pity. Suddenly Dynasian wasn't the least bit funny.

"Mardock?" The emperor's voice was high-pitched and nasal. "Why do you disturb me? Why have you brought these two dirty females to me?"

Mardock moved smoothly to his master's side, murmuring. Sheila caught the words *unicorns*, and *thieves*, and thought, *Uh-oh.*

Dynasian's face darkened.

"So! You would try to steal my unicorns, would you?"

"They aren't *your* unicorns." Illyria's voice was calm. "They belong to no one."

"Impudent wench," Dynasian spat.

"You don't understand. Haven't you noticed the signs of dawning disaster on the land? The scanty rains? The diseases?"

"Nonsense."

"It's truth, Dynasian. The unicorns aren't merely pretty beasts. They're living symbols of Light. Let them wander free as they will, and Campora will prosper. Keep them prisoner, and this city and all your kingdom will die."

The emperor frowned. "Do you dare to lecture me, woman? The beasts are mine, and I shall do with them as I will!"

"Sacrifice them, you mean? Dynasian, if you sacrifice the unicorns to the Dark Gods, you won't be gaining something as simple as a military alliance!"

"What do you mean?"

"Sacrifice symbols of Light to the Dark Gods, and you open a path for them into Campora!" Illyria's voice broke. "Oh, don't you

84 The Secret of the Unicorn QueenTHE SECRET OF THE UNICORN QUEEN

see? Dynasian, think! Kumuru's Dark Gods are demons! You'll be laying Campora open to evil beyond mortal comprehension!"

"Enough!" The single word was sharp as the crack of a whip. The emperor looked Illyria and Sheila up and down through his crystal. "Skinny things." His voice was as calm as though Illyria had never spoken. "Hardly worth the thought." He gave a casual wave of his hand. "Take them away, Mardock. Throw them into prison."

The sorcerer murmured something in his master's ear, and the fat man smiled coldly. "Why, yes. I agree. They will make fine participants in the games. Take them away!"

How nice of them to give us a moonlight tour of Campora, thought Sheila dryly, staring up at a grim, dark, ugly building that looked like some crouching monster in the night.

"Dynasian's prison," said Illyria shortly, and was slapped by one of the guards.

"No talking!"

"Gently," purred Mardock. "Don't hurt them. Yet."

Illyria and Sheila were forced down a dark, dank stairway, bare stone walls oozing moisture on either side. The sorcerer followed, picking his way delicately, holding his elegant black robes tightly around him to keep them from being soiled on the filthy steps. He watched, a smug smile on his saturnine face, as his prisoners were thrown into a small cell.

"Foolish little would-be sorceress," he sneered at Sheila, "and you, warrior-woman, do you see now how stupid it was to challenge my might?"

"*Your* might?" taunted Illyria. "You are nothing more than Dynasian's pet dog, sorcerer."

For a moment his eyes blazed with insulted rage. *Don't get him mad!* Sheila pleaded silently with Illyria. *I don't want to end up as a—a cockroach!*

But then the anger faded from Mardock's eyes.

"Did you think to enrage me enough to receive a swift death? Oh, no. You must wait your turn to die. Don't worry," he added mockingly. "You won't be here for long. The games start tomorrow. And you haven't a chance of winning. I shall see to that."

With that, he turned and swept out of the dungeon, followed by the guards. As Mardock's footsteps faded away, Illyria and Sheila were left alone in the heavy silence. Sheila looked about and shivered. There was nothing in the cell but a pile of moldy, foul-smelling straw. The door was of heavy iron, locked and bolted. The one window was little more than a crack in the thick wall. And the stray beam of moonlight that found its way into the cell only made it seem even more dark and damp.

They were trapped.

13

The Ghost

As soon as she was sure they were alone in the cell, and the jailor had wandered far enough away down the hall, Illyria sprang to her feet. As Sheila watched in bewilderment, the woman began going over every inch of their prison.

"No one could get through that crack of a window," she muttered. "No one in human form, that is." Illyria stopped, giving Sheila a speculative glance. "I don't suppose you know how to shape-shift?"

Sheila shook her head. "Sorry."

Illyria sighed. "I thought that might be too advanced a spell for a mere apprentice. Oh, I don't mean that as an insult! You just need a few more years of training, that's all, with the master sorcerer, Dr. Reit."

"Dr. Reit," murmured Sheila. All at once it hit her. They were trapped in this awful place. And tomorrow they were going to die! Sheila wrapped her arms tightly about herself, trying to hide her trembling, and bit her lip as hard as she could to keep from bursting into tears. She was never going to see Dr. Reit again, or her family and friends, or—

"Don't look so sad, Sheila! We're not lost yet." Illyria went back to searching the cell. "That was a brave thing you did back there, standing up to Mardock like that." She hesitated. "You weren't *really* thinking of joining him, were you?"

"No!"

"I thought not. After all, evil sorcerers have a tendency to sacrifice young apprentices who show too much ambition."

Sheila gulped. "I—I didn't know that."

"Mm-hmmm. Don't want those apprentices getting too uppity, you see, making dangerous pacts with demons, threatening their master—but you wouldn't know about things like that, since Dr. Reit's magic is good, not evil."

"Well, it's science, not sorcery," began Sheila, then hastily added, seeing Illyria raise an eyebrow, "but it's good."

The woman nodded and calmly continued her search. "Stone walls . . . good mortar between the blocks . . . stone floor . . . good mortar there, too. Too bad."

"I don't understand."

Illyria gave her a quick, rueful grin. "If the mortar were old and crumbling, we could lift one up and dig our way out."

"Dig? With what? They disarmed us."

Illyria grinned again. "Not quite," she said, and drew a thin little dagger from her boot. Letting the knife slide back into the hidden sheath, she shrugged. "It's better than nothing. But, curse it all, the door's solid, too, and well bolted. The hinges are on the outside, where we can't get at them."

She sank to the floor beside Sheila, tapping an impatient finger on the stone. "What about you, girl? Do you think you could work some manner of spell to get us out of here?"

"My—uh—magic backpack is out there with the guard," Sheila reminded her sadly.

"Ah." Illyria let out her breath in a long sigh. "At least Myno got away. And the others are free, too. They'll be able to help the unicorns. Even if we—Sheila, if it comes down to this, that we must enter the games, we still have a chance to help Campora, even if we die. Don't flinch, girl. I know it's a cruel choice for you to have to make, but hear me out.

"If we do enter the games, Dynasian is going to have to give us some sort of weapons. When he does, I mean to leap up to Dynasian's box and put an end to him. Do you think you can do the same to Mardock?"

"I—I don't know," said Sheila frankly. "I'll try."

"Brave girl! Then, even if we die, we die cleanly under the swords of the guards, knowing we've rid the land of two tyrants. Agreed?"

Sheila shuddered and nodded.

Silence fell. Sheila thought about the games and shuddered again. What if Illyria was wrong? What if she and Sheila couldn't reach Dynasian? They would have to take part in the games. There wouldn't be a choice. Would those games be anything like the ones she had read about in school, the ones the ancient Romans held? Was she going to have to fight trained warriors? Or beasts? Or . . . Mardock had promised she and Illyria wouldn't survive. Did that mean they were going to have to face something worse? Something that Mardock might summon from the Darkness just for this purpose?

"We aren't going to get out of this, are we?" she asked Illyria faintly.

"What's this, girl? Fear? Hey now, I've been in worse places than this!"

"How?" asked Sheila faintly.

"Ha, once I was in a situation where I didn't have a chance. Listen to this: I was climbing a mountain, looking for some lost sheep. Halfway up, it got really steep. I slipped and I slid, and I nearly fell all the long way down to my death. I was so high up that mountain that the clouds were below me! But the sheep were somewhere up above me, so up I went, watching each handhold carefully. All at once I heard this horrible roar above me and glanced up to see a *lyros*—Do you know what that is? No? It's a sort of mountain wolf, as big as a pony, with fangs as long as my arm. And it's always, always hungry.

"Well, this ravening *lyros* was standing right there on the ledge where I was just about to climb, just waiting for its dinner to come into its gaping jaws. And there I was, hanging on by one arm, wondering if I hadn't better forget the whole thing and go back down. But then I heard a hideous roar from just below. I glanced down and there, on the ledge below me, was a huge, ugly, mean-as-a-winter-storm cave bear, taller than a man and hungrier than anything but a *lyros*."

Illyria paused reflectively. "Picture that. There I was, hanging from one arm from the side of a mountain. I couldn't go up, because the *lyros* was waiting. I couldn't go down, because the bear was in the way. Now, have you ever heard of a worse predicament?"

"No!" Sheila waited eagerly for Illyria to continue. But the woman merely set about sorting through the moldy straw. "Ah—Illyria?"

"Smelly stuff. But some of it isn't too filthy. At least it should be better than sleeping on bare stone."

"Illyria!"

"Yes?"

"The story! Finish the story! How did you get out of that mess?"

"Oh, I didn't," the woman said blandly. "The bear ate me."

Sheila stared at her for a moment, then burst helplessly into laughter.

"That's better," Illyria said with a gentle smile. "Never give up, girl. Remember that. Now, come, let's try to get some sleep."

Sleep! thought Sheila in amazement. *How could I possibly ever fall asleep?*

But she obediently closed her eyes. She could at least rest, or try to rest . . .

Even if she couldn't sleep . . .

Sleep . . .

"Sheila . . ."

Sheila frowned. Here she was, having such a lovely dream, all about riding Morning Star through a flowery meadow. Why was this ghostly voice trying to intrude?

"Sheila . . ."

Go away, she told it. *Leave me alone.*

"Sheila . . . where are you . . . ?"

The voice wasn't going to go away. In fact, it was getting stronger and stronger—

Sheila came awake with a start, to find Illyria staring at her. "You hear it, too," said the woman.

"You mean, the voice is real? I wasn't just dreaming? And—and it wasn't you calling me?"

Illyria shook her head.

"Then who . . . ?" began Sheila uneasily.

"Sheila . . ." came the faint voice again. "Can you hear me?"

The girl tensed. "Wait a minute," she said slowly. "I know that voice . . . Dr. Reit! It sounds like Dr. Reit!"

"The sorcerer!" gasped Illyria.

"Can you hear me?" the voice repeated, more loudly this time.

"Yes!" Sheila cried joyfully. "I do! Dr. Reit, I hear you, but I can't see you."

There was a faint whirring sound, a crackling of electricity. Dr. Reit's voice muttered something that sounded like ". . . turning up the voltage . . . wait . . . aha!"

Illyria cried out in shock and shrank back against a wall, gasping, "Sorcery! High sorcery!"

A figure, shimmering and ghostly, was forming in the cell . . . a man's tall figure, dressed in a white laboratory apron and crowned by a mop of wild white hair. Sheila gave a soft laugh of relief.

"Don't be afraid," she whispered to Illyria. "It's Dr. Reit!"

"Sheila?" The scientist ran a hand through his hair, staring about him in bewilderment. "Are you all right?"

"Yes, yes, but—"

"Where is this place?"

"Shh! The guards will hear you!"

"Guards?" Dr. Reit looked about once more. "Why, Sheila, what have you been doing? This seems to be some sort of prison cell!"

"That's because it *is* a prison cell!" Sheila whispered. "Oh— don't go!"

"I'm trying not to go," he said apologetically. "But the power surge I've been able to create just isn't stable." He sighed. "Look at this. It's wavering all over again. I can't seem to get enough of a charge stabilized to let me materialize fully, and . . . Oh, dear. Here I go again. Wait a minute now. . . . Let me try . . ."

For an instant he disappeared completely. Sheila waited, chewing on her lower lip, hardly daring to breathe. He couldn't just vanish, not now, not when she'd started to hope!

There was a flicker of light, a faint crackling of electricity. And suddenly the ghostly figure of Dr. Reit was there in the cell with them once more. "I'm afraid the charge isn't going to last much longer, no matter what I do. I'll have to work on it some more. Quickly, now: Is there anything I can do?"

"Yes!" Sheila whispered frantically. "Get us out of here!"

"Oh, my dear girl, I wish I could! But the power surge is already starting to fade. . . . I don't know how much longer I can hold it before . . ."

His ghostly figure was starting to flicker and dissolve.

"Dr. Reit!" cried Sheila. "Please, don't leave us here. . . ."

In her misery she had forgotten all about whispering. "Hey, what's all the fuss?" came the jailor's rough voice.

And a sudden idea struck Sheila. "Help!" she screamed. "This—this cell is haunted!"

"Now, what sorta garbage are you trying to—"

"Come here! Look for yourself!"

The man peered into the cell, and his dirty face paled. He gasped in horror at the sight of Dr. Reit's slowly dissolving, shimmery, eerie figure. "Gods! You—you're right! I'm not hangin' around here!"

"Hey! You can't just run away!"

"No, no. I'm gonna go get help."

"No! Wait!" If he ran off now, she and Illyria might never have another chance. "You can't leave us here!"

"That's right," cut in Illyria. "Mardock will be furious if something happens to us. Do you want to be the one to tell him his precious prisoners were slain by a ghost?"

He hesitated, shaking. "Don't want a sorcerer mad at me," the man muttered, "not Mardock. The way he looks at you with those cold eyes, like he's figurin' which demons would like to eat you . . . Gods! He's worse than any ghost!"

Just then the last shimmer of Dr. Reit's figure winked out, trailing a haunting cry of: "I'll be back, Sheila, I promise!"

"You heard him!" Sheila cried to the jailor. Wait a minute! Dr. Reit had been speaking English, of course, and the jailor couldn't have understood him. The girl translated hastily, "He said he's coming back for me! Hurry! Get us out of here before it's too late!"

"Uh . . . yeah." The jailor fumbled with his keys, dropping them, mixing them up. "Right. Here we go. No tricks now!"

"Of course not," said Sheila innocently. She stepped meekly out of the cell, then froze, eyes wide, staring down the corridor. "Oh, no! Look! The—the ghost!"

The man whirled with a cry of terror. And Illyria calmly hit him on the back of the head with her clenched fists. As he fell limply to the floor, the woman and Sheila exchanged a fierce grin.

Together they dragged the unconscious jailor into the cell and locked the door. "Come on!" Illyria whispered. "Let's get out of here before someone notices he's missing."

Sheila scooped up her backpack and hastily shouldered it, then followed Illyria warily up the narrow stairway. The moon had set, and it was so dark in the dungeon that they had to carefully feel their way up every stair.

What if someone's at the top? What if Mardock's just waiting for us and—No! I'm not going to start scaring myself!

Just the same, she was glad when they reached a level floor once more. There was some light here, from flickering torches, and Sheila started forward, only to be dragged aside by Illyria.

"What—"

Illyria held a finger to her lips and pointed. There, in a small antechamber, amid a pile of other weapons, lay their swords.

"But there are two guards in there!" whispered Sheila.

They were seated at a small table, engrossed in a hot game of cards, but there was something about their hard-eyed faces that made the girl suspect they would leap to their feet, spears ready, at the first move she or Illyria made.

"I don't suppose you just want to forget about the swords?" asked Sheila hopefully.

"No! We'll need them."

"Yes, but—"

"Hush. Listen."

Hurriedly, Illyria whispered a plan in Sheila's ear. And after a moment Sheila grinned.

Wait till I tell Cookie about this, thought Sheila.

She moved forward so that the guards could see her. Neither one so much as glanced in her direction.

"Ahem."

No reaction.

"I said: *Ahem!*"

Both guards jumped. The cards went flying as the men snatched for their weapons, staring up in surprise.

"A girl!"

"Help me," Sheila wailed piteously. "Oh, please, help me."

"What are you doing here?" asked one man roughly.

"Please . . ." she repeated faintly, swaying gracefully. "Help me . . ."

"Hey, that's one of Mardock's prisoners!" cried the other guard. "How did she—Get her!"

Quickly Sheila gave a melodramatic groan, raised her hand to her head, and crumpled slowly to the floor. Peeking from under her lashes, she saw the guards hesitate, uncertain. She heard one of them mutter:

"Well, we can't just leave her lying there!"

He came out to kneel at her side . . . and Illyria sprang into action. With one catlike pounce, she struck down the other guard with two quick blows to stomach and head. As the first guard got to his feet, whirling, Illyria was on him, too, knocking him out before he could even yell. As he crumpled, Sheila hurriedly helped Illyria cushion his fall so that his armor didn't clash loudly against the stone floor.

"That was great!" Sheila whispered. "Nobody could have heard a thing."

The two warriors snatched up their swords and buckled on the swordbelts.

"That's better," said Illyria. "Now, let's get out of this place before someone thinks to sound an alarm!"

The corridor they were following fed out into the main hallway, a vast torchlit stone room off of which other prison corridors branched. At the far end of the room was the heavy, barred door that led out of the prison.

Sheila sighed. *As the saying goes: So near and yet so far!*

Between them and freedom was a whole troop of guards. They

were all fully armed. But half of them were lounging about lazily, and the other half were nearly asleep.

"Lax discipline," murmured Illyria in mock horror.

"Sure, but we're still not going to be able to slip past them," whispered Sheila. "And we can't get to the door unless we do. Unless . . ."

Off to one side was a window, a plain, unbarred window. She pointed at it, and Illyria nodded.

"Yes," she whispered. "That opens onto the outside world. But what about the soldiers?"

Sheila began rummaging around in her backpack. "Ah, here it is! I almost forgot I had this."

"More sorcery?"

"Well, no. Actually, it's Cookie's little traveling alarm clock, the one she was using till she got her watch fixed." She realized that Illyria was staring at her blankly, but there wasn't time to explain. "I hate to lose it, but—here goes!"

Sheila tiptoed into another corridor, praying one of the guards wouldn't happen to look over his shoulder and see her, set the little alarm clock carefully, and snuck back to Illyria's side.

"It should go off in about ten seconds . . ." she whispered, "nine . . . eight . . . seven . . ."

Just then the alarm went off, the shrill ringing echoing off the stone walls. The guards erupted into chaos, scrambling to their feet, grabbing for weapons, yelling in confusion. Sheila froze, shaken at how she had mistimed the alarm, realizing how close she had come to getting caught. Illyria grabbed her arm and nearly dragged her toward the window. Sheila shook off her fear and quickly scrambled through it.

For a moment she hung by her arms, afraid to let go. How far was it to the ground? The moon had set, and the dawn wasn't here yet, and the night was *dark!*

"Sheila!" hissed Illyria frantically. Sheila gulped and jumped blindly.

To her relief, it wasn't a long drop. She hit the ground, rolled, and got her feet under her.

"Come on!" she whispered up at Illyria. The woman leaped lightly down beside her.

"We still have to get over the outer wall," Illyria whispered. "But if we can't see any guards, they can't see us, either. Let's go."

Sheila found the wall first the hard way by running right into it in the darkness.

"It's too high!" she whispered in panic. "I can't find the top!"

"I'll help you. Ready . . . jump!"

With Illyria giving her a boost, Sheila jumped with all her might. Her hands closed over the top of the wall, and she pulled herself up on top of it, panting. She heard Illyria struggle up beside her.

It was only moments until the two warriors were letting themselves down on the far side of the prison wall, free again:

"We—we did it!" gasped Sheila.

"And it's about time, too!" said a voice suddenly.

14

Outnumbered

Sheila grabbed frantically for her flashlight. If only there was a little strength left in the batteries . . .

It flickered on for an instant, then died again. But that brief flash of light was just enough for the two warriors to see:

"Myno! You're all right!"

"Of course I am," she said gruffly. "Takes more than a few stupid soldiers to put an end to me. No need to get emotional about it." But she gave Sheila and Illyria a quick, fierce hug. "Let's get out of here. This neighborhood isn't going to be safe much longer."

They followed her in silence, stumbling in the darkness, through a tangle of narrow, foul-smelling alleyways. Once Sheila saw red eyes flash and heard small bodies scurry away. *Rats,* she told herself, *only a bunch of scared rats.* She didn't blame them for being scared. It *was* spooky here, in all this close, smelly darkness.

Myno and Illyria, apparently unafraid, were moving on.

"Hey, wait for me!" Sheila whispered.

Terrified that she would be left behind, she hurried after their forms, slipping and falling into a puddle of what she hoped was only water.

"Oh, ugh!"

However prettily Campora might shine in the sunlight, Sheila thought wryly, Dynasian had a thing or two to learn about some matters. Such as drains!

The two women ahead of her stopped, so suddenly that Sheila, in her rush to keep up, nearly crashed into them.

"Here we are," whispered Myno in triumph. "The main wall isn't too far from here, and we should be able to slip out without any—"

"Wait, Myno." Illyria's voice was grim. "We came to Campora for a purpose. I'm not leaving just yet."

"But Dynasian's whole army is going to be out looking for you!"

"Campora is a big maze of a city. They won't find us that quickly. And in the meantime . . . Myno, take us down to the harbor."

"Oh, come now, Illyria! You can't be expecting us to rescue the unicorns all by ourselves!"

"What choice have we?" asked Illyria quietly. "If we do nothing, the unicorns are as good as dead, and the Dark Gods will rise. We can, at least, try to prevent that."

Myno sighed. "I've been following you all these months. I've seen you risk your neck maybe a hundred times. But this has got to be the most harebrained stunt you've ever—"

"Do you want to leave?"

"Hey, no, I never said that! It's just . . . I mean . . ." Myno muttered something hot-tempered under her breath. "I guess I'm just as harebrained as you two," she said reluctantly. "But I don't like the idea of the unicorns being slaughtered, either. So be it. Come on. Follow me."

Myno seemed to know every alley, every passage, every hole in the wall in all of Campora. Sheila and Illyria struggled on in her wake as best they could.

At least the night's not so dark anymore, thought Sheila hopefully. *It must be nearly morning.*

Wait a minute. If it was nearly morning, that meant they didn't have much time left to save the unicorns!

Suddenly a shrill blare of trumpets split the silence.

"That's got to be the prison alarm!" gasped Sheila. "They know we've escaped!"

"They'll never find us." Myno sounded as calm as could be. "We're nearly at the harbor already, and—"

"By all the gods!" gasped Illyria. "Look at that!"

At first glance Sheila thought it was just a troupe of entertainers, clad in so many wild rags that the phrase "raggle-taggle gypsies-o" flashed through her mind. With them were their horses—

No! Those were unicorns—

No. Those were only horses, with silly, handmade cones tied onto their foreheads to make them look like unicorns, and—

Wait a minute! That handsome boy who was grinning at her . . .

"Illyria! That's Darian, and—and Pelu, and all the rest!" Sheila's heart was pounding! She was a little surprised to see how glad she was to see Darian. Illyria was already hurrying forward.

"Sheila!" crowed Darian joyfully. "Where did—"

"What are you doing here?" Illyria interrupted. "What are any of you doing here? I gave you an order—"

"We know," said Pelu gently. "But when you hear what happened, I think you'll understand."

Sheila looked around nervously, half expecting to see armed guards rushing toward them. "I'm sure it's going to be a fascinating story. But couldn't we find a safer place to talk?"

"Ah. Those alarm trumpets we heard were for you."

"They were," Myno said shortly.

Pelu glanced back at Darian and Dian and the rest of her wildly colorful companions, and grinned. "What better place to hide someone than right in the most conspicuous of places?" She handed Sheila, Illyria, and Myno three ragged, many-colored cloaks. "There, now you look like proper members of the Marvelous Magical Unicorn Troupe!"

"Pelu." Illyria's voice held a note of warning in it. "Your story?"

"Well, we were dividing our troop up, as you'd ordered, when suddenly it happened . . ." and Pelu explained how the eagles had forced them to change their plans.

"We got these rags from a good-natured merchant for whom we performed last night, outside the city gates," Dian explained.

Darian added with a hint of wounded pride, "We thought we were performing a drama. *He* thought we were doing a comedy! So much for our dreams of acting glory! At any rate, as soon as the gates were opened just before dawn, we came in with everyone else."

Illyria gave a soft laugh. "Now, *that* is a truly amazing story! If we all get out of this alive, I do think we had better do some investigating of certain more-than-mere-birds eagles." She glanced up at the rapidly brightening sky. "But we haven't got much time to waste."

Quickly she told the others of Dynasian's plans to send the captive unicorn herd to King Kumuru for sacrifice. As she finished her tale, there were gasps of horror from her listeners.

"How dare he!"

"Sacrifice unicorns to the Dark Gods—never!"

"We can't let Dynasian get away with that!" cried Darian.

"And we won't." Illyria's voice was strong with determination. "Dynasian will surely have his men begin loading the unicorns aboard ship just about now. . . ." She paused, smiling. "Perhaps we ought to let him finish the job."

"What!" burst out Myno. "You mean, we came all this way just to let that tyrant's men up and sail away with—"

"Did I say that?" asked Illyria. "But tell me this: Have any of you had a chance to actually see the ship?"

Darian nodded. "It's a big old thing, with oars and sails. Big enough to hold all the unicorns, I guess, with room left over."

Illyria nodded thoughtfully. "Nanine, you once told me you knew how to sail."

The princess nodded. "My land touches the sea, you know. And even those of royal blood are taught to master the way of ships and sails." She added dryly, "Even those who have the misfortune to have been born female."

"I see." Illyria turned to her brother. "Darian, I have a task for you. It . . . may be dangerous."

The boy straightened proudly. "I'm not afraid! What is it? Do you want me to fight somebody? Challenge the guards and—"

"I want you to take our unicorn friends here down to the dock where the others are being loaded."

His face fell. "That's all?"

"That's enough! You're going to have to convince the guards that you found these unicorns wandering in the city, and brought them to the ship out of loyalty to the emperor." She glanced severely at her brother. "Nothing more than that. No heroics, is that understood?"

"Yes, sure, but . . . do you really want Quiet Storm and all the rest on that ship?"

"I do," said Illyria, smiling faintly. "I do, indeed. My friends, I must say I'm glad you're here. Now let's go save those unicorns!"

The others cheered.

"Fine," muttered Myno. "Instead of *three* fools rushing off to disaster, we've got *seven*!"

Only Sheila overheard her. But she was glad to see that Myno, for all her complaining, moved just as eagerly as everybody else.

*   *   *

The ship on which the captive unicorns were to sail was a huge thing, just as Darian had said, a wide-beamed cargo ship with two banks of oars, a curving prow and stern, and two masts with a confusing amount of sail. It rocked serenely at its dock, while on that dock and the land from which it jutted, all was utter chaos.

The narrow streets rang with noise: the sharp cracking of whips, the cloppings of hoofs against cobblestones, equine screams of fear and anger, and shouts and curses from Dynasian's guards. The guards had taken over that corner of the city, blocking common folk, sailors, and merchants from the plain, whitewashed stone shops and taverns. Even so, the streets were crowded, what with guards and horse handlers—and the emperor's captive unicorns.

None of the guards realized that they were being watched. Illyria and her warriors had moved silently over the rooftops, unnoticed by anybody at that early hour, and were slipping softly down to hide in the shadow of a large stone warehouse.

"All right," whispered Dian eagerly. "We made it. We've got a ringside seat. Are we just going to sit here and watch?"

"Yes," said Illyria shortly.

"But—"

"Hush, now. Use your eyes. There are just too many enemies out there right now. We can't just boldly attack, not seven against an army."

"Now you're talking sense!" muttered Myno.

"But we're not giving up, either. If we can't attack, we'll use stealth, instead."

"Sure, but how?"

"Shh. Here comes Darian and our unicorns."

The warriors watched in tense silence as Darian, the very image of brash youth, sauntered over to the guard who seemed to be overseeing the ship. They couldn't hear everything that was said, but words drifted back to them:

"Guess your men let these unicorns loose."

The guard muttered something angrily.

"They didn't?" continued Darian blithely. "You mean it was an accident?" He grinned. "An accident like maybe too much drinking last night?"

Illyria winced. "Don't improvise, Darian," she muttered under her breath. "Just give him the unicorns and get out of there before he thinks to ask how you're controlling seven unbridled animals!"

Darian did his own wincing as the guard yelled at him. "Okay, okay," the boy said soothingly, "I get it. No drinking while on duty. The unicorns just got out by themselves." He shrugged. "If that's the way you want it, fine. Hey, don't get mad at me! *I* wasn't the one who let them out! Anyhow, here they are, all ready for loading. Long live the emperor and all that."

The unicorns weren't at all happy about being loaded brusquely onto something as unfamiliar as a ship. Quiet Storm rolled an eye back to where Illyria was hiding, as though asking, *You don't really mean this, do you?* But they obeyed, and soon were aboard.

"Now, get out of there, Darian!" murmured Illyria.

But no. He was lingering, plainly asking for a reward. That was too much for the irate guard. He snapped out an order. And then Darian was running for his life as soldiers chased him away. The women waited nervously until at last he managed to elude the men and slip back to join his sister.

"How was that?" he asked, panting and proud.

"Not bad," Illyria said dryly, frowning. Her brother's clever antics hadn't amused her at all. "Now all we have to do is wait till the other unicorns are on board, then create some sort of diversion . . . something to get the guards away from the ship. . . ."

Sheila straightened. "I think I've got just the thing!"

Hastily she whispered her idea to Illyria. "Beautiful, Sheila!" Illyria scanned the area with her sharp eyes. "Yes . . . Do you think you can slip over to that building, the one close to the loading dock, just around that bend in the street? More important, do you think you can get back to us in time without getting caught?"

Sheila hesitated, heart racing. The last thing she wanted was to wind up back in that dark prison! She could feel Dian's unfriendly gaze on her and realized that the girl expected her to fail. But she couldn't fail. Right now she was the only one who could help the unicorns. "Yes," Sheila said firmly.

Illyria clasped her hand briefly. "Then go, now, before any of the guards chance to look this way. When you get there, wait for my signal."

Sheila took a deep breath and summoned all her courage. Then she was off, trying to run down the narrow street without making a sound. The cobblestones were slippery and uneven, and she was sure she was going to fall with a crash that would alert all the guards. Somehow she managed to keep her footing, and reached the house Illyria had indicated without any problems. Quickly, re-membering one of the warrior's lessons she had been taught, Sheila checked for an escape route. . . .

Yes. She could swing herself up on that balcony easily enough, scramble along the roof, and jump down again to regain the oth-ers. Sheila waved to Illyria to show she was all right, then settled down to do the only thing she could right now: wait and watch.

There was a lot to see.

The unicorns weren't making it easy for the guards, not at all. Unlike Quiet Storm and the others, they didn't know that this was all part of a plan to save them. And so they fought every step of the way, terrified and furious, determined not to let themselves be led by these two-legged foes. But the sweating, swearing, equally furious men fought back, dragging them forward, foot by reluctant foot, pulling the ropes tight around the graceful necks and bodies.

The unicorns refused to yield. Sleek white or brown or chest-nut coats were wet and shining with the sweat of fear. Small ears were pinned flat back against lovely heads, and eyes rolled wildly. Now and again a unicorn, screaming in rage, would try to lunge, threatening a guard with horn or teeth. But each time the ropes would drag him back again.

Oh, the poor things! thought Sheila, remembering Morning Star running with the sheer joy of freedom. *I wish I could tell them it's going to be all right!*

The unicorns weren't completely defenseless. As the girl watched, wide-eyed, two of the guards yelped in pain and fell aside, swearing because sharp unicorn hoofs had kicked out and connected. For a second the other guards hesitated, startled at the thought that they, too, might get hurt.

But the men's fear of Dynasian's wrath was far greater than their fear of being kicked. And the slow, struggling procession continued, coming closer and closer to the waiting ship.

When the first of the unicorns stepped out onto the dock, and felt the hollowness under their hoofs, they stopped short, rearing in terror. The unicorns behind them screamed in sympathy and began fighting the ropes with all their strength. Guards were hurled off their feet, falling to the cobbles and wriggling frantically out of the way of flying hoofs. Some of those on the dock lost their footing on the wet, slippery wood and went plunging, splashing and cursing, into the sea.

"More men!" shouted the guards. "Get more men up here! Hurry!"

One by one they finally got the unicorns onto the ship and down into the storage area. Sheila, watching keenly, saw Illyria's hand rise and suddenly drop. The signal!

Okay, here we go!

She pressed a button. All at once the air was split by Michael Jackson singing "Beat It" at the tape player's full volume. Just as Sheila had hoped, the blaring music echoed off the walls. The twisted alleys and streets were like an echo chamber, bouncing the music back and forth along the narrow streets till it didn't even sound like music anymore. It sounded just like the shouts of a whole mob of angry people!

For a moment the guards froze in sheer shock. Then someone cried out, "We're being attacked!" And they all erupted into wild movement, swords out, spears at the ready, searching this way and that.

They can't tell where the music's coming from! Sheila realized.

But the guards' leader was barking out angry commands, and the men were splitting up into companies, each group starting grimly down a different street. One company was headed straight toward Sheila.

Uh-oh. Time to leave!

She climbed up to the roof as she had planned, ran to the end of it, and jumped down to rejoin the warrior-women.

"Well done, Sheila!" whispered Illyria. "But your magic trick isn't going to fool them for very long."

"They've left only a few men on board," said Pelu. "Just as we hoped! All we have to do is reach the gangplank without attracting any attention."

"Sure!" cut in Darian. "Then we can rush the ship and overpower them before they can fight back."

Nanine nodded. "The wind's in our favor. We should be able to cast off and sail safely out to sea before anyone can stop us."

Illyria grinned. "Come on. We have a ship to catch!"

It should have worked. It nearly did work. But just as the women were about to make their rush up the gang-plank, there was a crash and a blinding flash of light behind them.

Sheila whirled, blinking to clear her dazzled sight. "Mardock!" she gasped. "He's found us! And—and he's got a whole army of guards with him!"

15

The Battle

Even as Sheila shouted a warning, Kara drew her bow and loosed an arrow straight at Mardock. But the sorcerer merely raised his hand, murmured a word—and the arrow dissolved in a burst of flame!

"Oh. Well, it was worth a try," the archer muttered.

"Take them!" Mardock shouted to the soldiers. "Alive—or dead!"

With savage shouts the men charged. Quickly the warrior-women formed a circle, protecting their backs, and drew their swords. Blades flashed in an intricate dance, catching the enemy weapons, piercing leather armor and flesh.

Sheila, caught in the middle of all the noise and dust and danger, suddenly found herself facing a fiercely snarling soldier. She stared in shock as he loomed over her like a giant, his sword raised. As the heavy blade came plunging down at her, Sheila parried desperately, feeling the impact surge painfully all the way up her arm to the shoulder. She staggered back a step, and the man gave a cruel laugh as he brought his sword up again. And this time

Sheila didn't have room to parry! Instead, she did the only thing she could: she kicked out with all her strength. The guard yelped as her foot connected with his shin, and a laughing voice in her ear said:

"You're getting good at kicking people, aren't you?"

"Darian!"

"At your service, my lady!"

Quickly he moved forward to block the furious guard's attack. Even in the middle of danger, Sheila couldn't help but watch in wonder as Darian, graceful as a dancer, laughing as he fought, beat back his foe. There! The guard was falling back, clutching a wounded arm. But there wasn't any time for hero-worship, because now other foes were pushing forward to take the guard's place.

What about Mardock? Sheila wondered in sudden terror. *Why isn't he just wiping us all out with sorcery?*

She could see Mardock dancing angrily about behind the guards. Of course! He couldn't use his sorcery in such close quarters, because if he did, the force of it would destroy Dynasian's guards as well!

It didn't really matter. More and more of those guards were rushing forward. The unicorns, deep within the ship, hearing the sounds of battle, began screaming in alarm and fury, but they were trapped on board, helpless to come to the warriors' defense. Kara's arrows flew, each one striking down a foe, but all too soon her quiver was empty.

There are just too many enemies! thought Sheila in despair. *We haven't got a chance!*

Was she going to die here, with the morning sun shining down so brightly and the sky so blue? Was she going to die so far from home?

Suddenly a cloud seemed to pass overhead. Sheila glanced wildly up—and gasped.

"The eagles! The eagles are here!"

As the guards fell back in superstitious wonder, the huge birds came plummeting down to land beside the warrior-women. Their forms blurred and altered, faster than thought.

Suddenly they were eagles no longer, but men, tall, stalwart warriors, led by a handsome, fierce-eyed young man whose red cloak blazed in the sunlight. His armor gleamed with gold, and a thin golden circlet held back his long dark hair.

"Egael!" gasped Illyria in wonder.

Egael! thought Sheila. *That's the name of the man Illyria loves. Gosh, he's gorgeous!*

Dynasian's guards, stunned by the sudden transformation, had fallen back, staring.

"Go on!" Mardock prodded. "Fight them, you fools!"

Reluctantly the guards raised their swords. But this time they were facing more than one small band of seven. This time they found themselves confronted by grim, skillful warriors who fought as swiftly with swords and daggers as they had flown as eagles.

"Don't stop!" yelled the sorcerer. "They're only men, they can be slain! Fight them, curse you, fight them!"

I've had just about enough of you! thought Sheila. Falling back for a moment behind the other warriors, she fumbled about in her backpack and pulled out her now-useless flashlight. She tried the switch one last time, then shrugged. *Somehow I doubt I'll be able to buy any new batteries in this world. So . . .*

She drew back her arm and threw the flashlight with all her strength, as hard as though she were hurling the softball to the plate with a runner on third trying to steal home.

And she caught Mardock off guard! Before he could defend himself, the flashlight bonked the sorcerer hard, right on the forehead! Mardock staggered back, stunned, and there was a murmur of horror from the guards.

"Magic . . . eagles turning into men . . . and now a mere girl strikes down a master sorcerer . . . Let Mardock handle all this! We'll have none of it!"

As one, the guards turned and fled, leaving the warrior-women and the eagle-men triumphant!

"Oh, Sheila, that was wonderful!" said Illyria with a laugh. "Hurry, everybody! On board! We've got to set sail before Mardock recovers and the guards rally!"

They raced up the gangplank, pulling it up with them. Behind, Mardock was staggering to his feet, muttering, trying to get his scattered senses gathered enough so he could work a spell. For a moment blue-white bolts of magic swirled about him. Then the bright cracklings sputtered and fizzled, and Mardock swore in frustration.

"Cast off!" commanded Nanine. "You, eagle-men, do any of you know how to sail?"

"We all do," Egael told her, then, to his men, "Man the sails!"

Dynasian's guards had recovered their courage. Spears and arrows came clattering onto the deck. "Ammunition," murmured Kara calmly, and went about gathering the arrows up, refilling her quiver. Sheila, peering warily over the side of the ship, gasped.

"They've got boarding ladders! Oh, please, hurry, get us out of here!"

Just as the ladders fell with solid thunks against the ship's side, and guards began to swarm up, the sails caught the wind. The ship strained like a horse eager to run. But one last rope bound it to the dock. Illyria leaned boldly over the edge of the ship, ignoring arrows whizzing about her, and slashed at the thick rope with her sword. Once, twice, three times—

The rope parted with a snap. The ship darted sharply away from the dock, and Nanine and Pelu grabbed at Illyria, pulling her back onto the deck just in time.

"Thanks!" she gasped.

A series of loud splashes sounded behind them.

"That," said Myno, "must be the ladders falling into the water. Ah, and listen to those curses!" she added mildly. "*That* must be the guards falling into the water with them!"

Far behind them they could hear angry shouts. A bolt of lightning blazed out from the land, flashing right toward the ship. Sheila drew in her breath in horror. Mardock's sorcery was going to destroy them!

But long before it reached the ship, the bolt arched down to hiss harmlessly out into the ocean.

"Silly way to catch fish, isn't it?" asked Myno with a grin. "Looks like we're out of range."

And the ship sailed serenely out into the open sea, leaving the helplessly raging sorcerer and the guards far behind. Sheila hung over the rail, watching Campora growing smaller and smaller in the distance, and smiled.

"And so," she said with a sweep of her arm, imitating the syrupy voice of a travelogue narrator she had once heard on television, "we bid a fond farewell to beautiful, peaceful Campora, the gem of the empire."

16

Sailing Away

It was night on the open sea. There wasn't a sound save for the gentle slapping of water against the sides of the ship and the creaking of the rigging. Sheila leaned on the rail, bathed in moonlight, peacefully watching the silver light ripple on the gentle waves.

"Beautiful, isn't it?"

Darian had come silently forward to lean on the rail beside her. He looked very handsome in the moonlight. "Uh . . . yes," agreed Sheila. She suddenly felt very nervous, and for a moment she couldn't think of anything else to say. "I was afraid Dynasian was going to send warships after us. But it looks like our escape caught his navy off guard."

Darian grinned. "That's what happens when you've got a commander like Dynasian, I guess, someone who's so interested in his own pleasures he's gotten lazy."

"Where are we sailing?"

"South. There are rumors of rebel activities going on somewhere down there. If we can join up with these rebels, we'll have us some important allies. But . . . let's not talk about war and politics, not now. Okay?"

"Okay."

Silence fell. Then Darian said shyly, "Uh, Sheila . . ."

He was looking right at her, the moonlight bright in his eyes. Sheila felt her heart skip a beat. "Yes, Darian?"

"You . . . were very brave in the battle today."

"Oh. So were you."

They were silent once more. But Sheila thought suddenly, *Why, he's as nervous as I am!* and smiled to herself.

"Darian? Did—did you want to ask me anything?"

"I just wanted to say . . . Sheila, I've never met any girl like you. And I hope we can get a chance to—to—"

"Darian!" snapped a sudden voice.

Sheila jumped. Then she saw who had spoken, and sighed. "Hello, Dian."

The girl ignored her completely. "Darian, you promised to help me groom the unicorns!"

Darian sighed, too. "I did. Sheila, I'm sorry. Will you excuse me?"

"Go on."

Left alone at the rail, Sheila yawned and stretched her stiff muscles. It felt funny, not having anything to do after all the excitement of the day.

But I'm not complaining, really I'm not!

The ship, according to Nanine, wallowed like an old cow. It was too—what had she called it?—too broad of beam to cut through the water gracefully. But between Nanine's knowledge and the skill of those mysterious eagle-men, it was sailing smoothly under full canvas.

The unicorns weren't very happy about being stuck aboard a ship. Sheila had spent a long time trying to soothe Morning Star and the others. But at least they were finally tolerating the indignity of being cooped up in tight quarters.

And as soon as we're far enough from Campora, we'll be letting them go again.

She sighed, leaning on the rail again, resting her chin on her hands, wondering. Who were those eagle-men, anyhow? Maybe they could do something as amazing as turn into eagles, but they certainly didn't look very happy about it. They all had such sad, sad eyes. And their leader, Egael . . . he really *was* wonderful. Sheila couldn't blame Illyria at all for falling in love with him.

But—who is he?

Quiet voices caught her attention. She turned. There up on the raised platform of the stern stood Illyria and Egael, his red cloak whipping about them in the wind. Sheila hesitated, wondering if she was eavesdropping. Maybe she should just steal quietly away to the bow of the ship, where the other women were settling down for the night. But Egael's voice was so clear that she couldn't help but overhear.

". . . and so I had to leave you," he was saying.

"Why?"

The man paused, looking out over the ocean as though trying desperately to make up his mind about something. He turned to stare intently into Illyria's eyes. "Forgive me for not telling you the truth about myself from the beginning. You must understand, I—I didn't trust you—"

"What!"

"Not at first, anyhow." Egael sighed. "I had just been beaten by Dynasian's men. They had thought me only a fool of a beggar. But if they had known my true identity, I would have died, or been carried off in chains to Campora."

"But—"

"Illyria, love, for all I knew you might have been loyal to Dynasian."

"Never that!"

"Well, I didn't know. But then, once I . . . realized I loved you . . . how could I tell you the truth? I didn't want to hurt you."

"I'm not a silly little girl," said Illyria dryly.

The man bowed. "Indeed you are not. So. Love, my name isn't Egael. It's Laric, Prince of Perian. My father died fighting Dynasian's troops. When I and my own men tried to fight on, we were captured. And Mardock placed a terrible curse on us all.

"We must roam the sky as eagles, never able to transform to our rightful human shapes save for the five days and nights of the full moon." He glanced up at the radiant sky. "I'm only thankful the timing was right for me and my men to help you."

"Then that flock of giant eagles that seemed to follow us . . . that was you."

He nodded. "It was the only way I could be close to you."

"But isn't there any way to break the spell?"

"There must be! Illyria, right now my land and my poor people lie under Dynasian's tyranny, and I—I can do nothing to help them. But I have sworn an oath: I will force Mardock to lift his curse! And I will win back my throne and free my people!"

Prince Laric looked so noble and splendid there in the moonlight, his eyes blazing with determination, that Sheila shivered. But then he slumped.

"Till that day," he added sadly, "my men and I must take to the sky as eagles every time the phase of the full moon passes. Soon I must leave you again. But I will return to you, I promise."

"And I, my love, shall be waiting."

Prince Laric swept Illyria into his arms. As their lips met in a passionate kiss, Sheila sighed. The *romance* of it all!

Quietly she slipped away and settled down beside the other women, wrapping herself in her cloak. But for a long time she couldn't sleep. She lay staring up at the moon, thinking of all that had happened to her since that day—how long ago?—that she had first fallen into this world. Would she ever get out of it? Sheila sighed, homesick again. Would she ever see her family and friends again?

And yet . . . Sheila realized she wasn't quite ready to go home, not yet. Dynasian still ruled. Half the unicorns were still captive. And—and poor Laric and Illyria couldn't live happily ever after, not till Mardock's cruel spell was lifted.

I don't want to go home, not till I find out how this all comes out!

At least she knew one thing for sure: tomorrow would bring new and wondrous adventures. Smiling, rocked by the gentle motion of the ship, Sheila curled up in her cloak and fell asleep.

Sun Blind

With thanks to Suzanne Weyn
and Stephanie St. Pierre

1

Hunted

Someone shook Sheila McCarthy roughly from her sleep. "Wake up, we're moving out!"

With a groan, Sheila turned over and tried to burrow beneath the thin wool cloth that covered her. A moment later the blanket was pulled off and strong arms grabbed her, lifting her into a sitting position.

The dark-haired boy who held her spoke in a quiet, urgent voice. "Nanine has seen Dynasian's men in the village. We can't stay here any longer. We're breaking camp now."

"Where are we going?" Sheila mumbled, trying not to sound as groggy as she felt.

Darian sounded weary when he answered. "South, to Ansar, I think. I just wish that for once we could do this during the day."

"It'd be a change," Sheila agreed. In the month since she had been riding with Illyria, the Unicorn Queen, she had lost count of the number of times she had been wakened in the middle of the night to flee the tyrant Dynasian's soldiers. "All right," she said, as the familiar sense of danger set in, "I'm awake."

In spite of the situation Darian sounded amused.

"Well, then, stop looking so sleepy." He released her and stood up. "Get your things together and be ready to ride."

"I'll be ready in a minute," Sheila promised, but Darian had already moved on and was kneeling by the fire, gathering a battered assortment of copper pots and cooking utensils.

Sheila shivered in the cold night air and drew her worn blue tunic more tightly around her. She had arrived in this world wearing jeans and a shirt. Now the jeans were frayed cutoffs and her shirt, torn in a scuffle in the city of Campora, had been replaced by one of Darian's old tunics. It was big on her (Darian had almost collapsed laughing when she first tried it on and it fell to her knees) and needed mending, but it was woven of a soft, warm material. She adjusted the tunic, fastened a leather belt around her waist, and slipped a light sword into the sheath that hung from it.

Automatically she rolled up the wool blanket and began to scatter the pile of leaves she had used as a pillow. For the thousandth time she asked herself how she, a completely normal fourteen-year-old girl from the twentieth century, had wound up in this strange world of unicorns and warriors. *You fell into Dr. Reit's time machine, that's how,* she answered herself irritably, unable to stop the familiar wave of homesickness. No matter what adventures she had in this world, it seemed she always longed to return to her own. How could she forget her family and friends? And how could she let herself face the truth: unless Dr. Reit found a way to get her back to her world, she would never see any of them again. *So stop worrying over something you can't change,* she told herself. *There are more important things to deal with right now.*

Breaking camp meant leaving no trace that the unicorn riders had ever been in this place. On the night that Illyria and her warriors had freed the unicorns that Dynasian held captive, the tyrant had set a price on their heads. Sheila, who in her own time had never done anything more criminal than cut study hall, was now an official "enemy of the empire." If it weren't so real, it would be funny.

She used her hands to rake through the grass so there was no longer an imprint where she had lain. Around her, by the light of the dying fire, she could see the other riders working swiftly. And in the distance she could hear the soft, impatient whinnying of the unicorns. The animals knew they were moving out. They always knew.

Quickly Sheila gathered up the wool blanket and grabbed for the two things that had become her constant companions. The first, a light wooden spear with an iron tip, was from the world of the Unicorn Queen. The second item came from her own world. It was a simple green nylon backpack, filled with things that were ordinary in her own time—a tape player, a flashlight, a mirror, some bubble gum—but were considered "magic" here. Even among the riders of the Unicorn Queen there were some who still called her "sorceress" because of the backpack.

Stuffing her blanket into the pack, Sheila crossed the wooded camp. The moon was only about half-full, but the night was clear and the stars shone like a white swath across the sky. Though Sheila hadn't trained herself to move through the darkness the way Illyria's warriors had, she could see fairly well. That, of course, meant that Dynasian's men would also be able to see without trouble. It was a good night to hunt fugitives.

"Where's your saddle?" demanded a girl, coming up behind Sheila.

"Hidden with the others." Sheila tried to keep her voice calm. She was already feeling panicky at the thought of Dynasian's soldiers closing in on them. The last thing she needed was an argument with Dian.

"Well, find it, then, and stop standing around!" Dian ordered. Sixteen years old and the second youngest in Illyria's band, Dian had been resentful of Sheila from the start. "Dynasian's men will probably be here by the time you finally locate your saddle," she went on. "Do you think we have all night to wait for you?"

"I wasn't standing around—" Sheila began indignantly.

"Hush, both of you!" Myno, Illyria's lieutenant, clamped a powerful hand on each girl's shoulder and spoke in a fierce, low tone. "This is no time for arguing, and if either one of you lives till tomorrow, I swear I'll have your hides for it. Now, you know what you have to do. Don't make me speak to you again."

Both girls mumbled apologies, and Myno released them with a rough shake.

Sheila glared at Dian. Even when they were running for their lives, Dian managed to find a way to get her in trouble.

"You've done it now," Darian said matter-of-factly. He held out the worn leather saddle that Sheila had used ever since the unicorn Morning Star had accepted her as its rider. "I'd rather face Dynasian himself than an angry Myno."

Sheila took the saddle from him with a sigh. She was never sure whether Darian, Illyria's handsome sixteen-year-old brother, was the most intriguing boy she had ever met or the most irritating. Sometimes he had an absolute talent for saying the thing she least wanted to hear.

"Don't worry," he assured her, and she couldn't tell if he was teasing or not. "Illyria's never let Myno kill one of her riders."

Darian led the way into the sheltered glade where the others waited. As always, Sheila's breath caught at the sight of the warriors. In the center of the clearing, Illyria, her long silver-blond hair half-caught in thick braids, sat tall and regal on the magnificent Quiet Storm. Quiet Storm had been the first unicorn to appear in Illyria's homeland. Now his silver coat and horn shone in the starlight, as if he were somehow part of it—a creature spun out of stars and moon.

On Illyria's right, Myno, her sword drawn, sat astride a palomino unicorn. On her left was Kara, the archer, on a dark

brown unicorn with a white star across his forehead. Behind them
Sheila saw the other riders: Pelu, the healer; Nanine, the regal
black princess who had rebelled and fled her own court; and Dian.
A small herd of wild unicorns who ran with Illyria's warriors
moved restlessly among the mounted riders. All of the unicorns
and riders looked very beautiful—and very deadly.

Illyria watched, her gaze calm, as Sheila and Darian joined
them. A month ago, when Sheila had first stumbled through Dr.
Reit's time machine into this parallel universe, she hadn't even
known the front end of a saddle from the back. Now her hands
worked deftly to slip the saddle over Morning Star's back and fas-
ten the soft girth around the animal's stomach. In one smooth
movement she lifted herself onto the unicorn's back and ran a
hand through Morning Star's silky black mane. Then, with her
free hand, she reached for the spear she had set in the ground. Beside her Darian and Dian drew their own spears. At Illyria's signal
the small band of warriors raised their weapons in a brief salute,
then followed the unicorn queen into the night.

Illyria always chose her course carefully, and now she led her
band along a tangled path of narrow back roads that wound south.
They were riding inland, far from the busy ports and towns along
the coast. Sheila guessed that their route to Ansar would probably
take twice as long as the main roads. Then again, if they followed
the main roads, they probably wouldn't survive the night. Dynasian's men seemed to own the coast.

The cool night wind rushed through Sheila's hair as the road
widened and the unicorns broke into a full gallop, their hoofs
barely touching the ground. They were impossibly light when
they ran, and Sheila sometimes thought if they could only go a
little faster, they would be flying. Her pack bounced gently against
her back, and she leaned forward in the saddle, winding her left
hand more tightly through Morning Star's mane. Although unicorns accepted saddles, they were far too wild to let anyone fit

them with bridle or bit. Like the other riders, Sheila had learned to hold on to the thick, silky mane with one hand and carry her spear in the other. She still considered it a miracle that she managed to stay on at all, and suspected that most of the credit belonged to Morning Star.

The land rose up in a series of low hills, and the road narrowed again. At a signal from Illyria the unicorns slowed to a canter, and the riders fell in two by two. Sheila found Darian, who had been riding ahead near Illyria, at her side.

"Any sign of Dynasian's men?" she asked.

Darian shook his head. "Not yet. Which doesn't mean they haven't set a trap for us ahead. And if they have, we'll all ride straight into it. I don't know why we don't split up."

"Did you suggest it to Illyria?"

"Every time we go through this," he said, barely concealing his impatience. "I've told her I'm willing to go ahead as a scout, and that we should move in at least two groups. But my sister doesn't believe in splitting up her warriors when we're being pursued."

"Well," Sheila said uncertainly, "I'm sure Illyria has her reasons. I don't think I'd want to face a band of Dynasian's men without the others there. I mean, there aren't that many of us. Even when we're all together, there's a good chance we'll be outnumbered by the soldiers."

"Exactly," Darian said.

"What?"

Darian had the maddening habit of twisting her words around so it sounded as if she were arguing on his side. "We're going to be outnumbered anyway," he said logically, "so why give them the chance to finish us all off at once?"

"We're not giving anyone a chance to finish us off," said a very firm voice behind him. Illyria, whom Sheila could have sworn was riding at the head of the band, drew Quiet Storm even with Darian's unicorn and stared down at her dark-haired brother. "And when I need advice from a sixteen-year-old cub," she continued in a cold voice, "I'll ask for it. Let it go, Darian."

Darian said nothing but glared back, looking at that moment very much like his sister.

There was a moment of tense silence.

"That wasn't fair," Illyria admitted softly. "You've proven yourself a warrior. I shouldn't have called you a—"

"I'm sorry, too," Darian broke in. He shrugged apologetically. "It's just that I can't even look at a tree anymore without wondering if one of Dynasian's soldiers is hiding behind it."

"You, too?" Sheila looked at him in amazement. She had been positive she was the only one who was so paranoid. Sure that Dian would laugh her out of the camp, she hadn't dared tell anyone how nervous this whole "enemy of the state" business was making her.

"And me," Illyria confessed with a grin. "I'm tired of being hunted, which is why we ride to Ansar. Dynasian holds a fortress there. It's time I brought the hunt home to the hunter's door." Then, without another word, the Unicorn Queen pressed her heels into Quiet Storm and rode on ahead.

Sheila had no idea how long they had been riding. Ever since she had given her watch to Darian, she had been a little fuzzy on time. What had ever made her believe that, like the other riders, she would learn to tell the time from the positions of the sun and stars? Basically, she was only good at recognizing dawn, noon, and sunset, and on overcast days she lost noon altogether.

Now the night sky was turning a charcoal gray, and the road was becoming steeper. They were entering the southern mountains, an area known for its hot, dry lands. The trees along the side of the road were thinning already. There had been no sign of Dynasian's men, and the riders' careful pace on the narrow road was deceptively calm. Tired, Sheila let herself be rocked by Morning Star's gentle rhythm, almost forgetting that they were being pursued.

"No sleeping in the saddle!" called a teasing voice.

Sheila sat up with a start to find Pelu riding beside her. "Do you think we'll reach Ansar by dawn?" Sheila asked.

"Not unless it moves itself north. We're a good five days away from the city—and Dynasian's fortress."

"Oh," Sheila said, though what she really wanted to say was that she was very relieved. She had met Dynasian once before, and what she had seen in his eyes had terrified her. She wasn't exactly looking forward to riding straight into his stronghold.

She couldn't help glancing at Pelu to see if she felt the same way. Pelu looked inexplicably happy.

"What is it?" Sheila asked, puzzled.

Pelu pointed overhead. At first Sheila didn't see anything. The sun had barely started its ascent and the sky was still dark, but as she looked harder she saw deep shadows against the grayness— shadows of birds as large as men.

"The eagles," Sheila said in awe. "They're back!"

Pelu nodded, smiling as the harsh cries of the birds began to fill the air. "Illyria will be pleased," she said in a dreamy voice.

"And you?" Sheila teased.

Pelu blushed, answering her question.

"You fell in love with one of Laric's men?" Sheila said, eager for details.

"Hush!" Pelu's fair skin reddened. "Eagles have a very keen sense of hearing. They can probably hear every word we say."

"I don't believe this," Sheila muttered. Only in this world did someone have to worry about her boyfriend overhearing her because he happened to be transformed into an eagle and was presently flying overhead.

Everyone knew eagles didn't fly in flocks, and everyone knew that they didn't grow to the size of men, but the birds who flew overhead *were* men, enspelled by Mardock, Dynasian's evil sorcerer. In their human form the eagles were a warrior band led by Laric, prince of Perian, Illyria's love. Long ago Laric had angered Dynasian. The result was Mardock's curse: Except for five days and nights of the full moon, Laric and his men were condemned to roam the skies as eagles.

"Of all the things Mardock could have done, why did he curse them this way?" Sheila wondered aloud.

Pelu shrugged. "There are two things that matter to Prince Laric—stopping Dynasian and being with Illyria. Mardock's curse ensures that he has little chance of doing either."

"Then why does Mardock let them become men again under the full moon?"

"Let them?" Pelu gave an uncharacteristically bitter laugh. "He could not help it. Mardock's powers are weakest under the full moon, and fortunately, it is under the moon that the powers of Perian are strongest."

Sheila had never been clear about Perian. All she knew was that it was another country, entirely outside Dynasian's empire. And it was a magical land. She didn't know what sort of powers Laric and his men might have, but Laric had given Illyria Quiet Storm, and there was no doubt that the unicorns were magical creatures.

"Do you remember Cam?" Pelu asked, breaking into her thoughts.

Sheila thought back to the night Laric's men had arrived in the nick of time to help the riders steal one of Dynasian's ships and escape from Campora with half the captive unicorns aboard. At first she couldn't tell one warrior from another. They all looked strong and tall and incredibly fierce. But she remembered Cam. He was fair-haired, like Pelu, and had a warm, easy manner.

"Is he the one you like?" she asked Pelu.

The healer nodded.

"In Perian his family breeds horses. He says when we have defeated Dynasian, he would like me to visit."

It was perfect, Sheila thought. Pelu, who loved animals nearly as much as she loved her own life, falling in love with a man who bred horses.

Overhead the eagles wheeled against the sky, following the unicorns below. One of the golden birds called out in what sounded like harsh, angry protest.

"Oh, Sheila," Pelu said wistfully, "Mardock's curse is hard on them all. We cannot let Dynasian win."

Dawn had just broken, hotter than any dawn Sheila could remember. The sun was barely on the horizon, and already it felt as if it was ninety degrees. Pelu insisted that the riders stop often to give the unicorns water, and though they all carried leather water flasks, everyone knew that the supply wouldn't last long. Myno had even suggested to Illyria that perhaps there was another route they could take—one in which they would not all die of thirst. But Illyria had just frowned and said that they were going exactly as they should.

They were climbing higher and higher into a brown, dry landscape. In her own world Sheila's family had driven west one summer, and what she saw now reminded her of the mountains of northern New Mexico, except that in New Mexico the mountains had been covered with aspen and evergreen. Here there was no greenery at all. Everything looked as if the color had been baked right out of it.

The strange thing was that the higher they climbed and the more remote the land became, the more roads there were. The narrow road they were on branched and branched again, was crossed half a dozen times, and at one point seemed to lead in at least five different directions. They didn't see any houses. They didn't see any people. Never hesitating, Illyria led them as if she had memorized the way.

"What are all these roads for?" Sheila asked when she and Darian were riding alongside each other again.

"You mean *who* are all these roads for?" There was a wariness in his voice that made Sheila uneasy.

"Who, what . . . you know what I mean. There isn't anything up here."

"No," Darian replied thoughtfully. "But let's say all this land was yours, and you wanted to make sure that if you had to, you could get around it easily. You'd make sure there were roads."

"Not me. If I had the money to buy this much land, you can bet I'd spend it on some fancy villa overlooking the sea. Who in their right mind would buy all this desert and then carve roads into it? Even the unicorns have trouble in these mountains."

"He may not be in his right mind," Darian answered, "and I don't think he had to *buy* the land."

Despite the heat, Sheila felt a chill run through her as the meaning of Darian's words became clear. "What you mean," she said slowly, "is that we're in Dynasian's territory."

Morning Star's shrill whinny—a sound Sheila had come to recognize as the unicorn's warning of certain danger—was her answer.

2

A Battle and a Barn

Morning Star's warning was answered at once by the low, clear call of Illyria's battle cry. Sheila's grip on her spear tightened, and her heart began to pound as Myno drew her sword and gave the signal to fight. *Fight who?* Sheila wondered. The only people in sight were the unicorn riders, all of them holding their weapons ready. The unicorns were completely still, poised for action at a split second.

The silence seemed endless. Then suddenly, from behind, came the sound of thundering hoofbeats. Dynasian's soldiers were upon them.

Despite the heat, the tyrant's men wore thick leather armor and helmets with a narrow strip that went down the nose. There was something very sinister about them, and Sheila shuddered as she realized what it was—the helmets made the soldiers look like executioners.

Their leader, a broad man with heavily muscled arms, sent his spear flying. There was a reassuring *thunk* as the spear connected with Myno's shield, and Myno's voice rose above the noise of the

132

horses and the men. "Now," she cried, "*we* attack!"

Fearlessly Dian aimed her spear and hit a burly, bearded soldier. Darian, Nanine, and Pelu joined the attack, swords flying.

Sheila sat on Morning Star, paralyzed. A heavyset soldier aimed a spear at her, and instinctively she ducked, flattening herself against the unicorn's back. Another soldier, on foot, ran toward Morning Star's side. With a rising sense of terror, Sheila realized the soldier was going to pull her off the unicorn. She heard Myno's endless drills running through her head: "Give the enemy the spear or give him the blade, but don't give him a chance." Still, throwing a spear at a target was very different from throwing it at a man.

Sheila took a deep breath, aimed at the soldier who was charging her, and forced herself to throw. She was incredibly relieved when the spear sailed over his head. But her relief vanished as she realized that the only weapon she had left was her sword. She drew it from its sheath at her waist and prayed she wouldn't have to use it.

Time seemed to slow as she waited for the soldier to make his move, and Sheila wondered frantically if she would actually be able to use the blade.

She never had the chance to find out. Morning Star darted to the side of the road and reared up on her hind legs, sending her rider flying. Sheila landed hard on her backside. She wasn't sure what was worse—the jolt or the shock of Morning Star betraying her in the middle of a battle.

It took only seconds before she realized that Morning Star had not betrayed her. Rather, the unicorn had acted to get her out of harm's way. Now it was Morning Star who was doing the fighting, and the unicorn on her own was far more dangerous than she was with Sheila on her back. Morning Star made straight for the soldier who had come at Sheila. He swung his sword in a low arc, trying to cut the animal at the knees.

"*Stop!*" Sheila screamed, desperately trying to warn the man.

It was no use. Before his sword had completed its arc, Morning Star's horn had pierced his armor, lifted him into the air, and dropped him in a limp heap. Having dispatched that attacker, the unicorn eagerly sought the next enemy. Sheila had to look away as the unicorn tore into another soldier. She stood shakily, willing herself to go back into the battle, but her knees gave way, and she sat back down.

All around Sheila the unicorns and their riders were doing a thorough job of defeating the small troop of soldiers. Quiet Storm and Illyria plowed through a crescent of five archers who never even loosed their arrows. Myno rode her palomino like an avenging demon. Sheila could barely tell the unicorn's horn from Myno's sword; both were covered in blood. And Darian—he no longer seemed a teenage boy but a brave warrior, crossing swords with a soldier twice his size. From the movements of Dynasian's man, Sheila knew what the outcome would be. The soldier was obviously stronger, but Darian was little and quick and had unerring aim. His blade found its way home easily.

As the battle raged on, Sheila was sick.

It seemed like hours later that Illyria knelt by Sheila's side, offering her a leather flask filled with water. Illyria's silver braids were almost completely undone, and her face was grimy with dust and sweat. Her tunic, always ragged, looked even worse than usual.

"Is everyone all right?" Sheila asked as she gave back the flask.

"There are enough cuts and bruises to keep Pelu busy for a while, but we were lucky. No one was hurt badly. How are you?"

Sheila couldn't keep the bitterness out of her voice. "Great, for someone who fell off her unicorn and got sick to her stomach."

"You could not have fallen off if Morning Star had not deemed

it best," Illyria said gently. "Of the two of you, she is the more ex-
perienced fighter, and you must trust her judgment."

"You mean," Sheila said, "of the two of us, she is the *only*
fighter. . . . I'm sorry."

"There's nothing to be sorry for. You fought by my side in Campora," Illyria reminded her. "But that was a different kind of
fight." A smile played at the corner of the Unicorn Queen's
mouth. "If you promise not to tell, I'll let you in on a secret."

Sheila nodded.

"Swear," Illyria ordered with mock sternness.

"I swear. I'll never tell."

"Especially Darian," Illyria added with an unmistakable grin.

"Especially Darian."

"Well, then, you should know that the first year I fought I
shook before and after every battle. For hours. I used to have to
make up excuses to go off on my own afterward so no one would
see what awful shape I was in. Myno, of course, knew exactly
what was happening, but then, Myno misses very little. And she's
very good at keeping secrets."

Sheila smiled, only half-believing the story. Illyria was probably just trying to cheer her up.

Illyria's blue eyes held Sheila's in an unwavering gaze. "Sheila,
the taking of a man's life, even a man who fights for a tyrant, is a
very serious thing. It *ought* to affect you." The unicorn queen
stood up. "You come from a place and time where this sort of
bloodshed is not usual for girls your age."

The understatement of the year, Sheila thought, but to Illyria she
said, "Not too many of my friends back home are warriors."

Illyria shrugged. "Perhaps that is a good thing. In any case, you
need not be ashamed. But now, if you're feeling better, Morning
Star could use some attention. She has earned it."

Sheila took a curry brush and comb from her pack and went to attend to Morning Star. The unicorn nuzzled her gently, her nose velvety soft in Sheila's palm. "You're a lethal beast," Sheila said fondly, and then put an arm around the unicorn, hugging her. "Thanks for saving my life."

Five days later Illyria led her band to the southern coast of the empire. The dry mountains where they had fought Dynasian's soldiers had given way to hills covered with cedar, cypress, and olive trees. Even better, as far as Sheila was concerned, were the small villages that welcomed the unicorns and their riders.

Tonight they were in a place called Nolad, about a day's ride from Ansar. They hadn't planned to stop at all, but there had been a sudden downpour, and a woman named Yvere had offered to let them spend the night in her barn.

Whinnying softly, the unicorns immediately made friends with Yvere's horses, and the riders settled into the loft above the stalls. Considering that they were so close to Dynasian's stronghold, Sheila felt surprisingly content. It was good to be safe inside, listening to the rain fall on the thatched roof.

"This is luxury!" exclaimed Kara, stretching out in the sweet-smelling hay.

Nanine yawned. "In my land," she said, "this is not what we call luxury."

"What do you expect when you grow up in a palace?" Darian asked. Absently he toyed with the bandage that had covered his right wrist ever since the battle. He grinned at Nanine. "I told you you were spoiled."

"At least I grew up," Nanine retorted. Her golden necklace, inlaid with turquoise and coral, gleamed in the light of the barn's oil lamp. Even in a worn tunic covered with bits of straw, Nanine looked every inch the princess.

Sheila looked down at her own clothing. Somehow she had

managed to tear her tunic's right shoulder. Always too big, it was now threatening to slide off altogether. She tugged on it, wishing she had a few safety pins in her pack.

"Don't let it bother you," Illyria said, watching her. "We'll all have new clothing soon."

"We will?" Dian, who always tried to sound so cool, couldn't keep the excitement out of her voice.

Darian rolled his eyes.

"Tomorrow," Illyria said. "We'll make camp in the hills outside Ansar then. And we certainly can't ride into the city looking like this."

"We can't ride in at all," Darian pointed out. "Don't you think a band of warriors riding around with a herd of unicorns is just a little conspicuous?"

Illyria grinned and threw a fistful of hay at her brother. "Your faith in me is overwhelming. When I said we'd have new clothing, I meant disguises."

There was a soft knock at the barn door, and Yvere, a small, serious woman, came in. She lifted a shawl from her head, and Sheila saw that beneath it her hair and tunic were soaked. *If only they had umbrellas in this crazy place*, Sheila thought.

"Forgive me for interrupting," Yvere began.

"You didn't interrupt anything important," Illyria assured her, giving Darian a mock glare. "Will you join us, or would you rather I came down?"

Yvere hesitated, almost as if she were afraid.

Illyria climbed down the wooden ladder and stood before their hostess. Watching them together, Sheila didn't blame Yvere for feeling timid. Illyria was a good head taller than the woman and stood straight and strong. Yvere's small frame was hunched over from years of working in the fields.

"You are going to Ansar?" Yvere asked.

Illyria nodded.

"That is good," Yvere said, with the closest she had come to a smile.

Illyria sighed. "I mean to find Dynasian's fortress. I'm not sure that's so good."

"You'll have no trouble finding his fortress," Yvere said. "But I think you will find something else of interest." Quiet Storm came up behind the woman and playfully rubbed the side of his head against her shoulder. Yvere turned and ran her hand through his mane. "Yes, that's right," she murmured. "He knows."

"Knows what?" Dian called from the loft. Illyria turned and gave Dian a severe look, and Sheila was very relieved that Dian had been the one to ask.

"Oh!" Pelu said, with a soft gasp. "She means the unicorns."

Dynasian had committed countless crimes against his people, but among the worst was capture of the unicorns. It was known throughout the empire that the unicorns were a force of Light. Where the unicorns were free, the land and people prospered. When they were taken by the tyrant, disease and famine followed. Illyria and her riders had sworn to free the unicorns, and indeed, with the help of Laric's men, had freed half of those Dynasian held in Campora. But the tyrant still held half of the herd, and now Yvere was telling them that the unicorns were in Ansar.

At least some of them. "I don't know how many there are," Yvere went on, "but there are rumors all through the city that he hides them in his fortress."

"He always keeps them well guarded," Illyria said grimly. She looked up at her small troop in the loft. "Are you ready to storm a fortress?"

"In Campora it was his palace," Myno muttered. "In Ansar it's his fortress. He's going to get to know us awfully well."

"You needn't do it alone," Yvere said. "Ansar may be filled with Dynasian's men, but it's also filled with people who hate him. He has caused endless grief in that city." She paused again to stroke Quiet Storm, and Sheila saw her face lighten as she touched the unicorn. It was almost as if she looked younger, or as if she hadn't had such a hard life. Sheila had seen it happen before—the unicorns had that effect on almost everyone.

"I've heard rumors," Illyria said. "There's a rebel group. They call themselves—"

"The Sareen," Yvere finished.

"It means . . . something like . . . Warriors of the Sun," Illyria translated for Sheila's benefit.

When Sheila had first entered this world, Pelu had touched her with a gleaming blue stone she called the Gem of Speaking. Sheila had never figured out exactly what it was or how it worked. All she knew was that it allowed her to understand the language of Illyria and the riders. Unfortunately, it didn't work with any of the other languages in the empire. Or with many of the names, which didn't have an exact translation into English.

"The Sareen are very strong," Yvere went on. "They've attacked Dynasian many times."

"Where do we find them?" Illyria asked.

Yvere gave Quiet Storm a final pat, pulled her shawl over her head, and opened the barn door. Outside, the rain was still coming down in torrents. "Oh, you won't have to find the Sareen," she answered as she let herself out. "I guarantee they'll find you."

3

Dian's Plan

Sheila slid off Morning Star's back with a grateful sigh. They had left Yvere's barn just before dawn and ridden most of the day. Illyria had led them single file down a twisting mountain road and finally through a narrow pass to this—well, the best way Sheila could describe it was a miniature canyon. Two walls of solid brown rock rose up on either side, and between them ran a clear stream bordered with willow trees and high wild grasses. In this land where everything seemed carved out of dry brown rock, it was like they had found a little paradise.

Sheila took her bedroll from the unicorn's back and then removed the saddle. At once Morning Star ran to join the others by the stream. The unicorns clearly liked this place—they were frisking in the water, prancing with delight. Sheila grinned as she watched Darian, who was walking along the bank, get thoroughly splashed.

Myno's voice cracked through the camp. "Get yourself settled quickly. And then gather at Illyria's tent."

That was a surprise. They hadn't used the tents since they had

140

left Campora and Dynasian had declared them outlaws. The tents just took too long to take down when you had to strike camp and flee in the middle of the night. If they were using them again, it must mean they intended to stay for a few nights and that this place was relatively safe. Sheila, of course, had not come to this world carrying her own tent, and now she wondered whom she would be rooming with.

Kara solved the problem for her. "Help me set this up," she called to Sheila, "and then you can stay with me."

For a while Sheila and Kara wrestled with cloth flaps, leather ties, and at least fifteen wooden stakes.

"If you put that stake in there," Kara said calmly, "neither one of us is going to be able to sit up. You're pulling the top down flat."

"Oh," Sheila said, studying the tent with confusion.

"Try putting it in over here," Kara offered, pointing to the obvious place to nail in the stake.

How can this be so complicated? Sheila wondered. She couldn't help thinking about her own tent at home—an aluminum and nylon domelike thing that practically put itself up.

"We're home!" Kara said when the patched little tent was finally standing. She surveyed the canyon with a warrior's critical eye. "It's not bad," she declared. "We'll only need two people on watch." She pointed to the mouth of the canyon, where they had ridden in. "Someone guarding that pass and then someone walking the perimeter of the camp, just in case."

"I think it's great," Sheila said happily. The willow trees moved gently in the breeze, and the stream looked almost silver in the late afternoon light. Three other tents had already gone up, and Dian and Darian were starting a fire for the evening meal. For the first time since leaving Campora, there was an easy, relaxed feeling in the camp.

"Kara," Sheila began curiously, "how did Illyria find this place? The route we took—a homing pigeon would have gotten lost."

"She rides Quiet Storm," the archer answered simply.

"So?"

Kara took an arrow from her quiver and ran a finger along its shaft. "All of the unicorns have powers that go beyond the ordinary. You've seen that. But even among unicorns Quiet Storm is special. Ask Illyria about him sometime."

"Whatever you want to ask will have to wait," said Myno, coming up behind them. "Illyria wants to talk strategy now—with all of you."

Sheila followed Kara and Myno to Illyria's tent, where the other riders had gathered. They were sitting on the grass in front of the tent, as ragged a bunch as ever there was. Not one of them had a tunic that wasn't ripped, patched, stained, and faded. Dian, Sheila noticed, was sitting next to Darian, and Sheila couldn't help feeling an irrational stab of jealousy.

Illyria stepped out of her tent and the riders fell quiet. It might have been a trick of the light, but the Unicorn Queen looked even more beautiful than usual. Her thick braids of silver hair seemed to catch the afternoon sun and positively glowed. Her tanned skin looked even darker.

"Yes," she began, "we've come to a very pretty place. And I think we'll be here for a few nights, at least. But we have work to do. We're less than two hours from Ansar. I've never been there, but I'm told that the city lies at the foot of the mountain that is Dynasian's fortress."

"That means," Myno broke in, "that either he or his men see everything that goes on in the city."

"We've sworn a vow to free the unicorns," Illyria went on. "If what Yvere told us is true, then our course is clear. We must find a way into the fortress and free them." She looked at her band with a wry smile. "As my brother so accurately pointed out, we're not exactly an inconspicuous bunch. If we even approach the city looking like this—or riding the unicorns—we can expect to find ourselves in Dynasian's dungeons."

"But we need to find a way into that fortress," Myno added. "And we want to make contact with the rebel forces. So we'll need disguises."

"I can fashion disguises," Nanine said, "but not out of willow leaves. I'll need two or three bolts of cloth."

"That's easy," Dian said. "I'll slip into the marketplace and steal them."

"There's no need to steal," Kara said.

"You expect me to walk in looking like this and ask to buy cloth?" Dian demanded.

"She has a point," Darian said reasonably.

"There'll be no stealing," Illyria ruled. "However, Dian *does* have a point." She slipped into the tent and returned with a small leather pouch. "Here's twenty pieces of silver. I don't expect you to bargain for the cloth, but you can leave this as payment for the merchant. It will more than cover the cost."

She turned to Nanine. "Do you think you could work up something for her to wear into Ansar . . . maybe using one of the tents?"

Nanine gave a sullen nod. Tents obviously did not fit her idea of suitable fashion.

"You can use mine," Kara volunteered.

Sheila was torn between admiration for Kara's selflessness and being outraged at having to give up the tent they had worked so hard to assemble.

"I don't like this," Myno muttered. "It's too risky. What if she's caught? What if she gets lost?"

Dian began to sputter indignantly, but Illyria silenced her with a look. "Dian," she said, "I know your bravery, but perhaps this is one mission you should not undertake alone."

Myno flashed the Unicorn Queen a broad grin. "And I've got the perfect partner for her," she said. "Sheila, tonight you'll let Nanine do what she can about disguising you. Tomorrow at dawn you leave for Ansar with Dian."

4

In the Marketplace

Sheila tugged irritably at the thick dress that covered her. Although Nanine had done the best she could for them, both Sheila and Dian looked as if they were wearing small tents—which they were! The heavy, worn material was stiff with dust and dirt, and though Nanine had tried to make the garments shapely by adding belts, the fabric stuck out at weird angles from their bodies. Worse, the dresses, if you could call them that, were ankle length. After weeks in cutoffs and a tunic, Sheila felt as if she were walking in a bag. Also, she had grown so used to riding Morning Star that it had never even occurred to her that she and Dian would have to *walk* to Ansar.

Sheila was absolutely miserable. The sun was beating down on them, she was trapped in this horrible hot "dress," she was probably going to be arrested for stealing, and to top it all off, she was stuck with Dian.

Dian looked no happier than Sheila. And, except for growling "You'd better not get us caught," she hadn't said a word since they left the camp. Sheila suspected that if either one of them could have figured out a way to argue with Myno, Dian would have had a different partner.

The road that led into Ansar was broader than any road Sheila had ever seen and crowded with travelers on their way to the city markets. There were merchants driving donkeys, soldiers on their war horses, and families on foot. Animals were everywhere— goats, pigs, and dogs roamed freely, as if they were going to Ansar on their own. Sheila found herself darting out of the way of a cart loaded with chickens only to nearly collide with a woman balancing a huge basket of fruit on her shoulder. With relief, she realized that no one they had passed had given her knapsack a second look. It was just one more bundle on the way to market.

The sun was nearly overhead when Dian gasped, "There it is!"

Sheila, who had been staring at the road, wishing they had shopping malls in this place, looked up, startled.

She expected a city and what she saw was a huge wall built of thick sand-colored stones. And though the wall was high, it was completely dwarfed by the mountain that rose to the right of it. The odd thing about the mountain was that it looked as if its top was completely level. It figured that Dynasian would level a mountain for his own purposes.

"The city's inside the wall?" Sheila asked.

"Walled cities usually are," Dian replied.

Sheila decided to ignore the jibe. "How are we going to get in?"

"The same way everyone else is," Dian said in a bored tone. "There are gates into the city. We just go up to a gate, explain who we are and what we want, and then they let us in."

"Oh, great," Sheila muttered. "My name is Sheila McCarthy and I ride with the Unicorn Queen and I've come to Ansar to get some cloth for disguises so we can break into Dynasian's fortress."

Dian snorted with laughter. "Let me do the talking, all right?"

Sheila shrugged, but thought that for once it was probably a good idea.

A line had formed in front of an iron gate in the wall. Two of Dynasian's soldiers stood guard, and a shiver ran through Sheila as she recognized the menacing helmets and armor. The line moved slowly, and she began to get nervous. The soldiers were obviously questioning everyone carefully, and she hadn't even thought of a good alibi. She had always been a terrible liar. What if she slipped up and they caught her at it? What would happen if they questioned her and Dian separately and their stories didn't match?

"Listen," Dian said in a low voice, "if they question you, answer with words in your language that can't possibly translate in this time. Then I'll explain you're my cousin from across the sea who doesn't speak any of the languages of the empire. Understand?"

Sheila understood but didn't really believe it would work. Her stomach did somersaults as she waited. At last the elderly couple in front of them passed through the gate and it was Sheila and Dian's turn.

The guards asked a series of rapid-fire questions in what Sheila recognized as Miolan, the language spoken throughout the southern part of the empire. Sheila didn't understand it at all; the southern language was almost completely different from the northern tongue spoken by the riders. But Dian answered calmly, pointing to Sheila as she went through her explanations.

"Sheila?" one of the guards asked roughly. She nodded her head, and he said something that obviously was a question.

Sheila looked at Dian desperately and got the usual bored expression. It was entirely up to her, and her mind was going blank.

The guard repeated her name, then asked another sharp question.

Frantically, Sheila searched her mind for a phrase that they couldn't translate. Of course! The name of Dr. Reit's time machine, the device that had gotten her into this mess in the first place.

"Molecular Acceleration Transport Device," she answered clearly.

The two guards gave her a puzzled look, then held a hurried conference. With a grunt the taller guard waved the girls through.

"Where did you learn to speak Miolan?" Sheila asked.

"My mother was from the south," Dian answered brusquely. "Now, just keep walking."

Sheila was fascinated by the city that lay behind the walls. The first thing that hit her was the salt tang of the sea, but all she could see was the thick web of streets crowded with shops and houses.

"Where's the water?" she asked Dian.

"I think the harbor's south." Dian pointed down one of the wider streets that was paved with stone. Like all the other streets, it took a sudden curve, so it was impossible to see to its end. Ansar looked like a puzzle designed by a madman. A street would go straight for about twenty yards, then curve, curve again, and double back on itself.

"We've got to find a shop that sells cloth," Dian said.

Sheila looked at the colorful maze of shops and stalls that surrounded them. Rows of clay jars and bowls filled one doorway, fruits and vegetables another, gleaming brass bowls and lanterns a third. The sweet scent of fresh-baked bread wafted up from the end of the street, and Sheila realized she was starving. After all, they hadn't eaten since they left camp early this morning.

"I have an idea," Sheila said. "Why don't we buy some bread for lunch, and we can ask the shopkeeper where to find the cloth."

Dian shot her a scornful look. "We can't afford to attract any-one's attention. Tell your stomach to be patient."

"Look," Sheila began angrily. She was tired of Dian acting like such a know-it-all. But Dian ignored her and walked briskly ahead, turning the corner of yet another narrow lane. With a sigh, Sheila followed. She felt as if she was being led into the heart of a maze.

The street that Dian had entered was even narrower than the others, and smelled of leather goods. Here the crowded stalls were filled with sandals, tanned hides, and saddles. It didn't seem like the place to find cloth, but Dian turned another corner, and suddenly they were in a lane where the leather gave way to weavers' shops and stores that sold dye and sacks filled with raw cotton.

For a moment Sheila lost sight of Dian, and then Dian emerged from a small shop. She stood waiting for Sheila to catch up.

Sheila peered into the open doorway of the shop, where wooden shelves were piled high with neatly folded fabric. They had obviously come to the right place.

"Have you ever stolen anything?" Dian asked abruptly.

"No," Sheila admitted.

"That's what I thought. Of all the people for Myno to give me—"

"I wasn't *given* to anyone," Sheila retorted. "Besides, we're not actually stealing. You have the silver, don't you?"

Dian lifted the pouch at her side. "Here's what we'll do," she said. "You'll go into the shop first and distract the shopkeeper. Ask about cloth, the weather, anything. Just keep him busy. Meanwhile, I'll get the cloth and leave the money. When you hear me cough, you'll know I'm leaving. Wait a few seconds and then follow me out."

"What if he doesn't speak our language?"

"He does," Dian answered. "I went about halfway in and heard him. You won't have any problems as long as you don't say anything stupid."

That does it, Sheila thought. *One more remark like that, and you're on your own.*

"Go ahead," Dian said, giving her a push toward the shop. "Keep him busy."

Sheila resisted the impulse to punch Dian in the nose, and instead concentrated on pretending to shop for material. It wasn't hard to fake interest. The fabrics were beautiful. She found herself drawn to a shelf of silk—rich purples, emerald greens, and a red cloth edged with golden thread. She thought of the times she had bought material for home ec class—corduroys, denim, and once some horrible satiny stuff that kept getting stuck in the sewing machine. She had never seen anything like these silks. This was the kind of stuff that princesses in fairy tales wore.

"There's something you like?" asked a smooth voice behind her.

Sheila turned to see the shopkeeper, a round middle-aged man with dark hair slicked back from his face.

"Yes," Sheila said.

The shopkeeper looked at her expectantly. Clearly, he was waiting for a more specific answer.

"I mean, I—I like them all," Sheila said truthfully.

The shopkeeper raised his eyebrows.

Oh, this is going well, Sheila thought. *We're carrying on a great conversation here.* She forced herself to think of a question: "Where are the silks from?"

"From Ansar, of course," the man said in a voice that let her know she had just asked a dumb question. The merchant's eyes narrowed. "Do you want to buy?"

"I—I'm just looking now," Sheila said. "I want to buy a gift for my . . . my sister . . . and I've been looking all day."

"You're alone?" the shopkeeper asked in a surprisingly concerned tone.

Sheila wondered if she was making a mistake when she answered, "Yes." The shopkeeper was making her very nervous.

"Young girls shouldn't walk alone in this city," he said gruffly. "The people are uneasy . . . things have been seen."

Sheila turned her head to check on Dian. Near the back of the shop Dian was examining the cloth the way any customer might. For a supposedly accomplished thief she was certainly taking her sweet time about stealing.

Sheila brought her attention back to the shopkeeper and tried to sound interested in what he'd said last. "Why is the city uneasy?"

She fully expected to hear another story of Dynasian's soldiers harrassing the citizens and so was unprepared for his answer. "Our streets are haunted," the man said quietly.

"Haunted?" Sheila had seen a lot of strange things since entering this world, but ghosts were not among them.

The shopkeeper nodded. "An apparition of an old man. He appears and then vanishes and then reappears. Our seers say he is searching for something—or someone."

"Tell me"—Sheila could barely control her excitement—"do you know what he looks like?"

"Everyone knows. He is tall, thin, with white hair. He wears a strange white tunic and light leggings . . ."

It was Dr. Reit—Sheila was sure of it! It had been almost a month since Sheila had seen her friend. The last time the scientist had appeared in this world had been the night she and Illyria had been held in Dynasian's prison. It was Dr. Reit's ghostly form that had made their escape possible. And while Sheila had been incredibly glad to see him, she had been dismayed to learn that he didn't know how to get her back to her own world. Worse, he didn't know if he would ever be able to find her again. Now he had been seen in Ansar. That must mean he was searching for her.

"Where was the ghost last seen?" Sheila asked, trying to sound suitably scared.

But before the shopkeeper could answer, Sheila heard a furious coughing behind her. Dian had taken the cloth and was ready to leave.

"Um—I have to go now," she said hurriedly. "Thanks for warning me about the ghost."

Quickly she made her way toward Dian and almost started laughing. The slim, athletic girl had hidden the cloth inside her dress and now looked positively fat. Without speaking the girls left the shop. Dian was walking with a weird waddle.

"Did you leave the silver?" Sheila asked. She had grown to like the shopkeeper and felt bad about taking the cloth this way.

Dian looked pale. "I forgot."

"You what?"

"You try hiding enough material to clothe eight people, and see what you remember!"

"Then give it to me now," Sheila demanded as they rounded a corner onto a street that smelled of cinnamon and spices.

"Why? What are you going to do?"

"I'm going to leave it for him, of course."

Dian's strong hand gripped Sheila's wrist. "Are you crazy?" she demanded, shaking her. "We can't afford to go back in there."

Sheila had about had it with Dian. She reached out and ripped the leather purse from Dian's side, then before the other girl could protest, she ran back toward the shop.

"You, girl, stop!" bellowed an angry voice.

Sheila looked up in alarm to see the shopkeeper running toward her.

"Thief!" he screamed. "You leave my shop and my goods leave with you!"

Oh, no, Sheila thought. This was not the way things were supposed to turn out. Quickly she tossed the pouch of coins toward the shopkeeper, then never even knowing if he stopped to pick them up, she turned and ran.

She knew that she couldn't lead him to Dian—Dian who actually had the stolen goods. Cursing the bulky dress, she ran for all she was worth.

Behind her she could hear the shopkeeper's footsteps. She just prayed it was only the shopkeeper. If he called the soldiers, she wouldn't have a chance. She tore down the narrow streets, with no idea of where she was going. Then she saw it—a large coil of hemp on the side of the street, a perfect place to hide.

Sheila crouched down behind the coil of rope and caught her breath as the shopkeeper ran past. But the man realized almost at once that she was no longer ahead of him. He stopped and turned, eyeing the row of stalls suspiciously. Sheila scrunched even lower behind the rope. It was only a matter of time now before he found her unless . . . unless she distracted him. Sheila grinned as she remembered his being frightened of the ghost. Then she reached for her backpack and pulled out her tape player. She would need a man's voice, and the stronger the better. Quickly she grabbed a Springsteen tape and put it in, pressed the "on" button, turned the volume all the way up, and sauntered out into the street.

"There you are, you little—" The shopkeeper's angry words were cut off as Springsteen's voice began to pound out the words to "Born to Run." *Very funny, Bruce*, Sheila thought as she watched the shopkeeper back away from her.

"That ghost you spoke of," Sheila said, in what she hoped was her spookiest voice. "His spirit has found me. He travels with me now. Listen . . ."

She stepped closer to the man, the music moving with her. "He says," she went on, "to tell you that I haven't stolen anything, and you are to leave me alone."

The shopkeeper's face had gone completely white, and as Springsteen's voice rose in an urgent call to "run," Sheila decided it was time to take the Boss's advice. In as dignified a manner as possible, she turned her back on the frightened man and sought the nearest gate out of Ansar.

5

The Rebel Leader

Sheila never did meet up with Dian on her way out of the city. She half-expected that Dian had made it out of Ansar and would be waiting for her somewhere on the road. But as she walked toward the riders' camp, there was no sign of the other girl. In fact, there weren't many people at all once she was beyond the outskirts of the city. The road narrowed as it wound back into the hills, and Sheila began to feel completely alone. What if Dian hadn't made it? What if she had been captured? How would Sheila ever explain to Illyria?

It was late afternoon, as far she could tell, and the road still wound on. She hoped she would recognize the turn that led to the camp. She hoped she would make it back before dark.

Sheila looked up at the sound of hoofs—incredibly light hoofs. Wildwing, with Darian on his back, was racing toward her. Darian brought the white unicorn to a stop and looked down at her with an expression she couldn't figure out—happy, relieved, and a little angry all at once.

"Are you all right?" he asked.

"I'm fine," Sheila answered. "But what about Dian? We—we left Ansar separately."

"We noticed," he said dryly. "Dian's been back for a while. Nanine's already sewing disguises." He looked at Sheila's outfit and grinned. "I think the new ones are going to be an improvement over *that* thing."

"Thanks a lot," Sheila muttered, trying not to smile. Then she realized what Darian was risking. "What are you doing out on Wildwing? You know it's dangerous to ride so close to the city."

"I was looking for you," he answered gruffly. "Myno said you'd be fine, but . . . come on." He held out a hand to her. "It'll be nightfall before you get back if I let you keep walking."

To her surprise, Darian pulled her up so that she was sitting in front of him in the saddle. That meant she'd be the one riding Wildwing.

"Will he let me?" she asked Darian. Wildwing was a stallion and, as his name suggested, one of the wilder unicorns. She had seen him break into a careening gallop that even Darian had trouble controlling.

"Will you?" Darian asked the animal.

Wildwing whinnied in answer.

Darian smiled. "He says he'll give you a try."

Sheila leaned forward and stroked the unicorn's strong neck. "That's very kind of you," she told the animal. Then she gently pressed her knees into his side and the unicorn turned toward the camp.

Even with two riders on his back, Wildwing streaked effortlessly down the road. Sheila had never felt so much power in her life. With a laugh, she leaned forward and held on to the black mane, and the unicorn stretched out into a full gallop. Behind her, Darian's hands tightened around her waist, and he called out something she couldn't hear above the sound of the rushing wind.

This is freedom, Sheila thought. Not worrying about school or parents or any of the hundreds of perfectly boring things she used to worry about—just racing the wind, and knowing that whatever happened to her in this world would be an adventure.

When Wildwing finally stopped at the entrance to the canyon, Sheila's arms were trembling from holding on so tightly. Behind her, Darian's grip on her waist loosened, and she heard him draw a deep breath.

"That was great," she said, turning to look at him.

"Yeah. Great." He gave her a curious look. "Didn't you hear me shouting at you?"

She shook her head. "I couldn't hear anything over the wind. What'd you say?"

"I told you to slow down."

"Oh, that was helpful advice," Sheila said, grinning. "Do you really think I could have slowed him if I wanted to?" She slid off Wildwing and ran her hand along the unicorn's jaw.

"I don't know," Darian said, "but it didn't seem like you were trying very hard."

"Of course not." Sheila gave the unicorn a conspirator's wink. "It was too much fun."

As Sheila and Darian walked the unicorn into the camp, Sheila saw that Dian had indeed returned, and the women were eagerly experimenting with her purchases. Most of them stood by the edge of the stream in the last light of the day, staring at their reflections as they draped and arranged the material over themselves.

Sheila stopped short at the weird scene. She had never thought she would see this hardened band of warriors making such a fuss over themselves. Even Myno was holding a piece of saffron yellow cloth to her, as if to see whether or not it complemented her red hair. It did.

Pelu ran up to them, folds of pale blue cloth draped over her arm. "Can you believe it?" she asked. "We're actually going to look respectable again. I can't wait to see Myno in that saffron."

"I can't believe this," Sheila said. "They're all acting like . . ."

"Like women?" Pelu asked with a laugh. "There's nothing that says we can't be seasoned warriors and still like pretty new clothes."

"I guess," Sheila admitted, but somehow this didn't fit her image of the riders.

Pelu held the light blue cloth up against Darian. "No, I don't think it's quite your color," she teased, and was rewarded with a scowl. She turned to Sheila, trying to keep a straight face. "You'd better go down to the water and pick out something for yourself before it's all taken."

After her part in "buying" the cloth, Sheila would have been very happy never to have to look at the stuff again. As much as she wanted to get out of the horrible tent dress, she had no desire to wear the fabric she had almost gotten captured for.

"I think I'll just change into my old tunic," Sheila said, heading back to where her tent with Kara had stood the night before. There were a few things she wanted to think about anyway—like whether or not she would have to return to Ansar to find Dr. Reit.

With a smile Sheila realized that a small, neatly lashed lean-to had replaced the tent. Sheila's sleeping roll had been carefully laid out in its shadow, and Kara sat beside it, her braid hanging over her shoulder, as she concentrated on restringing one of her bows.

"Did you have a good time in Ansar?" Kara asked without looking up.

"I wouldn't exactly call it a good time. But we got the material."

"You mean Dian got the material." Kara finished stringing her bow and tossed her long braid over her back. When she looked up at Sheila, her eyes were hard with anger. "Dian told us you went back to pay the merchant. That was honest—and foolish. And it was even more foolish of Darian to go after you on Wildwing. We cannot afford such heroism from either of you. Do you understand me?"

Sheila couldn't believe what she hearing. Kara had never snapped at her before. In fact, except for an archery lesson when Sheila had been even more uncoordinated than usual, she had never seen Kara look irritated. Among the riders Kara was known for her unshakable calm.

"Do you understand?" Kara repeated.

"I wasn't trying to be heroic," Sheila replied stiffly. "I thought if we didn't pay the man, there was more risk we'd be caught as thieves."

"There's less risk of being caught the farther you are from Ansar. You should never have gone back." Kara's face paled. "They could have gotten you, too."

Sheila had no answer for that. She knew Kara was talking about her younger sister Lianne, who had been captured by Dynasian's soldiers. Lianne was the reason Kara had joined the riders. As Illyria had sworn to free the unicorns, Kara had sworn to find and free her sister. Sheila knew Kara had been sick with disappointment when no one had been able to find a trace of Lianne in Campora. She wondered if there was any possibility that the girl was in Ansar.

Kara stood up abruptly, as if impatient with the whole conversation. "And get out of that ridiculous dress. You're lucky you didn't have to fight in that thing."

"Whew!" Sheila breathed as the archer stalked away. She changed back into her cutoffs and Darian's ragged tunic and then went to help with dinner.

The riders took turns at various chores, and this week both Sheila and Nanine were assigned to prepare the fire for the evening meal. Starting the fire usually wasn't so bad, but it was always a pain to draw enough water to boil for cooking and cleaning up afterward.

Sheila reached the fire pit and found Darian edging it with stones. "Nanine's busy sewing," he explained. "So Illyria volunteered me as her substitute. I'll go get the water if you'll start the fire."

Sheila pulled a flint and a small piece of iron from the leather drawstring pouch that hung from her waist. When she had first been asked to help with the fires, she had "cheated"—by using the matches that had been in her backpack. Now she had exactly five matches left, and she knew better than to waste them on anything less than an emergency. With a sigh, she gathered a small pyramid of twigs on the ground and then began to strike the flint and iron together. This always took patience.

She had just gotten the first sparks from the flint when she heard the unicorns' shrill warning. The animals who had been at the stream's edge were suddenly moving toward the mouth of the canyon. And within an instant every rider had responded to their call. Without thinking, Sheila drew her knife and scanned the canyon walls, looking for a sign of the enemy. Nanine, Pelu, and Myno, who were already close to the canyon's entry, had their spears drawn. The unicorns moved in behind them in restless formation. Morning Star's horn was lowered, ready to charge. The stallions, Quiet Storm and Wildwing heading them, were rearing up, their forelegs lashing out in angry challenge.

Pelu turned to the herd, her eyes flashing. "No," she told them, "we'll handle this one on our own."

After Illyria, Pelu seemed to have the most influence over the animals, but no one could be sure of the unicorns' response. As much as they seemed to like and want to help the riders, they were creatures of the wild. Pelu looked slightly surprised when they quieted at her command. But the animals remained where they were, and it was clear that they would need little provocation to charge.

Cautiously the three riders went forward, their spears before them. Sheila watched them disappear into the mouth of the canyon. For a long moment there was silence. Then Pelu, Nanine, and Myno reappeared, and in their midst was a tall, muscular man with long red hair that streamed down past his shoulders. He wore a simple tunic, unadorned except for a gold clasp on the shoulder. He looked unimpressed by the three spears pointed at his throat.

Illyria, her sword drawn, pushed her way through the crowd of unicorns and riders. "Who are you?" she demanded.

The stranger motioned to the spears at his throat.

"Let him speak," she ordered.

The three warriors raised their spears slightly, and as they did the unicorns again prepared to fight.

"Please," he said, addressing the unicorns as much as the riders, "I come unarmed."

Illyria ignored the stranger for a moment, absorbed in the animals and whatever it was they were trying to tell her. She walked over to Quiet Storm, who danced nervously at the head of the herd. Speaking in a low voice, she managed to calm him and the others.

Then she turned to Myno. "Check him for weapons."

The stranger was searched. As he had said, he was unarmed.

"This is a warm welcome from comrades," he commented when Myno had done with him.

"Comrades?" The Unicorn Queen's voice was icy with contempt. "You haven't even told us who you are."

"I haven't been given much of a chance," he answered evenly. "My name is Nemor. I was a captain in Dynasian's armies. I led the Ninth Regiment." He hesitated a moment, as if seeing the past he described. "My troops won him many conquests. We took cities, villages, farms, captives . . . always captives. After a while, I became sickened by what I saw . . . and what I did. Finally I left Dynasian, but I'd spent my entire life fighting, and I grew bored without battles. I decided I would fight the tyrant himself. For the last two years I have led a band of rebels called the Sareen."

Yvere had said he would find them, and now here he was. Like the other riders, Sheila measured the man who claimed to lead the rebel forces. He was the kind of man she had come to recognize as belonging solely to this world. No matter how hard a guy from her time worked out, there was no way he could look quite like this. Nemor's tall frame was lean and muscled, and his arms bore the unmistakable scars of battle. He had the same "coiled" quality Sheila saw in Illyria and Kara, and sometimes in Darian—as if at any moment, from any position, he could explode, unleashing his power. If a man like Nemor was not an ally, he would be dangerous indeed.

Apparently, Illyria had come to the same conclusion. "I have heard of the Sareen," she told him, "but why should I believe you are their leader?"

"Lady," he answered softly, "you are not the only one with a price on your head. I come to your camp unarmed. All you need do is turn me over to the nearest soldier, and you would be rewarded with enough gold to"—he looked at the scruffy armed band that surrounded him—"to deck yourselves in jewels."

"We don't need jewels," Myno told him.

"That's good," Nemor said with a hint of a smile. "I was not counting on being turned in by my allies. I came unarmed, at substantial risk, to prove to you that I am not an enemy."

"That doesn't prove anything," said Kara.

"If you're a friend," Illyria said, "then tell me how you found us."

Nemor gestured again to the spears that were still aimed at his throat. "I promise I'll answer all your questions, but can't we at least talk in a friendlier manner?"

Sheila couldn't help smiling. The riders were not giving Nemor an easy time of it, yet he refused to be riled.

Illyria nodded and Nemor was led into the camp, where he and Illyria sat in front of her tent.

"Now," he began, "as to how I found you . . . I am skilled at tracking; it's something I've done since I was a child. And I had help from the people who know that the Sareen also seek to free the unicorns. There are over a hundred who fight with me, and many others who do not fight but aid us with food, shelter, and information."

A *hundred!* To Sheila, who was now used to the idea of fighting with a band of eight, the number was dizzying.

"With so many fighters of your own, what could you possibly want of us?" Illyria asked.

Nemor smiled, and Sheila realized how handsome he was. He had strong, broad cheekbones, and sparkling eyes that were nearly amber. His mane of red hair was streaked with gold, his skin tanned to a deep bronze. She began to understand the name "Warriors of the Sun." Nemor looked like some barbaric sun god, even in the simple brown tunic that wasn't in much better shape than her own.

"What I want," Nemor said, answering Illyria's question, "is to take Dynasian's fortress. You know he holds unicorns there. We can free them and break his hold on Ansar. There are two ways into the fortress—one is the road he has carved; the other is a footpath up the side of the mountain that few men know of." He laughed soundlessly. "Dynasian has a nasty habit of killing anyone who discovers the second route. I mean to take that route and throw open the gates to the Sareen. When I do, I want your riders and the unicorns to be the first through the gates, launching the attack." He eyed Quiet Storm with interest. "I have heard the unicorns are unmatched in battle. Even with a hundred men, I will need all the allies I can get if we're to have a chance of defeating Dynasian. We would make strong allies, Lady."

For a few moments there was only the sound of the stream running, cold and clear and having nothing to do with battles or tyrants.

"It's a bold plan," Illyria said at last.

Nemor shrugged. "I know of no subtle way to storm a fortress."

She laughed at that. "Well said. But I don't order my riders into missions. This is something that they will have to choose. Give us two days and I'll have an answer for you."

"That's too long," Nemor said. "I'll send for your answer tomorrow night."

Sheila couldn't be quite sure how it happened, but somewhere during that last exchange the power had shifted from Illyria to Nemor. It made her uneasy, and at the same time it made her admire Nemor even more. She had never seen anyone best the Unicorn Queen.

Nemor stood up with a smooth, animal grace. "I'll leave you now." With a slight inclination of his head he bowed to Illyria, and then began to walk toward the mouth of the canyon. He stopped for a moment as he passed Quiet Storm. "You *are* a beauty," he said, holding his hand out for the animal to sniff.

The unicorn tossed his head angrily, his silver horn nearly slicing open Nemor's hand. But the stranger moved with lightning reflexes and pulled his hand back before the unicorn could touch him.

"You're lucky you move quickly, Nemor. Still, if I were you, I wouldn't get so close." Illyria's soft warning held a note of mockery that took back whatever advantage Nemor had held.

He turned to her, still remarkably calm. "As you say, Lady." Then with another bow he left the camp.

6

Practice

Sheila rolled over on her side, trying to find a comfortable hollow for her shoulder. She was used to sleeping on the ground, but tonight she was restless. Maybe it was because Kara hadn't yet returned to the lean-to. She, Myno, and Nanine had been cloistered in Illyria's tent ever since Nemor had left the camp. Sheila wondered if Kara was still angry with her. She hoped not; she was dying to ask her what they were going to do about Nemor's offer.

There was a soft sound Sheila couldn't identify, and then someone sat down next to her. Sheila bolted up with a start.

"Relax," Kara said with a laugh. "It's just me."

Kara had taught herself to move soundlessly, which was great until she materialized out of the night beside you. Then it was positively spooky. The archer began to unlace a sandal. "Sorry. I forgot you're not used to it."

Well, at least she doesn't sound angry, Sheila thought with relief. Tentatively, she asked, "You're not mad anymore?"

Kara's dark eyes regarded her gravely. "What I said to you had

164

to be said, but if you'll do your best not to repeat the mistake, I think we can let the matter drop."

Sheila nodded her head in agreement.

"Besides," Kara added softly, "I was worried about you. I don't think I could stand it if the same thing happened to you that . . ." She let the sentence trail off, unable to finish it. "Now, tell me, what did you think of our new friend, Nemor?"

"He's impressive," Sheila replied honestly.

"I thought so, too," the archer admitted. "But then, I'd heard of him before. When Nemor led the Ninth Regiment, they were the most feared of all of Dynasian's troops."

"He seemed very sure of himself."

"That comes from being a fighter. And it's a safe bet he's a good one. Did you see how quickly he got his hand away from Quiet Storm? Anyone else would have been gored."

"But you don't trust him," Sheila guessed.

Kara loosened her braid and began to brush out her long, brown hair. "The point is the unicorns don't trust him. Pelu thinks he's poison."

Sheila knew that among the unicorns' powers was the unerring ability to sense danger. Illyria had not even trusted Sheila until Quiet Storm had given her his approval. The unicorn's violent reaction to Nemor was a warning that could not be ignored.

"Well, if we know he's dangerous, then what's the problem? Illyria can just say we're not going to join forces with him."

"It's not that simple," Kara answered. "Illyria doesn't trust him any more than Quiet Storm does, but she wants to get into Dynasian's fortress and free the unicorns. She thinks she can use Nemor to get us in."

"He doesn't look like the type who's easily used," Sheila said thoughtfully.

Kara gave her hair one last stroke and settled down to sleep. "That's the general opinion."

Sheila turned at the lazy tone. "You don't sound very worried."

In the moonlight she could see Kara's grin. "One enemy's like another . . . except this one's handsomer than most . . ." Her voice trailed off, and Sheila was sure she'd fallen asleep until she added, "There's only one thing about Nemor that worries me: How did he ever get so close to the camp before the unicorns sensed him?"

Sheila was up early the next morning, mostly because she was starving. With all the previous night's commotion about Nemor, no one had bothered to go hunting, and supper had consisted of flat loaves of bread and a stringy yellow plant that Pelu assured them was edible.

She found Darian cooking a porridge by the fire and giving Pelu dark looks. "And don't expect me to eat any more of whatever that was," he was saying to her. "You wouldn't dare feed anything that tasteless to the unicorns, and you know it."

"No one forced you to eat it," Pelu told him, grinning. She was wearing a tunic sewn from the new material. Its sky-blue weave brought out the blue of her eyes and that, combined with her delicate build, somehow made her look young and very innocent. No one would ever take her for a warrior.

"Want breakfast?" Darian asked Sheila. "I guarantee it's an improvement over last night."

Sheila accepted a bowl of the porridge as Pelu neatly stepped behind Darian, grabbed his wrist, and applied pressure.

"Do you apologize for all your nasty comments about dinner?" the healer asked sweetly.

Darian twisted against her grasp, found himself unable to break free, and swore under his breath.

Pelu waited patiently until he apologized.

"You'd better learn to choose your opponents more carefully," Illyria said with a laugh as she came upon Darian rubbing his wrist and glaring at Pelu. She sat down beside Sheila, helped herself to her brother's cooking, and winked at her youngest rider. "Well, at least he can cook."

Myno strode over to the group, a vision in saffron. Nanine had fashioned a longish tunic for her that hung in soft, graceful folds. But even Nanine's skill couldn't diminish Myno's powerful presence. Sheila was sure that if you dressed Myno in a twentieth-century lace wedding gown, she would still look as if she were about to charge into battle. "I want everyone over here now!" she barked.

Nanine and Dian came up from the stream, and Kara materialized from wherever she had been. Morning Star, her curiosity aroused, poked her head into the circle. "Not you," Sheila said fondly, and pushed her away.

Meanwhile Myno had begun. The day's mission, she announced, was for the band to split up, go into Ansar and the surrounding villages on foot, and gather as much information as they could about the Sareen, Nemor, and Dynasian's fortress. "Nanine and Pelu, you'll go into Ansar; Darian, the village just north of the city; Kara, Illyria, and I will cover the settlements in the hills. Dian and Sheila will remain in camp."

"Why?" both girls cried at once.

"Because," Illyria answered, "after yesterday, I'm not going to risk either one of you being recognized. And since Nemor found us, there's the possibility that someone else will. I don't want to leave the unicorns unguarded."

Sheila couldn't believe it. Two days in a row, stuck with Dian!

"Don't worry," Myno said, "I'll leave you plenty to keep you busy."

Within an hour the others had taken off and Sheila and Dian were left staring at a lengthy list of things to do. First they had to clean up after breakfast, then each girl was to do the sewing on the tunic that Nanine had cut out for her; there were saddle girths to be mended, and swords to be polished. And that was just the morning. The afternoon, Myno had specified, was to be spent in sword practice.

Sheila moaned as she envisioned the day ahead. "You know what this is, don't you?" she asked her fellow laborer. "This is Myno finally getting us back for that night when we were arguing about the saddles."

Dian shrugged. "It doesn't matter what it's for. Let's just get it over with."

They spent a good deal of time cleaning up after breakfast. Darian had managed to burn the porridge to the bottom of the pot, and it took forever to scrub it off in the cold stream.

As she had the day before, Dian barely spoke a word to Sheila, and as far as Sheila was concerned, that was just fine. But both girls had a pleasant surprise when they went to Nanine's tent and found the tunics she had cut for them. Nanine had worked hard to make sure that no two were the same, so that the riders wouldn't look like a troop.

Dian loved the color green and Nanine had left her a long, light green tunic, slit high at the sides. Even Sheila had to admit that Dian looked lovely when she slipped it on.

"I'll have to cut it," Dian said wistfully as she stared at her reflection in the water. "I mean once we really start riding again."

Sheila wouldn't have that problem. The tunic Nanine had cut for her was short and woven from a lavender fabric so soft it reminded her of flannel. Sheila had never really liked lavender before, but this shade seemed just right with her auburn hair, tanned skin, and hazel eyes. For the first time in weeks she felt pretty, and she couldn't help wondering what Darian would think when he saw her.

The afternoon was half gone by the time Sheila and Dian had worked their way down Myno's list to "sword practice." This was the part of the day Sheila had been dreading. The truth was, she liked sword lessons when they were with Illyria or even Myno. Illyria had given her Darian's old sword, and gradually Sheila had relaxed enough to realize that using the sword well had more to do with skill and speed than with strength. But she had never worked with Dian before. All she knew was that everyone in the camp agreed that when it came to weapons, Dian was a natural.

"We'll work down by the stream," Dian decided. "The ground's level there."

Grimly, Sheila tightened her hold on her sword and followed Dian. Both girls had remained in their old tunics for this, knowing they would wind up sweaty and probably dirty as well.

"Now," Dian said with a superior tone, "why don't we start with basic drills."

Sheila had done hours of basic drills with both Illyria and Myno, but she wasn't about to tell this to Dian.

"Front thrust, retreat, block, and upper cut," Dian ordered.

Sheila did as she was told, following Dian's motions. In spite of herself, she had to admit that Dian was really good. Like Illyria and Darian, her cuts were smooth and sure. The sword never wobbled or tilted at odd angles. And though they were practicing four separate moves, Dian had a way of blending them into a seamless whole.

They practiced basics until Sheila thought her arm was going to fall off.

"Good," Dian said at last. "Let's see you spar."

"Now?" Sheila panted. "Give me a minute to catch my breath."

"I can just see it," Dian scoffed. "In the middle of a battle you'll look up at Dynasian's soldiers and say, 'Could I have a minute to catch my breath, please?'"

"Forget I even asked," Sheila said angrily. "I'm ready whenever you are."

Usually when they sparred, the warriors would warm up with a set of prearranged moves, with one person attacking and the other defending. Dian dispensed with that as she announced, "No rules. Open fight."

"Fine," Sheila said, though the thought of going into an open match against Dian rattled her. She knew Dian was going to try something; it was just a question of what.

Dian took her by surprise by fighting fairly. The problem was, she was about five times better than Sheila and, unlike Illyria and Myno, had no qualms about using her full strength against a less-skilled opponent. Dian's sword whirled and met Sheila's with a ringing blow. Then before Sheila could counter the move, Dian was attacking again, relentless and tireless.

After a while Sheila lost count of the number of times she either had the sword knocked out of her hand or found herself knocked off her feet. When Dian finally managed to accomplish both with one move, Sheila decided she had had enough. Her teeth ached from being jarred so hard, and her left arm was shaking so badly she could barely close her hand around the sword's hilt. The worst part was that she hadn't scored a single hit on Dian. Not one.

She blinked back hot tears as Dian came to stand in front of her. "Get up," the other girl ordered, "you're not done."

"Yeah, but you are," said an angry voice behind them. "Maybe the reason she's having such a hard time is because her teacher isn't very good." Darian planted himself between Sheila and Dian, his sword drawn. "I don't think," he said to Dian, "that you'd like me to give *you* the kind of lesson you just gave her."

"You're interfering," Dian said angrily.

Sheila got to her feet, feeling a mixture of relief and embarrassment. The last thing she wanted was Dian thinking she needed Darian to protect her. "I'm fine," she announced. "And . . . and I'll continue, if you want."

"Why?" Darian asked. "So you can get even more worn out and discouraged?"

"Darian, please!" Sheila couldn't believe he was being so dense about this.

"I need practice, too," he announced with a cocky grin. "So I'll fight either one of you."

"You're acting like a bully, and you're pampering her!" Dian said.

"If you want to fight me, draw your sword," Darian replied, his own sword balanced lightly in front of him. "I'm waiting, O great teacher."

"Well, then, you'll wait!" Dian spat. Without another word, she grabbed her sword and stalked off toward her tent.

"I wish you hadn't done that," Sheila said when they were alone.

Darian now stood staring into the stream, as if the scene with Dian had never happened. "Catch your breath," he said, without looking at Sheila. "Then pick up your sword and we'll see that you learn something."

"Darian, I'm serious. If Dian thinks you're protecting me . . ."

"What Dian thinks doesn't matter." He turned to face her, and for once there was no spark of humor in Darian's dark eyes. "What matters is that you learn to fight without losing the confidence you've built so far. Beating you into the ground isn't the way to do it. Now, pick up that sword and stop wasting time."

Sighing, Sheila picked up the sword again. With a sense of surprise she realized that the blade felt completely natural in her hand, as if she had used one all her life. Illyria had once promised that eventually the sword would feel like an extension of her arm—and now it was happening.

Still, she was extremely relieved when Darian announced that they would start with the prearranged combinations. "I'll attack, you defend," he said.

He began slowly, so that Sheila could follow the movement of his sword and meet it with her own. Darian's sword carved precise lines through the air, and though Sheila could rarely anticipate where the next move would come from, the blade was so perfectly controlled that she felt safe. Darian could stop the sword a hairs-breadth from her skin. And though he could have easily disarmed her or knocked her off her feet, as Dian had, he never took advantage of his strength.

Gradually, as he saw that Sheila was calmer than she had been with Dian, Darian picked up speed. Sheila parried his blows as quickly as she could, whirling to meet the sword that darted at her from above, below, and all sides.

"Easy," Darian said, his voice reassuring. "Don't let me make you rush your own moves. Fight *your* fight, not mine."

Sheila took a deep breath and concentrated on controlling her pace. She had no sooner gotten a grip on that than Darian called a break to explain that she was giving him too many openings. Then he let her work the attack and, as he defended himself, showed her how to correct the mistakes she had been making.

Bit by bit they advanced to more complicated patterns. Occasionally Darian would throw in an unexpected strike or show her a different way to use the techniques she was already familiar with. Like Illyria, he was demanding without being intimidating. He never let her relax enough to be caught off guard and yet, Sheila realized with a sense of surprise, she was actually having fun.

When Darian called for a rest sometime later, Sheila was breathing hard, soaked with sweat, and even more sore than she had been with Dian. But her eyes were shining and she was laughing.

"Better?" Darian asked.

"Much better."

"If you keep practicing, you're going to be a terror," he predicted.

Sheila put her sword back in its sheath. "You're a good teacher."

"That's because I was lucky enough to have a good one."

"Illyria?"

"Not exactly," he said quietly. "But we had the same teacher. Our father."

Sheila didn't know what to say. Neither Darian nor Illyria talked much about their home. She had a feeling that every-thing—and everyone—had been destroyed by Dynasian's troops. Now, with Darian so quiet, she didn't dare ask.

Finally Darian broke the awkward silence. "You know," he said, the mischief back in his eyes, "one of the most important things my father taught me is that you've got to cool down properly after practice."

His glance slid from Sheila to the stream.

Sheila looked at the water and then back at Darian.

"Oh, no you don't," she said, understanding him all too well. She turned to run, but didn't get very far. She was exhausted and Darian was faster anyway.

"You won't need this now." Darian removed her sword from her belt as he caught her. Laughing, he picked her up and carried her to the stream.

"No!" she shrieked. "I'm too tired to swim. I'll drown. Darian, put me down now!"

"As you wish," he said with mock gallantry, and threw her into the stream.

Sheila felt the deliciously cool water close over her, and for a moment stayed beneath the surface, hoping to give Darian a scare. When she could no longer hold her breath, she sat up, sput-tering, and tried to look angry.

Darian stood on the bank watching her. "I don't think you drowned," he observed.

"No thanks to you." Sheila stood up, intent on vengeance, and sat down again with a splash as the weight of her soaked tunic combined with the current to bring her down.

Darian gave up all pretense of control and doubled over laughing.

"I don't care how good you are with a sword," Sheila said, hoping she sounded angrier than she actually was. "I'll get you for this."

"Yeah? What are you going to do? Hide my sandals?"

With a very undignified screech Sheila rose and lunged toward the shore, determined to at least soak him. But Darian beat her to it, arcing into the stream with a graceful dive.

"Show-off," Sheila muttered.

A moment later he surfaced beside her. Sheila sent a jet of water into his face and swam for the opposite bank.

It was no use. Darian pulled even with her, swimming with strong, smooth strokes. "Admit it," he told her in a smug tone. "You really wanted to go swimming with me."

Sheila just rolled her eyes. She was too tired to give him the satisfaction of an argument. But they swam together until it was nearly time for dinner, and secretly she couldn't help wondering if he was right.

7

Visitors

One by one the women returned to the camp. That evening they gathered around the fire to report on what they had found.

"Before any of you tell me about Nemor," Illyria began, "Kara has some news."

The archer's face was drawn as she spoke. "I spoke to a woman today who recognized my description of Lianne. She said that she had seen a chain of captives being led to Dynasian's fortress, and one of them looked like my sister."

"That's great!" Sheila said.

Kara shook her head. The others were silent.

"It's not great?" Sheila asked.

"We all know how Dynasian treats his captives," Myno said sharply. The tyrant was feared throughout the empire for his cruelty, and as an escaped slave herself, there were few who knew it better than Myno.

Illyria looked at Kara with both sympathy and a resolve to face the truth. "If we do take the fortress and find Lianne—"

"I'm not sure I want to see what we find," Kara finished, and strode from the fire.

Pelu started after her, but Illyria stopped the healer. "Let her go. Kara will be all right, but she needs time by herself. And I need to know what all of you found out about Nemor."

It seemed everything he had told them was true. He had been one of Dynasian's ablest and most trusted captains when he suddenly resigned. No one knew what explanation he gave the tyrant, but it must have been a good one, for few men left Dynasian's service alive. Nemor disappeared from sight for a while, then, approximately a year later, he showed up in one of the villages outside Ansar and began to build the rebel group the Sareen. Since then he had mounted a series of daring raids on Dynasian's troops. To Sheila, he sounded like some kind of Robin Hood, stealing from the tyrant's caravans and soldiers and giving to the poor. The people considered him a hero—and their only real hope for overthrowing Dynasian.

"Well," said Illyria when all of the riders had spoken. "It seems Nemor is beloved by the people. I, too, heard the same things wherever I asked. By all accounts, he's the perfect ally. Why, then, did Quiet Storm nearly rip him open?"

She stared into the fire, as if looking for her answer there. When she had disguised herself that morning, she had let Nanine paint lines and age spots on her face. She had assumed the hunched-over walk of an old woman, and she had taken her hair down. Now she had straightened and scrubbed off the makeup, but her hair still hung loose in waist-length silver waves. In the flickering firelight, Sheila saw a strange expression cross the Unicorn Queen's face. It was as if, just for a moment, Illyria wished she were doing anything in the world besides plotting battles and strategies. Sheila wondered if she was thinking of Laric.

"I think," Illyria said at last, "that we must work with Nemor."

"What?" Pelu was outraged. "How can you ignore the unicorns' warning?"

"I'm not ignoring anything. But if there is a way into that

fortress, Nemor will know it, and I mean to get it from him. Whatever it is he's up to, I want him to play out his hand."

"Even though this game may involve considerable danger," Nanine said, as if completing the thought.

Illyria stood, a sign that the council was over. "I meant what I told Nemor. I will not order any of you into this. Each of you must choose whether or not you will risk this partnership."

"Do you really think any of us would refuse?" Myno asked with an impatient grunt.

The Unicorn Queen smiled at her band. "I mean to get more information from Nemor himself before I commit any of us to battle. But if Nemor sends for my answer, I will tell him that we will join forces." She turned to Myno with one last instruction: "Make sure you double the watch tonight."

By the time dinner was over Sheila was nearly asleep on her feet. The sword lessons with Dian and Darian had worn her out completely. She crawled into her bedroll and was asleep as soon as her head touched the ground. So it was with a sense of bewilderment that she found herself wide awake in the middle of the night.

She sat up, trying to figure out what had awakened her. The sky was still black, and beside her, Kara's bedroll was empty. The archer was on watch. The camp was quiet. There were only the sounds of the stream and the soft whickering of the unicorns.

Without quite knowing why, Sheila pulled her blanket around her shoulders cloak-style and got up. She waited a few minutes until her eyes had adjusted to the darkness and then cautiously began to move through the camp—cautiously because she didn't want anyone on watch mistaking her for an enemy.

She walked toward the back of the canyon, away from the sleeping warriors. It wasn't a good night for walking. A steady, dry wind blew clouds across the waxing moon, so that she was able to see where she was going for about a minute, only to be plunged into darkness the next.

The clouds slid across the moon again and she stopped where she was, waiting for the light to return. And when it did, there in the moonlight was the ghostly figure of a tall, thin man with wild white hair.

"Dr. Reit!" Sheila cried. The scientist had been looking for her, after all. And now he'd found her. Did that mean he had also found a way to take her back to her own world?

"Shhhh!" he said, obviously delighted to see her. "You don't want to wake your friends, do you?"

"I'm so glad you're here!" Sheila lowered her voice just a fraction. If she could have hugged his shimmering form, she would have.

"Yes, well, I've been looking for you," he explained. "You are all right, aren't you?"

"Yes, but—" Suddenly Sheila was hit with a wave of homesickness so sharp it nearly undid her. At that moment she would have given anything to see her family. "Have—have you come to take me home?"

"Well, that's what I wanted to talk to you about," the scientist answered in his usual distracted manner. "Actually, it's pure luck that I found you. You might say I bounced right across your path."

Sheila couldn't exactly make sense of this, but that wasn't unusual with Dr. Reit. So she asked the same question she had asked him dozens of times: "What are you talking about?"

The scientist thrust his hands into the pockets of his lab coat with a sigh. "The problem with traveling between worlds, my dear, is crossing the molecular time warp. You just happened to fall into my time machine and wind up in this time. But for me to travel into this world and no other, I need a very specific form of acceleration—"

Sheila tried to picture the high-tech rocket Dr. Reit had probably constructed just for this purpose.

"I used a springboard," the scientist explained.

"You mean, like the kind you use in gymnastics?" Sheila asked in disbelief.

"Well, more or less. And it did get me here and will most probably get me back. However, I don't think it will do anything for your problem." Dr. Reit saw Sheila's crestfallen expression, and his form wavered with what might have been doubt. The moonlight shone straight through him. "Now, there's no reason to get downhearted," he said quickly. "You see, I'm working on a reverse mechanism that I think will get you back."

"You *think*?" Sheila echoed.

"Well, you know these things are never certain until they've been tested and retested. If I was doing this properly, I'd try it on mice first, then rats and guinea pigs, maybe rabbits . . ."

Sheila summoned all her patience. "Dr. Reit, have you found a way to get me home or not?"

"Well, that's what I've been trying to tell you, dear girl. I think I've found a way to reverse the molecular acceleration, but it requires a great deal more acceleration than I've been using up to now, and—"

"And I'm still stuck here," Sheila finished.

"Well, yes," the scientist admitted softly. "But only for a while. I promise you."

Sheila sank down against a tree. "What about my parents?" she asked in a small voice.

"They're fine, I'm sure."

Sheila wasn't sure this was good news. Of course, she didn't want anything bad to happen to her parents, but somehow she didn't like the idea of them being "fine" when she was missing.

"Oh, didn't I explain?" Distress filled his voice, and Dr. Reit's pale image wavered again and nearly vanished. "You're in a parallel universe, but the passage of time is not at all parallel. Time here has nothing to do with time back home. Though you've been here over a month now, at home it's still the same afternoon that you left. No one knows you're missing except me."

"Wonderful," Sheila said flatly. "I may get killed in some crazy battle, and no one will even know I'm gone."

"You're still trying to fight the tyrant, then?"

Sheila nodded and filled him in on all that had gone on.

"Fascinating," said Dr. Reit when she had finished. "Simply fascinating."

Sheila was about to tell him it wasn't nearly as fascinating as it was dangerous when the ghostly form before her flickered for a moment and then vanished as quickly as it had come.

Sheila let her head sink down on her knees. It had been nearly a month since Dr. Reit's last visit. Who knew when—or if—she would ever see him again. And even if she did, what was the use? He'd probably just vanish again.

"So that's the sorcerer," said a quiet voice.

Sheila jerked her head up with a start. Darian was standing beside her. He must have heard most of their conversation.

"I wish you'd stop sneaking up on me," she snapped, angry that he had spied on her. "You could have made a little noise, you know."

"I'm sorry," said the boy, sitting down next to her. "But I was on watch. I heard voices. . . . You want to go home, don't you?"

Sheila didn't answer. She was afraid that if she started talking about home, she would start crying.

"Are you so unhappy here?" he asked gently.

"I miss my family and my friends. Even my bedroom, sometimes."

Darian's hand reached out for hers. "I don't think I'd like it if I found myself in another world. I can't even imagine yours."

"You might like it," Sheila said, trying to picture him behind the wheel of a car. Darian's hand felt so good around hers— warm and strong and comforting. "And it's not that I hate this world," she went on, suddenly wanting him to understand. "It's funny. I used to daydream about living a life filled with heroic adventures. I guess that's why I always read a lot of science fiction and fantasy."

Darian looked at her blankly, and she realized he had no idea of what she was talking about. To him this world wasn't something out of a heroic daydream. It was simply his life.

"What I mean is," she tried again, "in a lot of ways, coming here—and meeting all of you—has been the best thing that ever happened to me. But—"

She never had a chance to finish, for at that moment there was a shrill, angry whinny. In the moonlight Sheila saw Quiet Storm rear up, his powerful forelegs lashing out in a furious attack.

Darian was up and running before Sheila even realized that a man was trying to approach the unicorn, a man carrying a halter.

Without thinking, Sheila took off after Darian. "Wake up!" she cried as she raced through the camp. "Someone's after Quiet Storm!"

Near the mouth of the canyon Darian took off in a flying leap, tackling the stranger. Both of them came down hard. There was a long scuffle and Sheila couldn't tell one from the other. Then, with a grunt, Darian pulled himself up on top of the stranger, his fist raised. Above them Quiet Storm's hoofs cut through the air. With a shout the stranger twisted violently, rolling Darian beneath him. Just as Sheila reached them the stranger's arm arced up, a knife gleaming in his hand.

"No!" Sheila didn't have time to draw her own knife. She just threw herself forward, grabbing the stranger's wrist and jerking it back.

There was a blur of motion beside her and then Illyria was

there, her knife at the man's throat. "Drop your weapon," she commanded, "and then get up, very slowly."

With a muttered curse, the stranger did as he was told.

"Let him go, Sheila," Illyria said.

Sheila stared at her own hand in surprise. Even though the stranger had dropped the knife, her fingers were still stiff around his wrist. With a shudder, she released him.

Myno stepped forward, grabbed the stranger's hands, and bound them tightly behind his back with a leather thong.

"Darian?" Illyria turned to her brother with concern.

Darian was on his feet, breathing hard, his head turned away from them. Sheila could see that he was cradling his right arm.

"Darian, let me see." Pelu tried to touch his arm, but he jerked away angrily, and Sheila saw the pain in his eyes. "Let me see," Pelu repeated gently.

"Do as she tells you," Illyria said, her words both a plea and a command.

With a sigh of defeat, Darian let Pelu take his arm.

She began to straighten it and then stopped. "It's broken."

Darian shrugged, as if to say, "I knew that."

"Can you set it?" Illyria asked.

Pelu's smile was grim. "I'll have to knock him out first."

"I can take the pain," Darian said gruffly.

"Not this much, you can't," Pelu told him. "Come. I'm going to brew a potion for you, and then you're going to sleep *very deeply*."

"Go with her." Illyria brushed a shock of dark hair from her brother's face. It was the tenderest gesture Sheila had ever seen between them. "I want you well soon."

Darian gave his sister a sly look. "All right, but first"—he turned to the stranger all but forgotten in the concern over his arm—"I want to hear what this snake has to say."

Illyria scowled for a moment at her brother, but when it was clear that he wouldn't give in, she turned to the stranger. Her voice was deadly calm as she asked, "Who are you?"

The man didn't reply but stared sullenly at the ground.

Behind him Kara grasped his long hair and jerked his head back. "You were asked a question," she hissed. "Now, answer before I put *my* knife in your throat."

Nanine's haughty voice cut through the night. "Does it matter who he is when we know who sent him?" She carried a makeshift torch that she now held close to the stranger's face. "Look at the necklace he wears."

A gold chain circled the man's neck and a pendant hung from it. Made of hammered gold, it looked like some sort of sun but with sharp geometric angles.

"Of course," Illyria said, with a sharp intake of breath. "He wears the same symbol Nemor wore on his tunic. He's Nemor's man. I, too, should have seen that."

"There's something else about that symbol," Nanine said, an unusual note of worry in her voice. "I could swear I've seen it before, only I can't remember where."

Illyria reached for the pendant and dropped it as soon as she touched it, almost as if she had been burned.

"Moon above," Nanine swore softly, "I know what that is, only"—she turned to the stranger, her voice acidic—"you've changed it, haven't you?"

The man remained silent, ignoring her.

Illyria's eyes widened in recognition, but she didn't respond to Nanine. Instead she turned to the stranger. "I suppose you are the one Nemor sent for my answer."

The man nodded his head.

"Why, then," Illyria continued, "did you bring a halter?"

Obstinately the intruder continued to stare at the ground. But for the first time he spoke. "Nemor sent me to find out if you will join him to take the fortress. If you agree, you must meet him at midday tomorrow in the village of Odelia." He fell silent again.

"I think that's as much as we'll get from him," Myno decreed impatiently. "Send him back to his master."

"What?" an outraged Darian protested. "He came into our camp armed, tried to take Quiet Storm—"

"Not now!" Illyria cut him off fiercely. She sent a questioning gaze to Nanine, who nodded her assent. "Very well, then," the Unicorn Queen agreed. "Return to Nemor and give him two messages from me. The first is that I will meet him in Odelia. The second is that if he ever crosses me again, he will not live to see the next dawn."

Myno grabbed the collar of the man's cloak and roughly began to pull him out of the canyon.

"My knife," the man protested. "You don't expect me to travel these roads unarmed?"

"That's a risk you'll have to take," Myno replied.

With Myno's spear against his ribs, the stranger left the camp.

"Let me see the knife," Nanine said as soon as he was out of sight.

Kara handed her the small bronze blade. "There it is again," Nanine said. Her finger traced the strange circular pattern engraved into the widest part of the blade. "He didn't need the knife; he just didn't want us to see this."

Sheila and Darian exchanged puzzled looks, and Dian spoke for them both, "It's more than Nemor's symbol, isn't it?"

"It's called a *krino*," Nanine answered. "The one that he and Nemor wear is slightly different from the original symbol, but it's essentially the same thing."

"As what?" Darian asked, clearly reaching the limits of his patience. "What's it a symbol of?"

"Evil," Illyria answered. "The *krino* is a very old, very powerful sign of dark magic. When we were in Campora, Mardock wore a ring that was similar. It's a protection, a calling on the Dark Gods. It explains why our visitor got past the watch and why Quiet Storm didn't do him any harm. The man is a mage."

Darian turned on his sister, his eyes blazing. "And knowing that, you released him?"

"Oh, Darian." Illyria's voice held none of the anger Sheila expected. "If he is even half as powerful as Nanine suspects, do you really think I could have kept him?" she chided. "However, it is entirely within my power to see that you have your arm attended to. Now, go with Pelu, and no more arguments!"

8

A Change of Plan

Odelia was one of the small hill towns on the outskirts of Ansar. It was far enough from the city for the riders to travel by unicorn, and Illyria had announced that with the exception of Darian, who was still nursing his broken arm, all of the riders would accompany her to Nemor's camp.

Her sword fastened to her waist and her backpack snugly on her back, Sheila readied Morning Star for the ride. She ran a brush along the unicorn's silky white coat. All of the unicorns were beautiful, but to Sheila Morning Star was the most beautiful of all. The mare nudged her with her head, as if impatient to leave. It had been two days since they had ridden together, and both of them had missed the other's companionship.

"Be patient a little longer," Sheila told the unicorn as she finished brushing out the thick, dark mane. "We'll be riding in just a few moments. I promise you."

"I'm afraid there's been a change of plan," Illyria said, walking up to them. She was holding a handful of greens which she offered to Morning Star. With a delicate shake of her head, the mare declined the offer.

186

Sheila looked at the Unicorn Queen. Illyria was dressed to ride, as were Nanine and Myno, who stood behind her. Things didn't *look* as if they had changed.

"I need to ask a favor of you, Sheila," Illyria began. "Will you let me ride Morning Star today?"

"You mean you ride Morning Star and I ride Quiet Storm?" Sheila asked. Riding Quiet Storm was probably a lot like riding Wildwing, except Quiet Storm was even bigger and probably more dangerous.

Illyria's blue eyes were troubled when she answered. "No. No one is going to ride Quiet Storm today. I went to saddle him and he reared up, panicked. He won't let me near him." She ran her hand down Morning Star's back. "I've never seen him like this before."

"It's no mystery," said Nanine, anger close to the surface. "It was the mage—he put Quiet Storm under a spell."

Illyria sighed. "I don't know how to lift the spell, and that's something I can't even attend to now. I need your help, Sheila. I must meet with Nemor this afternoon. Morning Star is the gentlest of the unicorns. I fear I would spend half a day convincing any of the others to accept me. Will you let me borrow her? Besides," she added with a smile, "I need you to stay with Darian and Quiet Storm. Whom else would I trust with my two dearest loves?"

Sheila was disappointed, but she knew she couldn't refuse. Resigning herself to the new plan, she ran her hand through Morning Star's mane. "You'll take Illyria where she wants to go, won't you?"

Morning Star gazed at her through long white lashes, as if to be sure she meant it.

"Please," Sheila urged the mare. "And you must protect her as you would me."

The unicorn gave her a slightly reproachful look, then turned toward Illyria. She lowered her black horn, and for a moment Sheila feared that the mare was preparing to charge.

Again, Illyria held out the greens. "Come, Morning Star," she said, her voice confident and gentle. "It's only till Quiet Storm is well again."

Sheila was relieved to see that, after a moment's hesitation, the unicorn munched down her gift and allowed Illyria to mount her.

Within minutes Illyria had summoned the other riders, and they had departed for Odelia. Sheila was left with Quiet Storm, Darian, and the wild unicorns. Despite Illyria's comforting words, she was sure she had been the one left behind because she was the least-experienced warrior. And having been left in the camp the day before, she was restless. The relentless rhythm of breaking camp every day and riding for miles must have gotten into her blood. Two days in one place and she longed to be riding again.

Feeling extremely grumpy, she surveyed the camp. Most of the herd stood by the edge of the stream, drinking quietly. But at the far end of the canyon, Quiet Storm stood alone. She saw immediately why the others wouldn't go near him. The stallion's eyes were wild and his sides were heaving. As if fighting an invisible enemy, he was caught in a furious pattern—rearing up, coming down and lowering his head for a charge, and then bucking as if a demon rode him. *Oh, you poor thing*, Sheila thought, *you're trying to break the spell on your own. If we don't get you cured, you'll probably die of exhaustion.*

She turned back to the camp. Darian sat by Illyria's tent, his back against a tree, his right arm splinted and in a sling. Pelu had assured her that he was no longer in pain. He might still be groggy from the sleeping potion, she explained, but if he didn't attempt anything too heroic, he would be fine. Sheila was supposed to make sure that he rested.

Reluctantly Sheila approached her charge. She had a feeling

that telling Darian to rest would be about as effective as telling Wildwing to slow down.

"Hi," she said. "Are you feeling better?"

Darian didn't look at her, but stared at the ground. "I'm fine," he answered in a flat voice. "Quiet Storm's going crazy, and I'm just sitting here. It feels great to be absolutely useless."

"You're not—" She stopped midsentence as he looked up, his eyes nearly black with anger.

"Tell me what it is I'm good for," he challenged. "I can't fight, can't ride. I can barely stand without feeling the ground spin."

"That's just the sleeping potion. Pelu said it would wear off."

"Pelu said it would wear off," he mimicked in mincing tones.

Sheila decided he had had enough sympathy. "I'm not exactly happy about staying here, either," she told him heatedly, "especially with *you* for company. I've seen six-year-olds who handled broken arms better. You get hurt and think it's an excuse to turn into a whining, sniveling, self-pitying—"

"All right, all right." There was the faintest trace of a smile on his mouth as he held up his good arm in a gesture of surrender. "I'm sorry . . . especially because I owe you my thanks."

"For what?"

"For saving my life last night. If you hadn't caught the intruder's knife hand and held it"—he gave her a dazzling grin—"I wouldn't be sitting here giving you such a rough time."

"Don't make me regret my heroism," Sheila muttered.

Unrepentant, Darian held out his good hand. "Friends again?"

Sheila looked at him in exasperation. She had never met anyone so moody. One minute he was ready to snap her head off, the next he was charming her.

"Friends," she agreed with mock reluctance.

Darian leaned back against the tree and regarded her with lazy curiosity. "So, since I'm your patient for the day, how do you intend to amuse me?"

"Amuse you?" she sputtered, getting to her feet. "You can amuse yourself, you obnoxious—"

"Oh, Sheila, don't get mad," he broke in. "I only meant maybe you had something in your backpack."

More than any of the others, Darian had been intrigued by the contents of Sheila's backpack. Everything from the twentieth century seemed to fascinate him. With the exception of his sword, the Mickey Mouse watch Sheila had given him had become his most valued possession.

"I think you've already seen it all," Sheila answered. She was still wearing the pack; after Illyria had told her she had to stay, she hadn't bothered to take it off. Now she zipped it open and peered inside. "Maybe listening to music will improve your mood." She took out the tape player and flipped it on.

Darian looked a little unnerved at the sound of Springsteen's voice booming out at him, but watched the tape player with fascination. Sheila had already tried to explain to him how it worked, but she got stuck when it came to how the voice actually got onto the tape. She wasn't too clear about that herself.

"Do you have anything else?" Darian asked hopefully.

Sheila rummaged in the bottom of the pack. No sense wasting the matches, flashlight, or Band-Aids to impress Darian. He had already seen the notebook and pen and her mirror. She smiled as her hands closed on a pack of bubble gum.

"I've got it," she declared triumphantly, holding out a stick of gum.

Darian examined the flat, paper-wrapped object. "What does it do?"

"You chew it. But don't swallow it."

He raised an eyebrow, then dutifully started to put it in his mouth.

"Take the paper off first," Sheila suggested, trying to keep a straight face. Just to make sure he got the idea, she unwrapped a piece for herself.

Darian did as he was told and began chewing. He chewed in silence for several minutes. "It tastes good," he announced at last, "but not like food."

"It's not food," Sheila assured him.

"Then why am I chewing it?" A look of betrayal crossed his face. "This is like Pelu's herbs, a medicine. You thought you could trick me!"

Sheila giggled helplessly. "It's not food and it's not medicine. It won't do you any good at all." He looked at her menacingly. "And it won't hurt you, either," she added quickly. "I promise. Gum is just something we chew because it tastes good. And with bubble gum, which is what this is, you can blow bubbles."

Darian looked mystified as she blew a perfect pink bubble and then popped it back into her mouth. He chewed harder as she blew another.

"You can't do it by chewing," Sheila said. "Here, I'll show you how." She figured a lesson in blowing bubbles might not exactly equal one in swordplay, but at least it would help pass the time and keep Darian out of trouble.

Half an hour later Sheila and Darian were laughing so hard they could barely sit up straight. Darian had tried valiantly to blow bubbles and had succeeded only in making terrible faces. Sheila had completely given up on trying to explain; blowing bubbles was more complicated than she had realized. Secretly she was amused to have discovered one thing Darian wasn't good at.

"Let me try one more time," he gasped as a last fit of laughter passed. With tremendous concentration he chewed some more— and blew the tiniest bubble Sheila had ever seen.

"You did it!" she shouted.

"Did what, dear girl?" asked a perplexed voice.

Darian's mouth dropped open and the gum, bubble and all, fell out.

"Dr. Reit?" Sheila couldn't believe what she was seeing. The apparition of the elderly scientist got weirder every time she saw him. "What are you doing on a skateboard? And wearing hightops?"

"Do you like them?" he asked, looking quite pleased with himself. "I was told by a reliable source that one must have hightops to skateboard properly."

Sheila just shook her head in amazement.

Darian nudged her. "Oh, Dr. Reit, this is Darian, Illyria's brother. He's been wanting to meet you."

"Sheila has told us that you are a powerful sorcerer," Darian said.

Dr. Reit nodded absently in the boy's direction. "Yes, well, I wouldn't phrase it that way myself, but the general idea is velocity."

"Velocity?" Sheila asked.

"That's why I'm here on the skateboard," Dr. Reit said, as if that explained everything. For the first time he noticed their blank expressions. "You see, I've discovered that the key to traveling through time is velocity—speed. This skateboard, with a little tinkering"—he pointed to a tiny jet attached to the base of the board—"provided the acceleration necessary to get me back here."

"And you've come to take Sheila home," Darian said in a hard voice.

"Oh, I am sorry, but no. There's simply not enough power on this skateboard."

"It figures," Sheila murmured.

"I'm working on it," the scientist said with a frown. "However, we'll deal with that problem when the time comes. I'm here on another matter entirely. When I left you last time, I had every intention of materializing in my laboratory. But I took a slight detour and wound up in the camp of that character you call Nemor. He certainly is a charismatic fellow. His followers think the world of him. But he's making plans that could be dangerous. Very dangerous indeed."

"You mean for the unicorn riders," Sheila said.

For once Dr. Reit gave a straightforward answer. "Sheila, I overheard a conversation between Nemor and a man named Valan, a man who fancies himself a wizard. Wears a gold necklace."

"He *is* a wizard," Darian said. "And a powerful one."

"Anyway, it became clear from their conversation that Nemor is not fighting Dynasian at all. Oh, I think he did for a while, but the tyrant has bought him back. The attack on the fortress you told me about is Dynasian's plan. He means not only to lure Illyria into his stronghold, but to destroy all of the riders as well. They said something about 'natural defenses,' but I couldn't quite catch their meaning. Perhaps I should return and investigate further. That will mean, of course, that I will have to recalculate my coordinates from here and—"

"It's a trap," Darian said quietly. "And even now my sister rides into the traitor's camp." Using the trees for support, he raised himself slowly and then stood for a moment, as if to be sure he had his balance back. He gave a soft, low whistle.

"Darian," Sheila said uneasily, "what are you doing?"

Darian ignored her question, instead turning to Dr. Reit. "The Sareen encampment, did you notice where it was—hidden by trees, in a valley, on a hillside?"

"Dear me"—the scientist's form began to waver—"I didn't really look. I was so absorbed in what Nemor and Valan were saying, not to mention my own coordinates of velocity and—" As he spoke his image gradually began to fade until by the time he said the word *velocity,* he was no more than a voice.

"Bye, Dr. Reit." Sheila tried not to sound hurt. She knew the scientist was doing his best to rescue her, but every time he left, she couldn't help wondering if he had left for good.

Darian took her mind off her problems by whistling again, this time a little louder. In answer, Wildwing ran toward them, clearly excited by the summons. Darian turned toward his tent.

"Darian," Sheila said, "where do you think you're going?"

"I'm going to get my saddle," he said casually. "Where did you think I was going?"

Sheila sighed. "You're in no shape to ride Wildwing. Pelu said you were to rest."

"Pelu didn't know that Nemor is fighting for Dynasian. I can't let Illyria ride into his camp without warning. And as for riding Wildwing, that won't be a problem."

"With one arm?" Sheila scoffed.

The boy shrugged and disappeared into his tent. He emerged a few moments later, holding both saddle and sword in one hand. Sheila watched with mixed feelings. She couldn't help but admire how well he was managing. At the same time he was taking a serious risk. After all, it wasn't like his arm was in a plaster cast; one good jolt on Wildwing could easily disturb the newly set bones. And after last night, she knew she couldn't stand to see him in pain again.

"Riding with my arm in a sling isn't that different from riding with a spear," Darian said reasonably. He fitted the saddle over the unicorn's back. "Besides, you're going to be the one riding him. Then all I have to do is hold on."

"You're out of your mind," Sheila said. "We can't leave Quiet Storm."

"We're leaving Quiet Storm guarded by the other unicorns. They're certainly better protection than either one of us. Besides, do you really think anyone could get near him in the state he's in?"

Quiet Storm was no longer bucking, but his head was lowered, his horn tearing violently through the air. Clearly, he was still in the midst of some invisible battle.

"Valan got near him last night," Sheila pointed out.

Awkwardly, Darian struggled to buckle his sword around his waist. Sheila didn't offer to help.

"Look," he said, "I don't feel good about leaving him, either,

but I think I can do more good by warning Illyria than by watching Quiet Storm wear himself out."

"Fine. You go."

"Oh, no. I'm not leaving you alone."

Sheila faced him furiously. "I don't need your protection!"

"But I need yours," he said with a disarming grin. His eyes went
wide with calculated innocence. "Didn't Illyria say you were supposed to take care of me?"

"She didn't tell me it would be like babysitting for a hyperactive toddler!" Sheila crossed her arms and turned away from him.
Briefly she wondered if the word *hyperactive* had translated into
his language.

Even with one arm in a sling, Darian mounted the unicorn easily. His pressed his knee against Wildwing's side, and the unicorn
walked around Sheila so that Darian was once again facing her.
He held out his left hand. "Please?"

"You'll go anyway, won't you?"

"I have to."

Sheila gave in with a groan and let him pull her into the saddle.
"All right," she said, "but if anyone asks, this was *your* idea."

9

Valan's Deal

Neither Darian nor Sheila knew exactly where Odelia was, but Darian had the general idea that it was about twelve miles northwest of the canyon. He was sure that once they reached Odelia, someone would tell them where to find the Sareen camp.

Sheila didn't have a better idea, so she followed his directions. She just hoped that they wouldn't encounter any of Dynasian's soldiers. The two of them alone, especially with Darian wounded, wouldn't stand a chance.

The noon sun burned hot as they rode, and Sheila leaned forward into the wind. The air was so hot and dry, it felt as if they were riding under a blow dryer. *Why,* Sheila wondered, *couldn't she have time traveled into a world where people did things like go to the beach?*

Darian broke into her thoughts as they came to a fork in the road. "I think you want to go right here."

"You *think?*"

"Just try it."

Darian hadn't said much since they had left camp. He had been too busy holding on and trying to keep his arm from being jostled. On a horse they wouldn't have gotten ten yards. But Wildwing moved with the near-psychic intuition Sheila had come to identify with the unicorns. The powerful stallion held himself in a smooth, even canter that was as close as he could come to cushioning his riders.

"To the *right*," Darian repeated in a tight voice.

Sheila wondered if he was in pain or just anxious about Illyria. Using her knee, she guided Wildwing to the right.

Ahead, the narrow road dipped down sharply, and as far as Sheila could tell, it was completely overgrown with a canopy of trees. In the dry southern lands of the empire, this was definitely weird. She half-expected Wildwing to turn and run in the opposite direction.

"Darian"—she tried to keep her voice calm—"are you sure this is the way we want to go?"

He leaned forward in the saddle, peering over her shoulder. "Keep going," he said quietly.

Wildwing walked at a steady, even pace, carrying them into what looked like a tunnel formed by the trees. A few narrow bands of sunlight slipped through the thick cover of branches. And yet there was no relief from the heat. If anything, it was hotter under the trees—and incredibly humid. Sheila brushed a soft green frond away from her face. The farther they went, the thicker the trees grew and the darker the road became. What had they done, suddenly ridden into the heart of a jungle?

"Darian," Sheila said, "I think we took a wrong turn."

"No, we didn't."

With considerable effort, she got Wildwing to halt. "Look at this place—all these trees. I haven't seen anything like this since I entered your world. It's all wrong for this climate."

Darian's voice was sharp with impatience. "Don't you think I know that?"

"Well, if you know it, why are we here?" Sheila tugged on the straps of her backpack. Beneath it, her tunic was soaked with sweat. Even the air was changed on this overgrown path. The air reeked with the smell of something sweet and decaying. Whatever this place was, it felt completely wrong.

Sheila made a quick decision. She wasn't going to argue with Darian on this one. She pressed her heels into Wildwing and brought his head around.

The unicorn looked at her for a moment, brought his head back, and remained exactly where he was. When she tried again to turn him, he walked forward deeper into the trees. Sheila felt her chest tighten with panic.

Darian leaned forward. "Keep going."

This time she brought Wildwing to a dead stop. "Darian, the land can't possibly be like this. Not when it was so dry just a little ways back."

"I know."

Sheila's voice rose higher than she meant it to. "I thought you were the one who didn't approve of riding straight into traps. What do you think we're doing now?"

Darian pressed his heels into Wildwing, and the stallion moved forward. Above them the thick cover of trees completely blocked sun and sky.

Sheila tried to keep her voice light but couldn't stop it from shaking. "This is worse than riding at night. I can't see at all."

"But Wildwing can." Darian gave her shoulders a quick squeeze. "We've got to trust him."

Sheila wound her fingers even more tightly through the black mane. She was holding on so hard she was sure her fingers would be cramped forever.

"There!" Darian's arm shot forward, pointing to a small point of red light blazing in the darkness.

The unicorn stopped, and Sheila felt him tense beneath her.

Ahead of them the point of light became larger—a small red orb spinning furiously in the darkness.

Oh, Dr. Reit, Sheila thought, *you never told me about anything like this.*

As they watched the light spin closer Sheila could see that it was not just a circle of red light, but red light racing in a geometric sunlike pattern. It was the *krino.*

Darian must have recognized it at the same moment Sheila did. She heard the metallic scrape of his sword being drawn.

"So you want to finish what you started last night?" There was a dry, hoarse laugh. Then the light spun out into the long lines of a man's form, and Valan, Nemor's mage, stood before them. His voice was mocking as he addressed Darian. "It is useless, you know. You've left Quiet Storm to die unprotected, and all for nothing. This time I will not be gentle with you," he promised with an evil laugh. "This time you will suffer more than a broken arm."

Sheila didn't know where she found the courage to speak, but when she did she was amazed to discover her voice no longer shook. "What do you want from us?"

Thin streaks of red light danced around Valan's form. Dr. Reit had often said that everyone gave off a certain level of energy. He even claimed his cat Einstein gave off the most calming energy he had ever encountered. It occurred to Sheila that she was watching Valan's energy, and it was anything but calming.

"I think," Valan said, "that the question should be turned around. After all, it was *you* who came to me this time."

"We don't want anything from you," Sheila replied.

"That's not true," Darian said quietly. "I did seek you. I want to know where my sister is. And I want your word that you won't use your power against her. We'll match Nemor, force against force, but no magic."

Valan laughed again, thin lines of red light darting into the treetops. Sheila was surprised nothing caught fire. "You know what this entails, young one," he taunted. "If you want my help, you'll have to pay."

Darian's breath caught, almost as if he was choking back a sob. "You want the unicorn."

"That's part of it, but not all. You can't buy magic that cheaply."

Sheila turned to see Darian sheathing his sword. "No!" she cried.

"Be quiet!" he snapped. To Valan he called, "The girl didn't know anything about this. Let her go and you can have your price."

The mage considered the proposition, the light about him growing more and more frantic. *He's calling up more energy*, Sheila realized. *He's getting ready to cast a spell.*

"The girl goes," he agreed at last. "She will leave you here. And she'll not get over it easily."

"I'm not going anywhere," Sheila told them both.

Darian's hand closed over her arm, gripping it so tightly it hurt. "You're going to get off Wildwing and walk out of here," he whispered fiercely. "Walk back the way we came in and don't look back."

"Stop giving me orders!" Sheila hissed. She turned away from him, concentrating instead on Valan. What was he going to do to Darian and Wildwing? And what made Darian think he would keep his word once they had paid his price? He would probably kill Wildwing and Darian, and then he would finish off Illyria and the riders. There *had* to be a way to fight the mage.

"Sheila." Darian's voice held a dangerous note of warning. If she hadn't been so terrified of Valan, it might have scared her. He swore furiously under his breath. "Do as I tell you. Now!"

And then Sheila had an idea. It might not work at all, but it was worth trying. "All right," she said to Darian. "I'll go, but since I may not see you again—" Her voice broke. She couldn't help it. If she was wrong, she never *would* see him again. "I want to give you something." She slipped the pack off her back and unzipped it.

The mage's voice cut through the darkness. "You've wasted too much time, girl. I can no longer let you go."

Three things happened at once. The first was not unexpected: Darian drew his sword. The second was a little more unusual: The streaks of light that flickered around Valan drew together in the burning red configuration of the *krino* and shot toward Sheila and Darian. And the third thing that happened was somewhere between a miracle and sheer luck: Sheila grabbed the mirror from her pack and held it up like a shield to the burning red light that was streaking toward them. There was a flash as the light met the mirror, bounced off it, and ricocheted backward. A bloodcurdling cry split the air, and then everything went dark.

For a long moment no one moved. Even the unicorn barely breathed.

"The *krino's* gone," Darian said at last. "And so is Valan . . . isn't he?"

Wildwing answered by snorting his agreement and walking past the spot where the mage had stood.

Still shaken, Sheila didn't answer. But the sweet, decaying scent was gone, and she knew that they were safe. At least for now.

10

Lightning

Wildwing stepped calmly out of the tree-covered valley where Sheila and Darian had confronted Valan. Beyond the tree line the sun was shining as brightly as ever. Sheila was actually happy to see the scorched landscape again.

She turned in the saddle. Behind her Darian sat looking unusually pale.

"Are you all right?" she asked.

He nodded his head.

"How about your arm?"

"I'm fine." He smiled, but his eyes were dark and serious. "You defeated a mage today. And you saved my life. Again. I'm indebted to you, Sheila McCarthy." He ran his hand lightly through her hair. "I think you must be a sorceress after all."

"You know I'm not," Sheila said quietly. She still felt shaken by the encounter. She would probably have nightmares about Valan for the rest of her life. And something he had said was bothering her.

Darian made a clicking sound with his tongue, and the unicorn began to move forward at a gentle walk. Sheila turned around quickly to grab a handful of mane.

"Darian, do you remember what Valan said about Quiet Storm?"

His reply was barely audible. "That we left him to die unprotected."

"We've got to go back to the camp," Sheila said. "Maybe it's not too late."

"And maybe it is." Darian's voice was drained of all emotion. "We've got to find the Sareen encampment and warn Illyria."

"No!" Sheila brought Wildwing to a halt. She turned to face Darian, who was looking at her as if she had lost her mind. "It's not that I don't care about Illyria," she explained, "but Illyria's got six riders with her and is very capable of taking care of herself."

Darian stared at her, unbelieving. "In case you don't remember," he said, "Illyria and that overwhelming company of six riders are about to be betrayed."

"I know that. But Darian, I can't stand the thought of Quiet Storm dying because we abandoned him. We've got to at least try and save him. Then we can ride to Odelia."

Darian's eyes were hard with barely controlled anger, and Sheila knew that she was about to be overruled. And with a sense of desperation, she also knew that this time Darian was wrong and she couldn't let that happen.

"You just told me you were indebted to me," she said quickly. "If you really mean that, then I'm calling in the debt."

"What?"

"I saved your life," she said. "Twice. But we'll call it even if you just do this one thing for me—we go back to the camp now."

For a long moment Darian stared at her. Sheila knew she was asking him to make an impossible choice. She was pitting his love for his sister against the warriors' unbreakable code of honor. And she was counting on the fact that like Illyria and the other riders, he would not be able to go back on his word, not when he had given it in thanks for his life.

"All right," he said at last. "We go back to attend to Quiet Storm, but if anything happens to Illyria—"

Sheila turned before he could complete the threat, and dug her heels into Wildwing's side. She would worry about the consequences of her decision later. Right now the only thing that mattered was getting to Quiet Storm.

Dusk was falling when Wildwing reached the mouth of the canyon. As fast as the stallion was, this time he hadn't been fast enough for Sheila. She leaped from the unicorn's back and raced into the riders' camp.

"He's still alive!" she called to Darian. She thought she would collapse from relief.

The silver unicorn stood alone at the far end of the canyon. He was no longer fighting his invisible opponent, but standing quietly with an odd, expectant air. *He's probably waiting for Illyria,* Sheila thought.

"He looks better, don't you think?" she asked Darian, who had walked Wildwing into the canyon, cooling him down. "He's much calmer. Maybe Valan was just bluffing. Or maybe we broke his spell back there."

"Stay here," Darian said. Slowly he approached the unicorn. "Quiet Storm," he called softly. "Will you let an old friend say hello?"

The unicorn watched warily as the boy advanced.

Darian had gotten within about ten yards of him when Quiet Storm began to rake the air with his horn. "Shhh," the boy said in a soothing voice. "It's all right. I'm not going to hurt you. I only want to take a look at you."

Quiet Storm began to buck with a frenzy, and Darian quickly

retreated. He turned to Sheila with a look of resignation. "I guess that just because Valan's gone doesn't mean his magic is."

"Do you think Quiet Storm is worse?"

"I don't know. The only thing that's certain is that he's still bound by magic." Darian put a hand on Sheila's shoulder. "Come on, let's get something to eat, and then we can figure out a way to feed Quiet Storm without getting too close."

The camp seemed unnaturally quiet as they worked to build a fire and heat the broth that Pelu had left for Darian. The night had fallen quickly, and Quiet Storm stood in a wash of moonlight, nearly motionless. Did that mean the spell was winning, since the unicorn no longer had the strength to fight it?

Sheila felt helpless. If she had really destroyed Valan, why was his spell still controlling the unicorn? Was the mage right—was Quiet Storm really dying? And if he was, what could Sheila do to stop it? She wished Illyria and Pelu were with them, and she was beginning to wish that she had gone to warn them.

"Here." Darian handed her a bowl of steaming broth.

She set it down without bothering to taste it. For the first time it occurred to Sheila that the others might not come back. Not ever. *Stop it,* she told herself fiercely. *Thinking like that won't help.*

Darian wasn't eating, either. He used his spoon to dig a shallow hole in the ground. "I wonder where they are now," he said. "If what your Dr. Reit told us was right, then they're probably safe until they actually attack the fortress. After all, Nemor won't ruin his own trap. The only problem is we don't know when the attack will take place."

"Maybe Illyria's—" began Sheila.

At the mention of Illyria's name Quiet Storm whinnied loudly and began to pace anxiously.

"He's worried, too," Darian said grimly. Then his head came up sharply and he pointed to Quiet Storm in amazement.

The unicorn had reared up on his two hind legs and now stood as if suspended in the air, his head cocked toward the back of the canyon. With a loud snort, Quiet Storm brought his forelegs down. He gave a last powerful buck and then tore toward the back of the canyon.

"What's he doing?" Sheila said. "There's only rock back there."

Darian didn't answer. He took off after the unicorn. Sheila was right behind him. Maybe the stallion really was going crazy. She had heard of "loco" horses, who tried to buck their way through walls. Was Quiet Storm going to try to tear through a wall of solid rock?

Ahead of her she heard Darian cry out. Quiet Storm had broken into a wild, headlong gallop. And each time his hoofs struck the ground, a blazing white light flashed up.

Moonlight met the unicorn's own lightning as the animal reached the end of the canyon. For a second the stallion paused, and the sight made Sheila dizzy with wonder. Quiet Storm stood bathed in light, his silver horn gleaming. Suddenly there was a tremendous flash as a bolt of lightning ripped into the hard rock wall. Sheila covered her ears to keep from being deafened by the terrific thunderclap that followed. Then it was quiet again. Quiet Storm gave a triumphant whinny as he galloped through a narrow pass, freshly cut into the canyon wall.

In unspoken agreement Sheila and Darian went after the unicorn despite the fact that they had no hope of keeping up with him. Illyria had once said that Quiet Storm could outrun the wind if he wanted to, and it wasn't an idle boast. Still, they couldn't just watch him disappear.

The pass through the canyon led to a narrow shelf of land that wound up behind the canyon walls. It meant running nearly straight uphill, and both Sheila and Darian were gasping for breath by the time they reached the top.

They stood for a minute, trying to control their breathing.

Sheila peered around. It looked like they had come out of the canyon and entered—an olive grove? A full moon illuminated the landscape. The land was flat as far as she could see. There were no houses or buildings, just thick, gnarled olive trees, growing in what might have a long time ago been rows. The trees themselves were spaced far apart with only a sparse covering of grass on the ground. There was no sign of Quiet Storm, but if he was still in the grove, sooner or later they would be able to see him.

Darian caught his breath first. "I don't even know what direction to go in," he admitted.

"Where are we?" Sheila asked. "I didn't see this grove today, or when I went into Ansar."

"No, I didn't, either. But look at the size of these trees—they're ancient. All of them. They've been here forever."

Something about Darian's tone made Sheila shiver. *Stop imagining things*, she told herself. *You've seen old trees before. How about the redwoods in California?* But it wasn't just the trees. It was the feeling that they had stumbled into a place that had been unchanged for thousands of years, unchanged for a reason.

A sudden flash of white light blazed through the grove.

"There he is!" Darian cried, and they were off again.

They ran for what seemed hours, and only rarely did they catch a glimpse of the silver unicorn. What they saw was the lightning he struck from the ground. It was almost as if Quiet Storm *wanted* them to follow him through the ancient grove, the grove that never seemed to end.

At last there came a point when Sheila and Darian thought they had lost Quiet Storm. It had been a long time since they had seen either the unicorn or the lightning.

Sheila slowed down and bent over, hands on knees, taking in deep gulps of the night air. "What are we chasing anyway?" she asked when her heart had slowed to an almost normal pace. "I mean, I'm beginning to think Quiet Storm isn't here at all." She looked up at Darian, unable to hide the fear in her eyes. "What if we've been chasing some sort of illusion. You know this grove is . . . is . . ."

"Magic," he said, letting the word hang between them. "I'm not sure whose or what kind, but you're right. It's a place of power."

"No," Sheila was almost pleading, "not after what happened with Valan." She stood up and wrapped her arms around her, as if for comfort. "Not again."

"I don't think it's quite the same," Darian said in a thoughtful tone.

A thin mist was rising from the ground. Quiet Storm was gone, and they were alone in a place that reeked of magic. The quiet was unbearable.

"What do we do now?" Sheila asked, not really expecting an answer.

The answer came from Quiet Storm. There was a blinding flash of light so bright that both Darian and Sheila covered their eyes. Then Quiet Storm stood before them as he had at the end of the canyon, bathed in the mingled rays of moonlight and the light he drew from the ground. The unicorn was staring intently into a pool of dark water. Then, as if suddenly aware that he had company, he lifted his head and looked straight at them with a clear, regal gaze.

"Come on." Darian took Sheila's hand. "I think he's waiting for us."

11

The Scrying Pool

Slowly Sheila and Darian approached Quiet Storm. This time the unicorn showed no sign of bolting. He stood calmly, waiting for them.

"Hey, Quiet Storm." Sheila held out her hand, but the unicorn brushed her off impatiently. He stood staring down into the pool of black water at his feet.

The pond was small; it couldn't have been more than six feet across. The full moon was reflected neatly in its center, and the strange thing was that the mist that rose from the ground didn't touch the pond at all. Its surface was perfectly clear. There was only black water framing a glowing, silver moon.

With a soft whinny Quiet Storm dipped his horn into the water. Sheila knew that unicorns were water conners—if they dipped their horns into water—even poisoned water—it became pure at once. Did Quiet Storm want them to drink from the pond?

Suddenly the surface of the pond began to cloud over. Sheila looked up quickly. The skies were clear; it wasn't a reflection. But an image was being formed in the water.

209

Darian sank to his knees, cradling his broken arm. "Illyria?" His voice was a hoarse whisper.

Sheila knelt beside him. The reflection of the moon had disappeared. In its place was a startlingly clear picture of Illyria entering a tent. Nemor followed close behind her. Illyria looked irritated and Nemor, exasperated. Sheila had a hunch that they were not getting along.

"I know you don't trust me," Nemor was saying, "but perhaps this will convince you of my intent." He crossed the tent, took a roll of parchment from the corner, and carefully opened it on a broad wooden table.

"Stars above!" Darian swore. They were staring at a detailed drawing of a mountain whose top had been leveled. A steep road had been cut into the side that faced the city of Ansar. What couldn't be seen from the city was the huge stone fortress that had been built on the mountaintop. Like the city, the fortress was surrounded by a stone wall.

Nemor pointed to the top of the wall. "There are guards posted here and here and here. No one can get up that road without being seen."

"You said there was another route," Illyria reminded him.

Nemor unrolled a second drawing. This one showed the side of the mountain that faced away from Ansar.

Sheila stared at it, puzzled. Although the drawing was detailed, all she saw was the side of a mountain with craggy and smooth rocks. She did not see anything that resembled a path.

"Here." Nemor's finger traced a line that ran up the steepest part of the mountain. "It's not what you'd call a road. It may not even qualify as a path, but it will get me up undetected and it's close to this gate. Once I'm inside the wall, I'll throw open the western gate, the one that opens to the road, to the Sareen and you and your riders. Then it's only a matter of a good, strong attack."

"Then it's only a matter of Dynasian destroying you," Darian translated. "I can't stand watching her agree to this."

"She has to free the unicorns," Sheila said, knowing that Illyria would not refuse a way into the fortress.

The Unicorn Queen studied the map with interest. "How do you plan to get over the wall?"

Nemor's voice was soft and chilling. "Treachery . . . I've planted my men among Dynasian's. They will help me."

"You mean *us*." Illyria nearly laughed as his eyes widened in astonishment. They were the color of amber, eyes like a lion's. "I'm not asking my riders to attack Dynasian's fortress unless I can personally guarantee that the gates will be open for them. If you want our help, you'll have to take me with you."

"He's going to kill her," Darian said. "And she's making it easy for him. All he has to do is push her off when they're climbing. Or give her to the soldiers on the wall. Or—"

"Sshhh!" Sheila cut him off as Illyria asked a short question: "When?"

Nemor's answer took them all by surprise. "Tomorrow. The longer we wait, the longer Dynasian has to uncover our plan. We'll start the climb before sunrise—the heat makes it impossible during the day. Given the time it will take us to get up the mountain, we should have our troops attack at midday."

"Tomorrow?" Sheila echoed hollowly. "How will we ever get to her in time?"

Darian groaned, and the mist that had not touched the pond now floated across its surface in a gauzy cloud. It cleared a few moments later and left only the reflection of the full, white moon floating in the still black water.

Sheila put a hand on Darian's shoulder and tried to think of something comforting to say. She noticed that neither she nor Darian nor Quiet Storm were reflected in the water, and the

strangeness of it unnerved her. What was it they had just seen—
the past, the future, or the present? And was it even real? In this
world it could easily be just another illusion, one of Valan's tricks.
Clearly, they had seen what they were meant to see. Now she
wanted to get out of this place fast.

She stood up and ran her hand along Quiet Storm's flank. "Will
you take us to Illyria?" she asked.

Quiet Storm whipped his head away with an angry snort.

"I think he just refused," Sheila said.

Darian stood up. "He probably doesn't know how to get out of
this place, either." He turned slowly. "It's the same in every direction. Just more trees. And it goes on for miles. You'd have to be a
bird to find a way out."

"Darian"—Sheila's voice suddenly filled with a wild hope—"I
think our way out just arrived." Against the moonlit sky she could
make out a flock of eagles swooping down through the grove.
They flew in a broad V formation, each bird the size of a man.

Quiet Storm lifted his head and called out in greeting, which
was immediately returned by the eagle that flew at the head of the
group.

They settled on the edge of the pond. In the light of the full
moon there was a stirring of the great wings and then their bodies
blurred. If Sheila hadn't seen the transformation once before, she
would have thought it a trick of the moonlight and mist. But the
eagles were gone, and she and Darian were now staring at a band
of stalwart warriors clad for battle.

A fierce-eyed young man, his long, black hair held back by a
silver circlet, stepped out from the mist and laid a hand on the
unicorn's neck.

Quiet Storm gave a nervous whinny.

"I know," the man said soothingly, "and I will help you. I
promise."

He turned to Sheila and Darian. "It has been a long time, my friends."

Sheila thought she would collapse with relief. The handsome warrior who stood before them was Laric, prince of Perian, and Illyria's love.

"Laric?" Darian sounded as if he was sure he was hallucinating.

"One and the same." The prince made a sweeping gesture with his red cloak. "You are welcome in this grove." He frowned at the two teenagers before him. "Though I would dearly love to know how you found it."

Sheila opened her mouth to explain, but Laric shook his head. "You can tell me later. Neither of you is going anywhere until Quiet Storm is free of the spell that holds him, and—"

"But Illyria's in danger!" Darian broke in angrily.

"I know that," Laric said with a sigh. "Believe me, if we are to help her, we will need Quiet Storm with us." He gave the unicorn a worried look. "He came here for help, and I will do what I can, but the spell that binds him is a powerful one. He's just lucky it was never completed. Something must have interrupted whoever cast it."

"Some*one*," Sheila said. "It was Darian."

Laric's eyes traveled to the boy's splinted arm. "And that was your payment?"

Darian nodded.

"Well, perhaps I can do something about that, too," Laric said. "But first, let me work on Quiet Storm."

Laric led the unicorn to a spot at the center point of four great trees and began an incantation.

Sheila and Darian waited with Laric's men. Sheila's eyes never left Laric. He was without question the most gorgeous man she had ever seen. *When* he was a man, that is. She wondered how Illyria could bear being in love with a man cursed to live in another form.

The prince raised his left hand and traced a circle around the unicorn's head, then another around the gleaming silver horn. All the while he spoke words of magic. After what seemed like an eternity to Sheila, Laric left the unicorn and came to sit beside her.

"So," he said, "how have you been, traveler from another world?"

Sheila blushed furiously. "Fine," she said.

"But your queen is not. Tell me what happened."

So Sheila told him all that had gone on and what she and Darian had just seen in the pond.

Laric listened silently as she poured out the whole story, but Sheila could feel him tense with fury.

"This is worse than I guessed," he said, getting to his feet. "We must go to her at once, but there is the matter of the spells. . . . Quiet Storm is not yet free, and to reach Illyria in time, I will have to lay a spell of my own on him. And I cannot do that until Valan's magic is gone." He gazed up at the full moon and sighed. "And all this before sunrise."

"Then what we saw in the pond was real?" Sheila asked. "Not just some illusion?"

"First of all," Laric said dryly, "it is not a pond. It is a scrying pool. Secondly, scrying pools are not capable of illusion. They reveal visions of reality to those who are ready for them. You may trust it completely."

He turned toward Darian. "Come. We must heal your arm. At least I will not waste the time we have."

Sheila watched as Laric carefully loosened the sling and removed the splint from Darian's arm. Gently he felt the break. "It's been skillfully set," he said. "Now we must ask it to knit faster." Holding Darian's arm between his hands, he murmured words in a language Sheila had never heard before.

Darian watched curiously.

"There will be some pain," said the prince, "but it will not last. Don't move your arm."

As Laric spoke Darian's face whitened and he shut his eyes. Sheila slipped her hand into his, and he clenched it so tightly she thought she might need to be healed as well.

"There." Laric released Darian's arm. He, too, was pale. "Now, turn your wrist. . . ."

On Laric's instructions Darian moved his arm through a series of exercises, the expression on his face changing from doubt to wonder to sheer delight.

"Yes, it will do," said Laric gruffly. "But don't tackle any more mages if you can possibly avoid it."

Darian's grin faded. "What you just did . . . that was no ordinary healing. You are a mage as well?" Though phrased as a question, it was a statement.

Laric shrugged. "Perian is not like your country. There, everyone is taught magic from childhood. And since I was raised in the palace, I was taught a bit more than others. Among your people it may be impressive. In my own land I am far from the rank of a true mage." He gave a bitter laugh. "And the proof is that I am unable to break Mardock's curse."

"But you brought Quiet Storm to Illyria," Sheila said. No matter what Laric thought, the coming of the unicorns was impressive.

The prince smiled. "I like unicorns," he said simply. "Illyria saved my life, and I didn't know if I'd ever see her again. Quiet Storm was the best gift I could leave her. And now I should see to him so I can send him back."

"Wait," Darian said. "Just one more thing. This grove . . . what is it?"

Laric hesitated, as if he wasn't sure he should answer.

"Yesterday we rode past the end of the canyon," Sheila said. "And yesterday there wasn't an olive grove here."

"This grove has nothing to do with time or place," Laric answered. "It does not lie within Dynasian's empire. And that's all I can tell you." He smiled and brushed a strand of auburn hair out of her eyes. "You should be used to strange travels by now, child of another time."

One of Laric's men joined them. "We've prepared places for you two to sleep," he said. "You will only have time for a nap, but Laric will be awhile with Quiet Storm and you should get what rest you can."

When Sheila turned for a last glimpse of Laric, she saw him working over Quiet Storm, both of them glowing in a haze of white light.

Sheila dreamed of Morning Star. She dreamed that Morning Star stood at the side of the scrying pool and dipped her black horn into its smooth depths. The pool began to cloud over . . . and Sheila sat upright, shaking herself awake. If it was possible to receive a message in your dreams, she was sure that Morning Star was trying to tell her to go to the scrying pool.

Most of Laric's men were sleeping and she didn't want to wake them. But she did wake Darian, and together they returned to the edge of the pool. Morning Star was, of course, nowhere in sight. But the pool was clouded over, as it had been in her dream.

At first they didn't recognize the image that formed in the black water, for the scene that was revealed was very dark.

"It's the mountain," Darian said. "Dynasian's mountain."

The wind caused the surface of the pool to ripple, and then Sheila and Darian could make out two human forms in the night, looking impossibly small against the massive wall of rock.

"Illyria and Nemor," said Laric, coming to stand beside them. "And it is dark on the mountain, as it is here. We are seeing the present."

They saw Nemor leading Illyria up the wall. Nemor moved up

the steep rock face as surely as if he had climbed it a thousand times. He never placed a foot or hand awkwardly. Illyria followed, not quite as adept, but easily holding her own.

Laric studied the image and drew a sharp breath. "He wears the *krino*," he said. "And there is something else. Do you see the way he moves—he has the lion's energy."

Sheila had always thought Nemor looked somewhat leonine, and it made him all the more attractive. "So?" she asked.

"Throughout time the lion and the unicorn have been deadly enemies," Laric answered. "When they meet, only one of them will survive. Dynasian could have not chosen a more lethal agent."

And yet, for all the danger she was in, Illyria seemed to be doing rather well. Though the wall of rock grew increasingly steep, she followed Nemor without hesitation. About halfway up, they stood together on a ledge that Sheila figured was all of four inches wide.

The rebel leader turned to Illyria and put a hand under her chin. "You are very beautiful, Lady," he said softly. Sheila thought she saw compassion in his eyes. "Are you sure you want to continue?"

Illyria shook off his touch. "I said that I would enter the fortress with you. I don't go back on my word. Do you?"

His voice was gentle when he answered. "I did not ask you to make this climb. There would be no disgrace in changing your mind."

"Do you want me to lead the way?" Illyria asked mockingly.

Nemor growled something unintelligible and moved on.

Sheila, Darian, and Laric watched, fascinated and helpless.

The full moon paled and the sun rose, and still Nemor and Illyria climbed. Soon the top of the mountain was in sight.

"Sunrise," Laric said, pulling himself away from the vision in the scrying pool. "Quiet Storm should be ready for you now."

Quiet Storm stood at the center of the four trees, looking calm and attentive. He nuzzled Laric affectionately as the prince laid a hand on his neck.

"You've cured him," Sheila said.

Laric smiled wearily. "That and a little more. Get on, both of you. He will take you to Illyria."

"He'll know how to get us out of this place?" Sheila asked uncertainly. In the gray dawn light the grove seemed to go on endlessly in all directions. Wherever she looked she saw only the thick, gnarled trees and, between them, wide stretches of grass.

It was Darian who answered. "That's Quiet Storm's gift. He always knows exactly where to go."

"He will bring you safely to Illyria," Laric agreed, "but you must leave now, for the journey from this place is a long one. . . . And you will not be traveling as you expect." He murmured a few words of enchantment to the unicorn.

Sheila and Darian watched open-mouthed as Quiet Storm lifted his front legs and leaped upward into the air. He didn't come down. He ran above them, frisking like a young colt, his silver cloven hoofs darting in and out of the treetops.

"That's enough," Laric said sternly.

The unicorn returned to earth at once, looking not at all chastened.

"Get on," the prince urged them. "We will follow you."

Darian mounted first, then Sheila in front of him. Both were too surprised to say anything at all. Laric spoke a few more words to the unicorn, and then Quiet Storm leaped into the air and flew straight toward the sunrise.

12

The Siege

Quiet Storm ran on the wind, his hoofs leaving faint silver streaks against the sky, his mane streaming out behind him. Sheila held on, awed by the dizzying landscape below. At first there had been endless miles of the ancient trees, as if the olive grove were a country unto itself. Then, when the sun was nearly at its zenith, there was a flash of light so bright that both Darian and Sheila had to shut their eyes. When they opened them again, the grove was gone and they were soaring over the city of Ansar. Behind them the eagles flew, a fierce winged guard.

Sheila suppressed a shiver as they neared Dynasian's mountain. It seemed as if the mountain lay in wait for them. One of the eagles darted below Quiet Storm's hoofs and ahead. Tracing the bird's flight, Sheila saw that the eagle was calling to a small band of warriors galloping down the road that led to the mountain.

"There are the riders!" she called to Darian above the sound of the wind.

There was no sign of the Sareen, but the riders were on their way to the fortress with the wild unicorns behind them. Sheila knew that they would soon be climbing the road that wound up the mountain—exactly as Nemor had planned.

Quiet Storm turned, heading for the other side of the mountain, the side that Illyria and Nemor had scaled. Sheila looked desperately for a sign of the Unicorn Queen. Was it possible that she and Nemor were still climbing?

"There!" Darian called.

Quiet Storm hovered in the air above the scene. Nemor stood just inside the surrounding wall, looking up at Illyria, who crouched on its top. Obviously, they had just reached the top of the mountain and were about to enter the fortress.

Sheila held her breath as Illyria dropped from the top of the wall to stand beside Nemor. She could see them talking, and then there was a flash of bright metal and Illyria was behind Nemor, her knife drawn across his throat. Without protest Nemor began to walk toward the fortress.

"Don't go inside!" Sheila screamed. "It's a trap!"

"She can't hear you. We're too far away!" Darian said furiously as a door in the fortress opened and Illyria and Nemor vanished inside. "Can't you make Quiet Storm land?"

Sheila knew how to get a unicorn to walk, canter, or gallop, but she couldn't imagine what signal she was supposed to use to make Quiet Storm start his descent. She pressed her knees and heels against his sides. She tugged on his mane. She leaned forward and explained exactly what she wanted him to do. The unicorn gave no sign of understanding.

Darian saw what was happening at once. "Never mind," he said gently. "He's not going anywhere until he's ready. I guess we've just got to be patient."

Since they were no longer moving forward, the sound of the wind rushing past had vanished. The sun was blazing and the air was hot and deathly still. Dynasian's soldiers marched in silent parade along the top of the fortress walls. It was a small comfort that when Illyria had entered the fortress Nemor had been her captive.

"I wish I knew what Dynasian has planned," Darian said restlessly. "What was it that Dr. Reit said—something about 'natural defenses'?"

"Yeah, but even Dr. Reit didn't know what Nemor meant," Sheila answered.

Since there was nothing else to do, she studied the scene below. The iron gate facing the road was open for the approaching riders, Sheila realized with a sinking sensation. The gate led into a wide, square courtyard, surrounded by thick outer walls and facing the front of the fortress. Like the mountain itself, the fortress and its walls were carved of a pale—almost white—rock that seemed to shimmer in the midday sun. Dynasian's fortress was immense. Sheila figured it had to be at least four stories high and big enough to cover an entire city block.

One of the eagles cried out in alarm as a door to the roof of the fortress suddenly opened, and Illyria was pushed out, her hands bound behind her back. Two soldiers followed and pulled her to the very edge of the ramparts overlooking the courtyard.

Then, from the other side of the ramparts, a carved stone door opened and a short, fat man dressed in gaudy robes emerged. Sheila would have recognized him anywhere. It was Dynasian himself. And Nemor was at his side.

Sheila tried to call out, hoping the sight of a flying unicorn would at least distract Dynasian, but her voice was paralyzed by the panic that gripped her. She felt Darian's arm around her, and then Quiet Storm and the eagles began to descend, dropping silently through the air toward the fortress below.

The unicorn and eagles slowed when they were a short distance from the fortress, hovering again, watching as the unicorn riders reached the top of the mountain and entered the open gates.

The riders couldn't have been more than ten feet beyond the wall when the iron gates swung shut behind them, and Dynasian's voice rose over the clamor.

"Welcome riders," he said, parading across the ramparts. There was an oily quality to his voice that made Sheila's stomach turn. "Do not come any farther unless you wish to be directly responsible for your queen's death."

Sheila saw the riders shield their eyes against the glare of the sun as they followed the sound of Dynasian's voice: "I've been planning this little get-together for over a month now, and it pleases me greatly that you are so prompt.

"I have only one regret," the tyrant went on. "You are unable to see your queen, who took the more difficult route up the mountain. Were the sun not so bright, you would see she stands by my side. She is, I am afraid, a little disheartened. For she has just learned that the story that unicorns are held captive here is just that—a story. Further, she now realizes that she has led you all into a trap."

Nanine's contemptuous voice carried clearly. "He is insufferable!"

"I believe she owes you an apology." Dynasian shoved Illyria forward, perilously close to the edge of the ramparts. "Speak to them!" he ordered. "Tell them how you have betrayed them."

Illyria ignored the command, her face proud and calm.

"Do as he says, Lady." Nemor, who stood on her other side, spoke in a persuasive voice. "He does not like disobedience."

"Too late," Dynasian announced in a peevish tone. "You're not following orders, Unicorn Queen." He turned to Nemor and uttered two succinct words: "Kill her."

Nemor hesitated just a moment. Horrified, Sheila screamed as Nemor stepped forward and pushed Illyria off the ramparts. Time seemed to stop as the Unicorn Queen plunged toward certain death.

Suddenly Quiet Storm moved with a speed that Sheila doubted

a plane could equal. He swept down in front of the fortress beneath Illyria, catching her across his back as she fell.

Sheila hadn't even recovered from the surprise of it before Darian handed her his knife, telling her to cut the rope that bound Illyria's hands. Quiet Storm touched down lightly in the courtyard, and Darian and Sheila slipped from his back. Illyria remained on the unicorn's back, ready for the battle ahead.

Myno gave a loud, ringing cry, drew her sword—and then stopped dead in her tracks. The other riders also remained where they were, and Sheila knew why. The sun, now directly overhead, turned the fortress and its walls into a giant, glaring reflector, blinding anyone who stood in the courtyard. This was what Nemor had meant by natural defenses. They couldn't fight. They were sun-blind.

The riders shielded their eyes uselessly, unable to do anything but look at the ground. The wild part of the herd raced around them. Sheila wasn't sure whether or not the sun had the same effect on the unicorns. But there were no enemies for them to attack. The soldiers all stood safely on the walls, jeering at the helpless warriors below. Sheila knew it was only a matter of moments before the soldiers would begin picking the warriors off with well-placed arrows.

Suddenly a series of long dark shadows fell across the fortress. A terrible high scream was heard. The soldiers looked up to see a formation of golden eagles circling the fortress. As the largest eagle cried out again, the flock dived for the men on the ramparts. They tore into the guards, knocking them from the walls, attacking until the ranks broke, panic-stricken.

There were the sounds of men running, swords being drawn, and the unicorns charging in a frenzy. Sheila had a feeling that more of Dynasian's reinforcements were pouring out of the fortress, but she couldn't be sure. All she could see was glare. *I've got to get out of this courtyard so I can see what's going on*, she told herself. She did the first thing she could think of—she took the pack from her back and held it to her forehead, using it as an oversized visor.

It took a moment to sort out what was going on. More soldiers, wearing visors on their helmets, had indeed rushed out and were heading for the riders. Both the eagles and unicorns were doing an impressive job of fighting the soldiers, but they were greatly outnumbered. Then the strangest combatant of all joined the fray. Pedaling like a madman on a ten-speed bicycle, and carrying a huge plastic garbage bag, Dr. Reit zoomed into the courtyard. The sun didn't bother him. He was wearing black Wayfarer sunglasses. He looked like an extra from *Miami Vice*, Sheila thought with astonishment.

Oblivious to the swords and arrows flashing through the air, Dr. Reit pedaled straight toward her. "There you are, dear girl!" he cried. "I've brought you supplies." He thrust the plastic garbage bag into Sheila's hand.

Sheila opened it and gave a loud whoop of laughter. The bag was filled with Ray-Ban sunglasses. Without missing a beat, she took a pair for herself and then dodged through the battle, distributing the sunglasses to the other riders and Laric's men, who, one by one, were changing into their human forms.

Dian actually smiled at Sheila as she put on her shades, but before Sheila could wonder about that, she found herself staring at the edge of a sword. And holding the sword was one of Dynasian's soldiers. Sheila couldn't make out the face beneath the helmet, but the man was at least six feet two, and from the arrogant way he moved, she could tell that he had marked her as easy prey.

Reflexively Sheila drew her own blade and blocked his first blow.

What am I doing? she wondered frantically as she dodged his next strike. *He's going to total me!*

She should have gone to the backpack instead of trying to fight with a weapon, but it was too late to change tactics now. This was one fight she would have to finish.

The soldier advanced with steady, deliberate blows. He didn't seem to be trying very hard to actually get through her guard, and with a sense of surprise, Sheila realized that he wasn't. He was simply going to wear her out. He would keep up his attack until she could no longer lift the sword against him.

Suddenly she heard Darian's words: "Easy . . . fight *your* fight," and understood that the soldier had been making her fight *his* fight—and he wasn't going to do it any longer.

His blade slashed down against her own, and then rose, preparing for the next swing. Sheila knew that he was counting on her to block it. So before his blade could complete its downward arc, she stepped in close and sliced the heavy leather armor open. The soldier looked at her in amazement, and, as he hesitated, she moved in again, taking the offense. He stumbled backward, trying to avoid her sword, and Sheila lost all fear. She went after the soldier with the sweet certainty of a victory, and only realized how thoroughly their roles had changed when he fled from her.

She was standing there feeling pleased with herself when a strong arm yanked her out of a spear's path. Darian pulled her against a wall, out of harm's way. "I told you you'd be a terror," he said with an approving grin. His grin faded as he looked straight ahead of them and caught sight of Dr. Reit. "What's he *doing?*" Darian asked.

Dr. Reit was, in fact, coming to Dian's rescue, though not in any way that Darian would have recognized. Having decided to run interference between Dian and an advancing soldier, the elderly scientist hunched down ("better aerodynamics," he would later explain) and rode over the amazed soldier's sandaled foot.

"Way to go, Dr. Reit!" Sheila cheered.

The scientist brought the bike to a rather jerky halt directly in front of her. "Yes, well . . . ," he mumbled in his usual flustered tone. He looked around at the battle that was still raging. It was impossible to tell who was winning. "I realize this may not be the best time to exit," he began, "but I'm going to fade any second now. I can feel it."

"Okay," Sheila said, determined not to get all upset again. "Thanks for helping us. But how did you know to bring the sunglasses?"

"I told you I had to go back and investigate those 'natural defenses' Nemor mentioned," Dr. Reit explained. "It didn't take me long to figure out they were counting on the sun as their most powerful weapon. But let's get going. I'm starting to fade."

"What do you mean, 'let's'?" Sheila asked, confused. "Thanks for helping us. Come back when you can."

"You don't understand," Dr. Reit said. "This time you can fade with me. The bicycle will take us both."

Sheila couldn't believe what she was hearing. "You mean you're finally going to take me home?"

"Only if you get on the bike!" he shouted above the din. "There's not much time. Hurry!"

A lump rose in Sheila's throat. This was it. She was finally going home. It was what she had wanted ever since that crazy day when she fell into the time machine. Then why did she suddenly feel so sad? She scanned the courtyard, trying to get one last glimpse of each of her friends. Her eyes met Darian's and she had to look away.

"Sheila!" Dr. Reit's voice was weaker, and his image was wavering. "I can't stay much longer. You've got to get on *now!*"

"I know." Sheila brushed back a tear and reached for the bike— and at that moment she saw Illyria surrounded by three soldiers and fighting desperately for her life.

Before she had a chance to think about the consequences, she drew her sword and ran to Illyria's side. She and Darian each took on one of the soldiers. A jolt ran through her arm as she parried a blow meant for Illyria, giving the Unicorn Queen time to recover and fend off the first man. Laric, his sword moving with lightning speed, suddenly appeared and dispensed of the third soldier, who was matching blades with Darian. Sheila didn't mind at all when Laric then finished off her opponent.

Illyria finished her own fight, and Sheila breathed a sigh of relief. She turned back to where she had last seen Dr. Reit, but it was too late. The scientist was gone. How could she have let this happen? She had given up her only chance to go home. For the first time since the battle began, Sheila broke down and cried.

13

The Fortress

The rest of the battle passed in a blur. After helping Illyria, the only thing Sheila remembered clearly was the moment when Quiet Storm repaid Nemor for his treachery. The powerful unicorn had torn into the mercenary, goring and then trampling him as he lay wounded. The unicorns were all fierce, but Sheila had never seen anything this savage. Laric had said the lion and the unicorn could not meet without one of them dying. Quiet Storm gave Nemor no chance to survive.

A short time later it was over. The sun was beginning to set as the riders, the unicorns, and Laric's men stood grouped by the entrance to the fortress. Pelu was already applying bandages.

"Is everyone here?" Myno asked with a frown.

"Everyone except Dynasian," Nanine said darkly. "The pig has escaped."

"And the captive unicorns," Illyria added. She shook her head wearily. "They were never here. It was all a ruse to trap us. Dynasian spread the rumor throughout the countryside and I believed it."

"What happened to the Sareen?" Darian asked. "Weren't they supposed to ride up to the fortress with all of you?"

"Another lie. Nemor never told them about this," Illyria answered. "They didn't know he was a traitor, and I don't think he wanted them to find out. Maybe that was his saving grace—he could have sent them into the trap and didn't. Maybe he felt some responsibility to them after all."

Sheila stood listening, one arm around Morning Star's neck. She was exhausted and numb from all that had happened. She looked around at the group of riders, thinking, *This is my world now. This is as close as I'll come to family.* And then she realized that one very important member of the family wasn't there. "Illyria," she said, "Kara's missing."

The group fell quiet. They all knew where Kara was—somewhere inside the fortress, searching for Lianne.

"I'll find her," Sheila volunteered. She really didn't know why she said it, except she couldn't stand the idea of Kara in there alone searching for a sister who might not even be alive.

She patted Morning Star and walked toward the massive stone building. There were footsteps behind her, and she turned to see Darian.

"Thought I'd come along," he said as they stepped inside the building.

Together they walked through Dynasian's stronghold. For a building belonging to a man with such fussy taste, the inside of the fortress was surprisingly barren. Except for weapons on every wall, storerooms, and living quarters for the soldiers, there was little beyond empty, high-ceilinged hallways.

Their footsteps echoed in the hallways as they walked. There was no sign of Kara, Lianne, or any other slaves for that matter. Sheila was beginning to wonder if the story about Lianne was like the story of the captive unicorns—a lie designed to sweeten the bait.

At last they came to a passage that branched into another hallway. A woman's sobbing could be heard somewhere in the distance.

"There she is!" Sheila and Darian cried at once, each of them pointing in opposite directions.

They looked at each other with sheepish smiles. The inside of the fort was like a giant echo chamber. Either one of them could be right.

"I have an idea," said Darian. "Why don't I go in that direction—"

"And I'll go in this one," Sheila finished.

Darian nodded. "Look," he said, "I know you can take care of yourself, but be careful. Okay?"

"I will," Sheila promised. "You, too."

She turned and headed left, toward the sound of the sobbing. She was sure that she was getting closer. As she walked farther down the hall the sound became louder.

She kept going and soon realized it was fading. That meant that whoever was crying wasn't in the hallway but in a room off the hall, and she had passed it. Patiently she doubled back, this time trying every door she passed.

The doors were all locked—all except one. Sheila pushed against a low doorway, and it swung open into a small, dark room.

Cautiously she stepped inside and stopped. Kara knelt at the far end of the room, cradling a sobbing figure.

"You found her?" Sheila asked.

The archer looked up. It was too dark for Sheila to read her expression. "Yes, I've found her, but she's been badly frightened. She's been hiding in this room for weeks and doesn't want to leave. She's afraid the soldiers will hurt her. Maybe you can help me persuade her that it's safe to leave."

Sheila approached Lianne, a pretty, delicate girl who looked to be about seventeen. In spite of the situation Sheila couldn't help making a snap judgment: Lianne would never make it as a rider. Almost at once she realized that anyone who had seen her on her first day in this world would have said the same thing about her. Remembering what it felt like to be scared and lost and confused, Sheila gently began to help coax the girl out of the room.

In the three weeks that Lianne had been hiding out, she had barely eaten. Kara and Sheila had to support her on either side for her to be able to walk, so leaving the fortress was a slow process. They had almost gotten Lianne to the main door when Darian found them. Sheila expected Lianne to be afraid of him, but Lianne gave Darian a shy smile and he immediately offered to help carry her.

Sheila stepped back and watched the trio move ahead. Lianne would heal, she thought, and like all the riders she would grow strong.

Kara, Lianne, and Darian opened the fortress door and stepped outside. Sheila was about to follow when suddenly the door slammed shut behind them. Sheila was alone in the fortress, and spinning wildly in the darkened hallway were the red lines of the *krino*. She had been right. Valan wasn't dead. He was here in the fortress with her.

Sheila felt strangely calm. Too much had happened that day for her to feel much more. She was simply wrung dry of all emotion. "What do you want?" she asked tonelessly.

The mage materialized at the sound of her voice. It occurred to her that she had given up her one chance to return home, and now Valan was going to kill her, and she was too exhausted to do anything about it. Some warrior she turned out to be.

"I seek only to make something clear to you, time traveler," he answered. "You and your friends have won today's battle. Despite my protection Nemor lies dead. But despite your sorcerer friend and your own magic"—he indicated her backpack—"you will not win. And you will all pay for Nemor's death." He spoke in the voice of prophecy, and Sheila felt herself grow cold as he continued. "Laric and his men will soon remain eagles never to transform, and the unicorns will be destroyed."

Believe him and you fight his fight, Sheila told herself.

She shrugged and made her voice as sure and steady as she could. "You've been stopped before. You can be stopped again."

"Let me show you, then, what you're really up against," said Valan softly. The *krino* began to spin furiously. Sheila reached toward her pack for the mirror, knowing that she didn't have time to find it, much less use it.

But this time Valan did not use the *krino* as a weapon. Instead, the glowing red light spun around his own form, weaving a network of fine red lines that shimmered in the darkness, completely covering his figure.

There was a hissing sound, and then Valan was gone. Sheila gasped and took a step back. As the red of the *krino* faded she saw him—Mardock. Mardock, with his long, black curls and elegant silk robe. Mardock, whose magic drew the Dark Gods' power to Dynasian.

"Valan," he explained smoothly, "was just an amusing game I chose to play with you. But I was not pleased with the outcome of that game. When my wounds have healed, I am the one you will deal with, Sheila McCarthy. Do not forget that."

Sheila saw that his face was marred by a deep red welt. *The mirror,* she thought. *It burned him.*

And then as suddenly as he had appeared Mardock was gone. Sheila was truly alone in the fortress with only her fear and silence echoing through the empty halls. It took her a moment to collect herself and then Sheila flung the door open and ran—straight into Illyria and Laric.

The Unicorn Queen caught her, placing her hands on Sheila's shoulders. "What's the hurry? Are you all right?"

"I'm fine," Sheila answered, "but I just ran into Valan . . . I mean, Mardock . . ."

"All the better," said Laric when she had finished. "Then there is only one mage I must destroy." He didn't look at all intimidated by Mardock's threats. Actually, he had his arm around Illyria and was looking extremely romantic.

"I came looking for you because I wanted to thank you," Illyria said, not even addressing the question of Mardock. "Darian told me what you did—that you gave up the chance to return to your home in order to save my life."

Sheila didn't know what to say.

"I know that wasn't easy," Illyria went on. "You come from a different time and world, and yet you have proved yourself the equal of my best warriors." The Unicorn Queen smiled. "A fighter who doesn't like to fight—you have great courage, Sheila McCarthy. I want you to know that for as long as you remain in this world, you have a home with us."

Sheila said the only thing she could. "Thank you." But she had never felt prouder.

Myno barked an order to prepare to ride. Smiling, Sheila called to Morning Star and lifted herself into the saddle. Feeling tired, but strong and happy, she joined the other unicorn warriors and rode out to adventure beneath the rising moon.